FATHERS OF CAMBODIAN TIME-TRAVEL SCIENCE

BRADLEY BAZZLE

C&R Press
Conscious & Responsible

Winston-Salem, NC

FATHERS OF CAMBODIAN TIME-TRAVEL SCIENCE

STORIES

TABLE OF CONTENTS

Stories from this collection appear in the following publications: *Web Conjunctions* ("The Beard of Human Weakness"), *Beloit Fiction Journal* ("The Milkman" and "Legendary Americans on Wheels"), *Epoch* ("The Mask of Cajolo"), *The Iowa Review* ("Magellan"), and *Copper Nickel* ("In the Presence of the Actor").

For Andrea

THE BEARD OF HUMAN WEAKNESS

Whenever we get a new client looking for a big cheap parcel, we show her 26 Seagoville Highway. It helps if the client doesn't know the DFW Metroplex too well, because 26 Seagoville isn't exactly high traffic. It's an unfinished subdivision with mini-castle-shaped pink brick houses. There's zero landscaping so it looks pretty weird.

Today I'm showing it to some guys from Pakistan who want to do a Horror World franchise. The Pakistani guys tell me location doesn't matter for Horror Worlds because their target customer, the American teen, loves long drives where he can guzzle beer in secret with his pals and busty American girlfriend. I'm not too sure about all that, having been an American teen myself not too long ago, but I laugh and say don't I know it.

We walk the perimeter so the Pakistani guys can get a feel for just how big the parcel is. That's part of the routine. Each parcel has its own choreography, developed by Mr. Hamilton and whichever junior agent is in charge of that particular parcel, in this case me. According to the routine for 26 Seagoville, I'm supposed to cut over to the best preserved house before we get to the scummy creek that runs behind the parcel, though I'm not, under any circumstances, supposed to show the client *inside* the house, since onetime a vagrant squatter popped out of an en-suite bathroom brandishing a rusty chef's knife. So I try to cut over to the houses but one of the Pakistani guys is already pointing at the creek and the other guys start following him like bushwhackers through the tall grass. I'm bringing up the rear. We're way off script, but I have to go with it. Mr. Hamilton has coached me to be flexible.

Down by the creek, bugs whizz from weed to weed beneath a low canopy of crooked Live Oak branches. One guy rolls up his pants and starts wading into the murky water. I'd tell him he shouldn't go in there except I don't want him to ask why not. Plus he looks like he's having fun. The other guys are laughing. I guess they don't have much nature back in Pakistan.

After I show them the rest of the parcel, the Pakistani guys are pumped, so I call Mr. Hamilton to ask if he wants to join us for lunch. I suggest Taco Brothers, which is code for "we can close this deal today." Mr. Hamilton likes to close deals at Taco Brothers over peach-a-ritas, and he gets a deal on the peach-a-ritas because he hooked up the franchisee of this particular Taco Brothers with the empty lot next door for extra parking. When I call him, he's pumped as hell.

Then, at the Taco Brothers, we discover that the Pakistani guys don't drink alcohol. So Mr. Hamilton and I are drinking peach-a-ritas the size of goldfish bowls while the Pakistani guys are nibbling on chips. The guy with the gray handlebar mustache keeps trying salsa and frowning. All is lost, I think, until Mr. Hamilton asks if they've checked out the new Bollywood movie theater in Carrollton. The guys say sure, of course, and suddenly Mr. Hamilton is talking to them about Bollywood movies, about somebody named Krishnamurthy, who's like the Bollywood Chuck Norris, I guess, because Mr. Hamilton is doing his hands in karate chops and the Pakistani guys are doing snatches of dialogue in Pakistani or Indian or whatever and Mr. Hamilton is laughing like hell, like he un-derstands them. And maybe he *does* understand them. He's like a genius almost. Sometimes I try to imagine taking over the business from him, since he doesn't have any kids, but in moments like this I can't picture it. All that joking and talking. Mr. Hamilton just really likes other people, I guess, even ones he's about to screw over. Me, I'd rather be alone—or with Uncle Mitch.

Mr. Hamilton is still laughing when the guy with the gray handlebar mustache asks about the water table. He hasn't spoken the whole day except in Pakistani. Turns out his English is perfect. He says that Horror Worlds require basements, but that those pink brick houses don't have basements, clearly.

Mr. Hamilton glances at me like maybe I showed the handlebar mustache guy inside a house, but I didn't. No, the handlebar mustache guy either did recon in secret or just knows his stuff: in Dallas, cheap subdivision houses tend not to have basements, because of the clay layer.

Mr. Hamilton launches into a speech about the clay layer and how the trees are shrimpy because of it and how, no matter what property they decide to go with for their Horror World, they better come up with an alternative to digging a basement.

The handlebar mustache guy nods. He says that they need to reach out to their investors, that they'll be in touch. The meeting is over.

Out in the car, Mr. Hamilton seems pretty bummed, so I start talking about how we'll get 'em next time and whatnot but Mr. Hamilton tells me to cut the crap. I'm surprised. Usually he lays on crap thicker than anybody. He's positive to an almost manic degree. A self-made man. A Christian. The problem, he explains, is that 26 Seagoville is up for inspection. If it's on the roster, we clean it. Normally, cleaning a property isn't a big deal, but in the case of 26 Seagoville there's runoff from a chicken parts factory, plus ancient tannery juice runoff from way back, and also something kind of sludgy that nobody knows what it is. The sludgy stuff has collected on the clay layer like blue dish-soap on a countertop. If the inspector digs deep enough, Mr. Hamilton tells me, his eyebrows might fall off his face.

At home that night, Uncle Mitch is in the kitchen with a hairnet over his bushy white beard. He's making breakfast for dinner: pancakes, fried eggs, and sweet potato hash browns. Mitch is a wizard in the kitchen and seems to know exactly what I want, and when I'll be home each night. I don't even have to call.

Over dinner, Mitch asks about Claudia, a girl at work. He's kind of obsessed with Claudia. He's always telling me to ask her out and hanging on my every word whenever I mention her, like "Claudia said *what?* Oh no she didn't!" For a while I thought Mitch was pervy but now I think he wants what's best for me. He says Claudia reminds him of someone he used to know. The one that got away, I guess.

I tell Mitch that Claudia is fine.

"That Claudia," he says, "what a special lady."

"Whatever," I say.

"What a grumpy gus you are tonight. Something on your mind?"

I don't want to talk about what's on my mind, but I find it impossible to keep anything from Mitch, who knows me inside-out, so I tell him about the Pakistani guys. How close I was. How I called Mr. Hamilton to do the deal over peach-a-ritas but ended up wasting his time.

"Don't worry about Hamilton," Mitch says. "He'll die soon."

"I don't wanna hear it," I say.

"Of a heart attack."

I don't ask Mitch why he predicts Mr. Hamilton will die of a heart attack. Mitch makes lots of predictions. He has a website, unclemitchsez.com, where he blogs them. Prophecies too. Like how, in the year 2027, fourteen will die on a rollercoaster called the Texecutioner, or how in 2041 the microwave will be revealed to cause 19% of cancers in America and its manufacture prohibited, or how by the year 2050 there will be so many little plastic balls in the ocean, from emulsifying face cream, that predator fish such as tuna will accumulate enough to become poisonous to humans. Plastic emulsifying face cream balls are the new mercury, according to Mitch.

Mitch says he knows all that stuff because he's from the future. For proof he told me I should switch my 401k to a different mutual fund because it was about to go up, and it did go up. Then he told me a big oil spill would happen in the Gulf of Mexico, and it did. Not all of his predictions come true, though. When one doesn't, he says it's because his presence in the past is fucking with the future. He says that's good, though. He says his mission is to fuck with the future in a *good* way.

Now, do I believe Uncle Mitch is from the future? Sometimes yes, sometimes no. Depends on my mood. He says he's related to me, though, and that much I do believe. The family resemblance is undeniable. We have the same big hands and feet, the same sort of oversized tadpole head that hangs forward while we walk. Plus we have lots in common. We like to smoke pot and watch movies, for instance, and eat ice cream. Sometimes we have an ice cream challenge where we race through pints but you lose if you barf.

At work the next day, Mr. Hamilton is on the phone with an EPA guy named Dirk Johnston, who was Mr. Hamilton's frat brother at A&M and owes him a couple hundred favors, according to Mr. Hamilton. Mr. Hamilton is smiling and going down memory lane, conversation wise, meanwhile pacing around the office grabbing random papers, looking at them, then crumpling them into balls and pitching them in wastebaskets. He's fixated on the cleanliness of desktops. He considers the desktop a metaphor for the mind. At Claudia's desk he starts to grab some papers but she gently and insistently pulls them out of his hand until he moves on, catching up Dirk Johnston on a woman they used to know who married a Mormon and has five kids with names like Orem. He says, "I know, right!?" then paces, guffawing, into the conference room.

Claudia used to be the receptionist but now she has the same job as I do. Our desks face each other awkwardly. Hers has all kinds of calendars and photos of her and her cousins and nieces and nephews and a signed photo of Tony Romo with a sleazy grin on his face. Mine has a photo of me and Uncle Mitch at Six Flags.

Claudia asks what I'm working on and I tell her 26 Seagoville, what else? She tells me she might have a tip for me. "I know a guy who wants something big like that," she says, "bigger than anything I got on my roster."

This is unprecedented. Junior agents never exchange tips, so either Claudia is greener than I thought or Uncle Mitch is right: she really does like me. Claudia is Mexican and I never imagined myself with a Mexican girl, but I guess it doesn't matter. Except what if her dad and brothers are real macho and want to test my mettle somehow, by wrestling me, say, or shooting off guns in a ravine? It'll never work. Besides, she's pretty. Too pretty for me. And wholesome! On take your daughter to work day she brought her niece and put the girl's juice in a coffee mug, to be like Mr. Hamilton, and made an overturned cardboard box into a little desk where the girl could do drawings.

For now I thank Claudia and she says no problem, she'll e-mail me the contact. I don't have high hopes. Why should this guy be any different than the Pakistani Horror World guys, or the Yeshiva guys before them, or the Super China Buffet guys before that? Those Super China guys would have done the deal for sure if it weren't for the lacquered drainage hole they had to dig for kitchen grease. One of them did a probe and his probe melted. Mr. Hamilton had to pay him off to keep quiet.

I open the e-mail from Claudia and study the contact attached: Jorge Bergman, President of Book Lovers Inc., LLC, out of Euless. I Google "Book Lovers Inc" but find nothing. "Jorge Bergman" gives me court proceedings from 1994. I can't tell what the case is about, the language is so arcane, but the word "indecency" is prominent. I take a few breaths, put a smile on my face, and dial.

"Jorge Bergman speaking." He pronounces Jorge *Yorge*, like it rhymes with George. "What can I do you for?"

"Well, sir," I say, then introduce myself and enter stage one of my routine about 26 Seagoville Highway, which is the verbal stage.

"I like it, I like it," he says, not even disguising his enthusiasm. "Seagoville, though, it's a bit far. A bit family oriented. In my business, I need to attract a certain city element, if you know what I mean."

I don't, but I explain how, even though the parcel is on the Seagoville Highway, it's closer to Dallas than to Seagoville. "Do you have a computer in front of you?" I ask, hoping he can map it.

"No computers."

"Sure, well, we can meet out there if you want to see it for yourself."

"Can I meet Claudia instead?"

"Um—"

"She isn't returning my calls."

"Huh. Well, I'll ask if she'll come out there with me, but she's pretty busy with her own roster so I don't know if—"

"Busy? She doesn't know the meaning. You and me, we can keep her busy, know what I'm saying?"

I laugh uncomfortably.

"You probably heard of me, kid, but whatever you know, that's the old me. Forget that me. Jorge Bergman is looking to take it up a notch. We're talking big time. The big top. Getting paper like Walt fucking Disney."

"Paper?"

"Stacks. Cream."

We set a time to meet tomorrow and I hang up, confused.

Across the desk, Claudia is watching me expectantly. I thank her again for the tip and ask her if maybe, just maybe, she can come with me to meet Jorge Bergman tomorrow.

"Absolutely not," she says, which I understand completely.

"What line of work is he in?" I ask.

"Adult bookstores."

At home Uncle Mitch is at the kitchen table blogging prophecies. Veggie patties and burger fixings are laid out on the counter, so I slide open the back door and step onto the little cement patio where the Weber is. I fill the charcoal chimney with crumpled newspaper to light some charcoals, then I go back inside.

"Seven will die in Chicago," Mitch says, typing.

"When?"

"A week from today."

"Shouldn't you do something? Call the police or something?"

"Already did. They thought I was a quack."

"You *are* a quack."

Mitch laughs. "You're in a good mood. Finally work up the nerve to ask out Claudia?"

"No, but she did me a favor." I tell him about my conversation with the weird potential client, how I'm going out to 26 Seagoville the next day. I start to tell him about my misgivings but he interrupts: "So you've contacted Jorge Bergman?" He looks up from the computer. His big beard climbs up to his cheekbones and mostly covers his mouth, but I can tell from his eyes that he's smiling. "And so it begins," he says.

"And so *what* begins?"

"Nothing. You'll show him the parcel tomorrow, I presume?"

"I don't know if I want to. He's kind of a sleazebag. He keeps calling Claudia and—"

"After you and Claudia are married, do you think she'll care about a couple dirty phone calls?"

"The phone calls are dirty?"

Mitch closes his eyes and nods. "Disgusting," he whispers. "Shawn, if you don't sell this parcel to Jorge Bergman, it won't ever get sold. The EPA inspection will happen, the parcel will become an albatross, mucked up in lawsuits, and Hamilton Commercial Realty will be bankrupt within two years."

"Okay, okay," I say, to get Mitch off my back. I don't want to tell him that my misgivings go beyond Jorge Bergman; that sometimes I worry Hamilton Commercial Realty and everybody involved in it, me especially, is making the Metroplex kind of shitty. Do we really need another strip mall? Another replicable pod drugstore or chain restaurant? Another shuttered big box store converted into a quasi-postapocalyptic warzone for paintball? Sometimes I think it would be better if we let the weeds and critters do their work. The toxins will go away eventually. Even the blue sludge, it has to go somewhere, or get metabolized by some yet-to-evolve bacteria.

"What's on your mind, grumpy gus?" Mitch asks.

I tell him about the blue sludge.

"Metroplex aesthetics are the least of our worries," he says, then launches into his usual rigmarole about the machine wars and how the extreme heat of modern warfare will liquefy carbon-based life forms, which is why the drones and simulacra will have a distinct advantage against us. He goes into confusing detail on the nature and use of simulacra before concluding, "If Hamilton Realty goes bankrupt, you'll never take over for Mr. Hamilton. You'll—" He hesitates.

"I'll what? What'll happen to me?"

"Nothing. Never mind."

I remind myself that Mitch only *claims* to be from the future. I don't have to believe him. When I first met him, shuffling around Grandma's funeral in his dark coveralls, he told me he was one of Grandpa's brothers from West Texas. That's what he told everybody, and nobody could challenge him since there'd been six or seven brothers, too many to keep track of. It wasn't until Mitch showed up at Grandma and Grandpa's house, the house they left me, the house he and I share now, that he told me the so-called truth. At the time, I laughed, but deep down I think I believed him. I trusted him. He seemed to *know* me. For peace of mind I tried not to think about him being from the future and whatnot; I just thought of him as a really smart guy who thought seriously about the trajectory of human affairs, and it made me feel good to be friends with a person so smart and doing important blogs.

Looking at Mitch, him looking back at me, I get the feeling he knows I'm thinking all this. It's kind of creepy.

Mitch closes my laptop and proposes we "relax a bit," so we eat our veggie burgers then get high and watch *Heavenly Milkman*, where an alien disguised as a milkman rekindles the romance between an estranged husband and wife via carefully forged love notes tucked under the caps of milk bottles. The milk itself contains an aphrodisiac from Betelgeuse.

On the way to 26 Seagoville Highway I prepare myself for the worst, which, to me, is a big fat white guy who blows cigar smoke in my face. No matter how repellent I find Jorge "Yorge" Bergman to be, I have to be able to put myself in his shoes. That's something Mr. Hamilton taught me. When Jorge Bergman said he wanted to "take it up a notch," maybe he meant something like an adult book superstore, like the Barnes and Noble of adult bookstores, with a big parking lot and an outdoor café, and why not? Pornography isn't illegal.

By the time I get to the parcel, fifteen minutes early, a Lexus SUV is parked on the crumbling road meant to serve the imagined residents of the pink brick houses. There's no sign of Bergman, but a man can be heard yelling in the distance. Is somebody with him? Is he on the phone? I hesitate to call out, to interrupt the conversation, so it takes me a while to locate the voice. When I do, I see a man (Bergman?) with a phone at his ear as he peers through the front window of the most dilapidated house in the entire parcel. The second floor of this house is totally missing except for studs, so it looks like a dinosaur walked by and took a big bite out of the top. Not a great start.

When the man sees me he says into the phone, "Sorry, gotta go, I got a guy here," then hangs up and comes at me with his hand out. He's wearing a three-piece suit without the jacket, with a fat red necktie bursting from the vest like a cravat. His hair is so black it's almost purple. He seems friendly, though. We shake. His hand has three jeweled rings on it.

"Jorge Bergman," he says. "You probably heard of me but in case you haven't, I'll tell you what I'm about: adult bookstores. But forget all that."

"Forget what?"

"Exactly. I gotta take it up a notch. This place is dynamite. Now, is it raggedy? Sure. Way far out here? Sure. But for what I got in mind, it can be far as hell. Raggedy too. This place has theme park written all over it."

I'm confused. "Like, an adult theme park?"

"Adult *bookstore* theme park."

"Sounds interesting."

"You bet it is. The working man needs to blow off steam. He needs hobbies. And this, my friend, is the oldest hobby in the book. Everybody has it. Everything *serves* it: TV, movies, stage plays, you name it. A man goes to a strip club, okay, but what does he do after?"

"Go home?"

"Maybe he goes home to do it, maybe he does it in his car, maybe he does it in a gas station parking lot then buys a soda. Either way, and no matter what, he does it. Well, my friend, what if I told you I could give you the tiptop jerkoff experience, and at a place where people come to jerk off from miles around? The Disneyland of jerkoffs?"

"Sounds good."

"Sounds *great*. And I can tell you think so. The real die-hards always have a look like you do, a sort of decent-but-lonely look. No offense. You got a girlfriend?"

"No."

"You live alone?"

I'm getting uncomfortable. I'd tell him no, I live with my uncle, but I never tell people about Mitch. Our relationship is too personal, like a secret part of me, even though Mitch is a person, not a part of me—it's confusing. I mutter something about "my uncle" and Jorge Bergman says family is important. He speaks passionately on the subject of his grandfather, somebody named Jack Rubinstein who I guess I'm supposed to know.

"My dream is my grandfather's dream," he says. "My grandfather was just a Jewish kid from Chicago. He had nothing when he came down here. When he started his first joint, it wasn't much, but it was his. The girls called him pops. They loved him, everybody did. Animals especially. The man had a way with dogs, a way of touching them around the ears and flanks, a sort of secret communication known only to great dog lovers and the dogs themselves. Now he's famous for other reasons, but first and foremost he was a great club man, and a great lover of this city. The people who love Dallas most are the people who come from somewhere else. In Dallas, you can be anything you wanna be." He goes on and on about Dallas while I walk him to the pink brick house I'm supposed to show him. The good one. I'm trying to get back on routine. But Jorge Bergman opens the door without asking and strides into the house.

"Hey," I say feebly.

Now he's standing in the large front room, the so-called "great room." I had to tear out the rotten carpet so the subfloor is exposed, but it's still a pretty nice room. High ceilings, lots of light.

"We'll have live girls down here," he says, "to get the guests fired up, sort of like a strip joint, and upstairs we'll have the animatronics."

I struggle not to frown. I try to stay positive, to channel my inner Mr. Hamilton. At least he isn't dealing in live hookers, right?

"Of course," he says, "for the man with a little extra cash there'll be an extra special room." He winks at me then wipes his lips with the hairy back of his hand.

I can't stand it anymore. "Mr. Bergman—"

"Call me Jorge."

"Jorge, I should tell you something about this place. If you buy it, when you have it inspected, the inspector might—"

"I don't give a shit about the inspector. I'll buy it right now."

"But your customers—"

"I don't give a shit about them either. I mean I love the fuckers, don't get me wrong, but a man who patronizes an adult bookstore theme park feels too guilty to press charges. A shark could pop out of that creek and bite his balls off—worst case, I peel off a couple k and lose a customer."

"But—" I hesitate. I don't know if I have it in me to talk a client *out* of buying a parcel. It isn't right. Think of Mr. Hamilton, I tell myself, and I'm still thinking of him when Jorge Bergman picks up a rock and pitches it at a high window. The window shatters.

"Hey!" I say.

"What? I'm buying this shithole, I can do what I want."

There. He said it. He's going to buy the parcel. I could call Mr. Hamilton and tell him to meet us for lunch at Taco Brothers. But I don't. Jorge Bergman is just too sleazy. His vision, for lack of a better word, is too soulless even for Hamilton Commercial Realty. It stops here. I tell Jorge Bergman that I need to reach out to Mr. Hamilton, that I'll be in touch.

Bergman seems confused. "Call him. I'll wait."

"I'll be in touch," I repeat. The meeting is over.

Bergman turns away in a huff and heads for his Lexus SUV. While I wait, to give Bergman a head start, I look around at the great room. Then I wander through the other empty rooms. The walls have water damage but most of the windows are intact. Except for the second floor, the place is still inhabitable. Uncle Mitch says that when the dollar collapses, empty houses such as this will become prime real estate for squatters, but why wait? Maybe we could throw a blue tarp over the top and lease it on the cheap to a homeless shelter or something. I could pitch the idea to Mr. Hamilton as a way to save money on the low-rent security guard we pay to check the place twice a night.

When I call, Mr. Hamilton picks up the phone so quickly that I know he's been waiting to hear from me. I tell him the bad news. Whatever brief thrill I got from rejecting Jorge Bergman deserts me when I hear Mr. Hamilton sigh deeply, crestfallen. I can almost hear him pinching the bridge of his nose, squinting as though in pain.

"What about Dirk Johnston," I say, "your friend at the EPA?"

Mr. Hamilton explains that Johnston is the backup inspector for the Metroplex region so the only chance of getting Johnston is if the main inspector, a man named Rogelio Gomez, calls in sick that day. Mr. Hamilton pauses, like he wonders if I'm thinking what he's thinking, but I have no idea what he's thinking, and that makes me nervous.

Uncle Mitch is even more distraught than Mr. Hamilton was. He stops blogging prophecies and paces around the kitchen with his head slung forward, muttering. I stir the chili he's been cooking and say, "Maybe Dirk Johnston will come through for us."

"Dirk Johnston isn't the inspector," Mitch says. "Rogelio Gomez is the inspector."

I stop stirring the chili. "How did you know that?"

"You know how I know that."

"But even if you *are* from the future, how do you know a little detail like that?"

"We don't have time for this. We have to stop Claudia from moving to San Antonio."

"Why is Claudia moving to San Antonio?"

"When Hamilton Commercial Realty closes, she takes a job in San Antonio."

"What about me? Do I take another job?"

"Yes."

"Is the pay good?"

"It's the same. It's the exact same fucking job, pretty much."

"Then what's the problem?"

"Claudia! Haven't you been listening? And Mr. Hamilton..." His voice trails off, like he's thinking about what happens to Mr. Hamilton.

"Mitch," I say, "Mr. Hamilton isn't going to do something rash, is he?"

Mitch stops pacing. He looks at me, thinking. His face is familiar but strange. I've seen him every day for two years, but I never look very hard at his face. His wrinkly eyes and big white beard, his wild white eyebrows, make me think about my own future decrepitude. He seems so lively, so young, but his body is so obviously deteriorating. It's kind of gross. I feel bad for thinking that, but maybe it's normal to think that. Maybe it's why people avoid the elderly, why people ghetto them off into old folks homes.

Later that night, after we eat Mitch's chili, after we're good and high and watching an erotic thriller called *Taxi Dancers*, Mitch starts muttering about his beard. He says how it was "weakness" that made him "don the beard."

"Okay, okay," I say. I'm trying to watch the movie.

"Weakness," he repeats, "human weakness."

"You're way high right now."

Later, when the credits roll, Uncle Mitch stands up and turns off the TV. He comes back to me and puts a hand on my shoulder, leaning on it, still wobbly from the pot. I feel wobbly too. His hand tingles on my shoulder. I imagine energy shooting from the hand into my blood—the blood we share—and warming it.

"Don't quit your job," Mitch says.

"Yeah," I say. "Yeah. You're right."

"Don't quit your job," he repeats, "until you've got something else lined up. I'll think of something. I have to think." His eyes close. His head tips forward.

I take his hand from my shoulder and stand up. I mean to walk him to the guest bedroom, where he sleeps, but we're so similar in height that I don't know whether to wrap my arm around his shoulders or his waist. I opt for the latter. As we walk, I can feel Mitch's ribs under thin layers of shirt and skin, and I wonder when my own body will begin to make that change.

In the days leading up to the inspection, I keep a close eye on Mr. Hamilton. I find out from his assistant, Nancy, when exactly the inspection is happening, and I ask Mr. Hamilton if I can handle it alone. He says no way. He has to be there "to get the details straight," he says, which sounds like bullshit to me. He tells me I could skip it, but I insist on being there too. "It's on my roster," I say, which may sound like bullshit to *him*. It's a like a game between us.

On the day of the inspection we drive out to 26 Seagoville in Mr. Hamilton's truck. He puts on talk radio and whenever there's a break in the talking he flips the stations until he hears somebody else talking. Maybe he has to hear voices to take his mind off his own voice, in his head.

We get there half an hour early so we putter around pulling weeds away from doors, sweeping broken glass into a heavy-duty trash bags, etc. None of that stuff matters, though. It's just to have something to do, to have the illusion of control.

A little pickup truck rolls onto the driveway, parks, and out steps Rogelio Gomez. He's small, wearing khakis and a short-sleeved dress shirt. Before he greets us, he opens his briefcase on the hood of the truck and removes a clipboard.

Mr. Hamilton goes toward him, me following, and greets him with his usual bluster. He starts telling Rogelio Gomez what a mess the parcel is, how he's sorry ever to have taken it on and will probably die with it. He laughs, like this is a joke, so I laugh too, to amplify the joke, but Rogelio Gomez doesn't get the joke or doesn't care. He says, "Let's start with the creek."

Mr. Hamilton leads Rogelio Gomez through the tall grass down to the creek, and I watch from a distance as Mr. Hamilton stands there arms akimbo while Rogelio Gomez takes water samples in a prissy little test tubes, and it occurs to me, watching them, how far away we are from civilization. If someone screamed, would anybody hear?

Gomez takes some soil samples and puts them in baggies, then we march back through the grass to the pink brick houses. Mr. Hamilton tries to lead him into the usual house but Gomez strides defiantly toward a different house, and Mr. Hamilton seems so flustered by this that I wonder if he rigged up a beam to collapse. It's possible. He's handy, and the parcel is indemnified against accidents. But maybe he's just nervous. He hates to be off script.

Next to me, Mr. Hamilton digs his foot in the dirt while Gomez uses a pen to chisel a tiny strip of white paint off the door. Then Gomez collects some dust from a windowsill and puts it in a dime bag. Then he collects a soil sample from an overgrown flower bed. Then he takes a big green leaf. He never looks at us.

Mr. Hamilton watches all this, his smile bending out of shape.

I shouldn't be worried, I tell myself. Uncle Mitch never said anything about Mr. Hamilton doing anything crazy. But Mitch has gotten things wrong. Things are changing. He's fucking with the future. Plus, Mr. Hamilton keeps glancing at me, and I can't tell if the glances are conspiratorial or just plain weird. His smile has exhausted itself into something wretched, almost menacing, like the death grimace of a craven animal ready to lash out with one last desperate strike.

Eventually Rogelio Gomez goes back to his truck to get a probe, and we lead him to a spot where the infill makes the soil softer so it'll be easier to dig. For once, Gomez thanks us. But this is the same spot where the Super China guy found blue sludge, so I know Mr. Hamilton is shitting bricks. I check his hands—they're balled into fists. He's so much bigger than Gomez that he could grab the probe and use it to skewer the guy, leave him piked there as a warning to all other inspectors. Then what would I do? Call the police? Of course not, but keeping silent would make me an accessory to murder, or attempted murder, or aggravated assault at the very least. Does a person do time for accessory to aggravated assault?

Rogelio Gomez sets up a machine that'll drill the long metal probe into the soil, and he wipes the tip of the metal tube with some kind of oil. Beside me, Mr. Hamilton is breathing heavy. When Gomez starts threading the tube into the machine, I glance at Hamilton. His face is red. Is he having a heart attack? Is that what Uncle Mitch predicted? I scoot closer so I can ask discreetly if he's okay, but there's a *bong!* and a scream and Mr. Hamilton's eyes get big and I turn just in time to see Rogelio Gomez fall forward like a bag of potatoes. There's blood. An old man disappears behind the nearest pink brick house. A vagrant? A thug? Did Mr. Hamilton pay a thug to do his dirty work?

"Shawn?" Mr. Hamilton says.

"Yeah," I say, but I'm sort of behind Mr. Hamilton so maybe he can't hear me. He staggers forward hollering "Shawn! Shawn!"

I follow him, trying not to look back at Rogelio Gomez, who's groaning on the ground and clutching his bloody head.

We're running now. The old man is far ahead of us. He's wearing coveralls. Mr. Hamilton keeps yelling "Shawn!" and I keep yelling I'm right behind him but he ignores me; it's more like he's yelling "Shawn!" at the old man, which makes no sense. I struggle to keep up. Mr. Hamilton is fast for such a big guy, way faster than the old man, whose coveralls start to look familiar, like Uncle Mitch's coveralls, the ones he wore to Grandma's funeral: top-of-the-line coveralls from the future, he said, with stain-resistant nanosilver. I'm confused. Even when Mr. Hamilton catches the old man by the collar of the coveralls and spins him around, it takes me a moment to understand what's happening. That's because the beard is gone. It's Uncle Mitch, but it isn't.

It's me.

"Shawn," Mr. Hamilton says to Mitch, "what have you done? What is this ridiculous makeup?"

"Never mind that now," Mitch says. "Call nine-one-one. Tell them a vagrant squatter popped out of the house and attacked him."

"But what about you?" Hamilton asks.

"I'm here," I say behind him.

Mr. Hamilton turns, and his face bears an expression of such surprise that he looks almost tranquil, like his brain just short-circuited.

"We're twins," Mitch lies. "I have a pituitary gland disease. I'm too embarrassed to leave the house, which is why you've never met me. No one has. If pressed, Shawn says I'm his uncle. There's a photo of us on his desk. At Six Flags."

Mr. Hamilton releases Mitch, as though revolted. Maybe he's revolted by the pituitary disease, or maybe—and this is what Mitch would say—by the uncanny doubling, what Mitch calls "the doppelganger effect," common in Teutonic culture, in which a sinister double presages death.

"I'm sorry," Mr. Hamilton says, looking first at Mitch, then at me. "I don't know what to say."

What Mr. Hamilton says, to the police and to everybody else who asks, is that a vagrant came out of nowhere and attacked Rogelio Gomez. Gomez confirms it. His skull isn't even fractured. That's because Mitch knows just how hard to bonk people on the head to draw blood and scare them without seriously hurting them. In the future people learn to use violence as a tool, he explains, what with the marauders and whatnot.

The police records confirm aggressive vagrant activity on the parcel, so everything is pretty tidy. The inspection is postponed two weeks, and Mr. Hamilton tells me Dirk Johnston will probably step in, to spare Rogelio Gomez the trauma of returning to the scene of the attack. But I don't want to risk pinning the company's future to Dirk Johnston.

I tell Claudia she needs to call Jorge Bergman. If he hears from her, I explain, he might still do the deal, and if she's going to move up, she has to get used to dealing with sleazebags. "Better a few sleazebags than a machine war," I say. "Better a few soulless chain restaurants than a post-nuclear wasteland."

"That seems like a false dichotomy," Claudia says.

"All I'm saying is we have better things to worry about than an adult bookstore theme park." I'm lying, of course. I worry all the time about sleazy crap like adult bookstore theme parks, crap whose spread I've facilitated. But I don't think Claudia worries. Claudia seems like a goal-oriented person. A self-made person. If only Mr. Hamilton had detected, years ago, that Claudia was more like him than I was.

"When you meet him, try to think of it as a game," I say, "or a test of your mettle." It's advice Mr. Hamilton used to give me, with mixed results.

As I predict, Claudia closes the deal with Jorge Bergman. Mr. Hamilton throws a party to celebrate. After the party, I tell him I'm quitting. He isn't surprised but he's sad. I tell him he's sad because he likes me, not because I'm a good commercial real estate agent, and I tell him we can still have peach-a-ritas whenever he wants. "As long as you're paying," I add, which, as a joke, is pure Hamilton, so he laughs like hell and slaps my back.

Mr. Hamilton may have taken the news okay, but Uncle Mitch doesn't.

"What the fuck?" he says. He's madder than I've ever seen him, which would be scary, considering I just saw him beat a man with a pipe, if I didn't know that Mitch, like me, tends toward sullen anger. He shakes his head and mutters about how this isn't supposed to be what happened. "If you don't become boss, how will you get Claudia?"

I try to tell him one doesn't "get" another person, like a prize, but he stops talking to me. He writes on a notepad that he won't speak again until I ask her out.

I shrug and resume cleaning kale. It's the first of the season, from a bed Mitch planted after he tore out Grandma's ornamentals. Mitch says kale and other crucifers are key to a long and healthy life.

I don't know if I'll ever get Claudia in the larger sense of Mitch's parlance, but I do get her to go out with me. She sees me putting my desk stuff into boxes and says, "I can't believe it. I just can't believe it. What will you do?"

"Who knows what the future holds," I say, "but maybe we can hang out sometime, you know, outside of work?"

She says she'd like that.

For our first date we have lunch at a chain restaurant called Topsy's with one of her nieces, who got into trouble at school for putting gum in another girl's hair. The niece just sits there disconsolately twirling her milkshake straw while Claudia tells me that Mr. Hamilton told her that Jorge Bergman, who's breaking ground as we speak, almost certainly bribed Dirk Johnston.

The presence of the niece is kind of weird to me, but the date goes well. Later, Mitch tells me that the niece was a good sign, that Claudia must consider me a potential role model for young people.

"Why?" I ask.

"Deckle knows," Mitch says.

"Who's Deckle?"

"Roger Deckle is a guru who rises to prominence during the first machine war. In the future, diminution will be regarded as a sign of wisdom, and Roger Deckle is the size of a juvenile chimpanzee."

Uncle Mitch has gotten looser lipped about the future. He says he misses it, but that he isn't going back, though he does plan to move out of the house after Claudia moves in, to give us some privacy. I try to tell him we haven't even been on our second date yet but he won't hear it. He says he's going down to Austin for a prophecy conference. He fixed up his website. Now there's a photo of us two together with our hair done exactly the same. It's eerie. Under the photo it says, *"The two me's,"* then: *"As we journey into the future together, Shawn and Shawn, one (left) for the first time and the other (right/me) for the second, we take solace in the knowledge that the future is correctable and the world, perhaps, not completely degenerate."*

But Uncle Mitch never comes back from Austin. The most likely explanation is that he got in a car crash, since he hadn't driven for years, but maybe—and this is what I hope—he fucked with the future to such a degree that he, we, no longer felt the need to go back in time, either because we fixed the future or, more likely, because we fixed our own life. I like to imagine Mitch on a porch somewhere with Claudia or whoever I end up with, maybe a few kids or grandkids, braving the noxious vapors for the sake of the cool night air and a few noxious-vapor-proof lighting bugs.

As I continue on my journey toward becoming Uncle Mitch, it occurs to me I'll be a different Mitch. Less restless, maybe, but less dynamic too. Not the type of person to go back in time and hatch a scheme to change the future. Sometimes it makes me sad to think I won't become that person. I admired him. Which gives me hope that one day I'll admire myself.

THE MILKMAN

If you're expecting a motivational book for customer service professionals, I'm sorry. To write a seventh such book was my intention. My sixth, *Positive Thinking in Retail and Beyond*, won an award from Business Book Review Online and was translated into Spanish. On its heels I flew all over Texas and New Mexico giving motivational talks based on the breakthrough service precepts I'd formulated, and soon I could afford the luxury home of my dreams, with a swimming pool, a wraparound porch, and a bedroom for each of my sons, who live with me summers and either Christmas break or both Thanksgiving and spring breaks, depending on the year. My dream house had lots of things I wanted back then, like built-in shoe cubbies and one of those fireplaces you can see from both sides. And also, a milkman.

It was a Tuesday evening in June when my new neighbors rang the doorbell to tell me the milkman was coming the next morning, so I should wake up early to meet him.

"I'm afraid I buy my milk at the store," I told them.

"Not anymore," they said.

I invited them in for a drink, but they said something about adjusting their milk order and withdrew into the darkness.

Sure enough, the doorbell rang at five the next morning.

Startled, I slid on my robe and house shoes, hoping the children hadn't been woken. Their mother had dropped them off the week before (two days late, of course) and I wanted their acclimation to the new house to go as smoothly as possible.

I hurried the considerable distance to the front door and opened it to find, in the harsh yellow porch light, a skinny young man in a crisp white button-down shirt and dark jeans. He had bushy sideburns and a white hat like an envelope.

He smiled. "Good morning, sir."

"Good morning," I said, charmed.

"My name's Cliff and I'm a purveyor of milk. Would you care to discuss a milk plan?" He fished through a leather satchel at his side. "I have several options, all of which can be tailored to your family's needs."

Though I knew immediately I wanted Cliff's milk, I hoped to hear his spiel for professional reasons, so I rubbed my chin and tried to look thoughtful. "Hmm," I said, "I usually buy my milk at the grocery store—"

"Please." He closed his eyes and moved his mouth strangely, as though struggling not to grimace. "Store milk is full of hormones, steroids and genetic poisons. It wastes plastic and abuses our animal neighbors, whose milk, which they're willing to *give* to us, is among life's few true blessings."

The sell was a bit hard for my taste, but Cliff's passion was obvious. "How much will it cost?" I asked coolly.

"A lot less than what you pay now."

And so that morning over the kitchen table, Cliff spent half an hour laying out different milk plans for my family. There was the matter of quantity, of course, but also of variety. There were different fat contents (whole, two percent, etc.) and different blends of these, as well as different salt and sugar levels. I asked if the milk was rated—Grade A, Grade B, something like that. Cliff said only pasteurized milk was rated, but that he recommended raw milk, whose health benefits were compromised in the pasteurization process. The FDA, he explained, had been hoodwinked by the milk lobby, which went out of its way to protect the interests of giant industrial dairies. He gave me test-tube-sized samples from a cooler. I was impressed.

Soon the boys emerged from their bedrooms and began to drift in and out of the kitchen, and Cliff retreated to a corner by the pantry. From there, he observed their milk consumption with the studied eye of a true service professional. He jotted notes in a small memo pad after Hunter, seven but small for his age, put his cereal bowl in the sink and carefully overturned it, sloshing milk down the drain.

"Don't waste milk," I chastized Hunter.

Hunter looked at me, confused. I'd never told my children not to waste milk, which I thought of as a nearly bottomless resource, like water.

After Hunter left to watch TV, Cliff offered me a tip: "Give them sugary cereal to sweeten the milk. No child can resist the taste of sweet milk." He said this as if it were one word: *sweetmilk*.

Our morning together was full of useful tips like that, and I marveled at Cliff's commitment to his job. Clearly he believed I needed his product. In my experience, that type of sincerity cannot be taught. I marveled again when Cliff calculated our weekly milk payment to be a mere five dollars and twenty cents.

Over the next few weeks, my boys and I would put our three jars on the porch Tuesday evening and, by the time we rose Wednesday morning, two of the jars would be full and one would be three-fifths full. Three-fifths! I don't drink much milk, but my boys assured me that Cliff's was exceptional: creamy, flavorful, and white as Elmer's glue.

The quality of Cliff's service made a strong impression on me. In my books I often point out what's wrong with customer service, as well as with human interaction in general, but rarely am I confronted so blatantly with what's *right*. I began mentioning Cliff in my talks. At first, audiences were baffled. Few were old enough to remember milkmen, and those who did remembered surly men bundled against the dawn with cigarettes dangling from their lips. But after the initial confusion, audiences were thrilled to hear of someone performing a seemingly mundane job with such aplomb.

One Wednesday a few weeks into our milk plan, I woke to find Dan, the earliest riser of my kids, on the porch with Cliff. Each sat in an Adirondack chair with his legs crossed, Dan with a tall glass of milk and Cliff with his notepad and a pen. Their conversation wove through moments of solemnity and bright bursts of laughter. Dan, who had grown taciturn with adolescence, slapped his thigh several times.

When Dan returned to the kitchen with our full jars of milk, I asked him what he and Cliff had been talking about so animatedly.

"Milk flavor," Dan said.

"Milk flavor?"

"Cliff says different milks taste different sometimes."

"Did he explain why?"

"What the cows eat and what kind of cows they are."

I shook my head, incredulous. Would Cliff ever tire of delivering quality customer service?

*

One week the milk tasted kind of weird. I told Dan to write Cliff a note explaining that we preferred the milk we had before; that regular old milk was just fine by us, though we appreciated Cliff's effort at fine-tuning our milk order. Dan wrote the note and we left it under an empty bottle the following Tuesday.

The next morning we found, under one of the full bottles, a page of notebook paper covered front and back with Cliff's tiny cursive script. In the note, Cliff apologized for "*getting showy*" with his milk choices and placing "*creativity over quality.*" He explained that he was giving the cows special homeopathic medicine to make them stronger and their milk more healthy for kids, but that he hadn't yet gotten the formula quite right. Then, in a reflective turn of striking rhetorical power, he blamed his own scrawny build and yellowish teeth on poor quality milk: "*milk drawn from cows treated as slaves, left to wallow in their considerable filth.*"

At last I began to understand Cliff's commitment to his craft, and I added this fold to my talks: if each of us can find something personal in his or her work, I explained, then he or she will perform that work with much more care. This resonated with my audience, many of whom were in customer service out of a deep desire to connect with other people. Many of them, like Cliff, were in sales. I told them that if they believed in the products they sold then the *selling* would take care of itself. The same idea applied to me and my books!

Soon Cliff was the most popular part of my talks. Audiences clapped at the very mention of his name. When, after a talk I gave in Round Rock, a blurb appeared in the *Austin American Statesman*, I decided to tell Cliff just how popular he'd become. With luck, it might cause him to tell me more about himself.

That Wednesday morning I waited on the porch until Cliff walked up with his crate of bottles. He shook my hand, and I told him how his work was inspiring others. He seemed confused. "They want to be milkmen?"

"They want to be the best they can be!" I said, laughing.

Cliff looked at me with a mixture of curiosity and burning introspection. "Am *I* the best I can be?"

"Of course," I said, a little startled by the question. "I can't imagine a better milkman. Can you?"

"I reckon I can."

Cliff proceeded to tell the lengthy, somewhat troubling story of his great uncle Josef, born in a particularly impoverished corner of the Texas Hill Country to immigrant Czech ranchers, Cliff's great grandparents. "They thought he was a mongoloid," Cliff said. The word made me wince, but Cliff didn't notice. He described Josef as a sort of malformed bumpkin, mute and walleyed. "Had a withered little right hand," Cliff said, raising his own hand to his shoulder in an awkward fist, "sort of hard, like a nutcracker. He lived in the barn with the cows and pigs, milking them constantly."

"Milking the pigs?"

"I think so."

I tried to picture this.

"No one understood how he got so much milk out of the animals," Cliff said. "They bought some goats and he milked them too."

"With the withered hand?"

"Possibly, but nobody had the guts to go in the barn—Josef was real territorial. Anyhow there was more milk than his folks knew what to do with, so they dressed him up in white and sent him 'round town selling it. That was common in the old world, but in Texas most families had their own cows, or at least a goat or two. The country people laughed at Josef, but he kept thrusting his jars of milk at them, confused, and my daddy says when Josef got confused his face went slack in a way that could be pretty scary." Cliff paused, as though conjuring memories of the face and his father's words. "Some people tried his milk, out of pity or fear or just to make him go away, and boy were they glad they did. Josef's milk was sweet, fragrant, and white as the belly of a fish. People saved their coins to pay him for more, and soon he had a delivery service. Some people even gave him their own animals, wanting him to milk his beautiful milk from them and thereby put the cows and goats to a use worthy of the lives God gave them. His folks had to build a bigger barn." Cliff shook his head. "Well, I should get back to work."

I tried to say wait, don't go, but the story had amazed me. Overlaid on Cliff's thin body, as he slouched toward his dirty white van, I saw the specter of this earlier milkman, Josef, whom I imagined with a broad Bohemian mustache. Finally I mustered a hoarse "Cliff!"

Cliff stopped and turned around.

"What happened to him?" I asked. "To Josef?"

Cliff shrugged. "He heard some cows go through town on a train, and when somebody told him they were on their way to a slaughterhouse in Fort Worth, he hanged himself."

The questions that had been gathering in my mind—if Josef was Cliff's inspiration, if Cliff studied his great uncle's methods—vanished into the dark fact of suicide.

Over the next few months I tried to write my seventh book, to be called *Milkman Power!* or, perhaps more elegantly, *Lessons from a Milkman*. I tried to compartmentalize what made Cliff so effective into short chapters with inspirational titles like "Be Passionate About What You Do" and "Stickle For Service," but the whole enterprise was haunted by Josef and his untimely death. It was impossible not to imagine Josef as an enterprising young man like Cliff, and why would Cliff, master of his tiny corner of the retail industry, ever kill himself? And yet there was an inscrutable quality in Cliff, a distracted look that suggested a cryptic inner world. It was this quality that made Cliff special, but also somewhat frightening. Was it genius? If so, how could I communicate that to my readers? Should I scrap the book and write, simply, "Be a genius"?

Wrestling with such questions, my prose grew strange. Gone were the aphorisms and frequent exclamations. In their place, a serpentine quality crept into my sentences, as if all of them skirted a dark, unnameable core. To read them, I was sure, would be a joyless, even harrowing experience.

I had been up all night working on a concluding chapter that would at least gloss the element of Cliff's personality that exceeded my understanding, when I heard footsteps on the porch. I wondered if it could possibly be Wednesday morning already. Had I lost track of the days and nights?

I hurried to the door and saw Cliff hunched over three full bottles and framed by the dim blue light of dawn.

"I'm putting you in my new book," I blurted.

Cliff noticed me and said, "I'm marginally increasing your milk order because Hunter is growing so fast."

"Thanks. Great. Listen, the book isn't quite right. I want to"—the truth is I had no idea what I wanted to do, but a thought came to me in a confused flash—"to see where you do it. Your business. I need to see you inside your business."

Cliff gathered the empty bottles without looking at me.

"Didn't you hear me?" I asked with a mixture of petulance and mild panic. "I'm an author. Don't you know what I can do for your business?"

Cliff looked at me intensely. I noticed that he'd rolled up his sleeves, maybe because of the heat. This, the first ever compromise in his otherwise flawless uniform, revealed dark tattoos that twisted along his veiny forearms. In the swirling blacks and greens were what looked like sets of eyes—animal eyes.

The screen door opened and closed with a clap.

"Dad?" It was Zach, my middle son. "We're out of cereal."

"Go back inside," I said.

"But what am I supposed to eat? I'm calling Mom."

I bristled at this but didn't reply. I didn't want to show weakness in front of Cliff.

"Zach," Cliff said, "your dad has a lot on his mind right now. He's finishing a new book, and that's what puts food on your table."

Zach froze, clearly startled to hear Cliff speak of anything but milk. By now, Hunter had pressed his face to the screen door and was watching. Finally Zach nodded. "I guess you're right," he said. "Sorry, Dad."

I put my arm around Zach's shoulders before he retreated into the house.

"There are granola bars in the pantry!" I shouted after him. I didn't know if there were granola bars, but I didn't want Cliff to think I was the sort of parent who got so wrapped up in his own work that he failed to "put food on the table," as Cliff put it.

"Ever crushed up a granola bar and poured milk on it?" Cliff asked.

I shook my head.

"It's good. Like regular granola, almost."

"I'm sure the pantry is stocked," I said, but Cliff had already started for his van.

When I followed him onto the driveway, Cliff stopped. His neck stiffened in a way that made the word *hackle* flash in my mind. Even though his back was to me, Cliff seemed to know where I was standing, and after a moment of tense silence he continued on his way.

I avoided Cliff for a few weeks after that, which was as simple as staying in my bedroom on Wednesday mornings, but his words haunted me, as did the dark swirls of animals on his forearms. Cliff's was a past, a history, I could not begin to comprehend.

I scrapped the insipid final chapter and considered sending my publisher the other chapters. I had written six full-length books, so couldn't I get away with one short one, even at full price? But I imagined the shame I would feel before Cliff's rigid countenance as I handed him a signed copy of the half-assed case study he had inspired. It would make me a hypocrite, I decided, to provide such poor service to the service professionals who made up my readership. No, I would finish my book the right way.

Following Cliff wouldn't be easy. Early in the morning, when he made his rounds, there were so few cars on the highways and country roads that Cliff would have noticed me immediately. I had to use my bicycle. With luck, the milk deliveries would slow Cliff down so I could follow him. And with the help of binoculars I might maintain such a distance that, if he did notice me, he'd mistake me for a spindly tree.

On a Wednesday morning in late August, the first Wednesday after my kids left for their mother's house in Dallas, I woke up well before dawn, put on the dark spandex riding gear I'd purchased for this foolhardy endeavor, and waited by the side of the house with my bicycle. Cliff's van pulled into the driveway, and after he replaced our milk bottles, I followed him back to the road.

The cool morning air was invigorating. I trailed Cliff up and down hills, and along the edges of rocky uplifts. I was feeling a little proud of my endurance when I realized I had been concentrating so hard on Cliff that I'd lost track of where I was. I pulled out my phone to map my location, but the phone wasn't getting any signal. I was lost. So when Cliff disappeared beyond an unfamiliar hill, I panicked. I pedaled as fast as I could to crest the hill quickly, but Cliff wasn't on the other side. I crested another and another until at last I saw the van's red taillights peering at me through the dust.

My heart was beating so hard that the taillights wiggled, as if taunting me. I hesitated to follow them, but it was too late to turn back.

From the position of the sun I knew we were headed northwest. The trees got shorter and less frequent, the landscape flattened, and the dirt grew red and cracked. To my left I fancied I saw, gray with distance, the glittering dome of the granite uplift known as Enchanted Rock. At least I hoped it was Enchanted Rock. Enchanted Rock meant I was somewhere on a map and not lost in a maze of Cliff's secret world and my own confused intention.

Cliff turned onto a dirt road lined with gnarled posts and lazily strung barbed wire, and the cloud of red dust the van kicked up made him easy to follow. Two buildings rose in the distance. The larger of the two was white and had an arched roof like a barn. The other, across a patch of dirt from the first, was long and yellow. I stopped behind a tree and watched through my binoculars as Cliff parked his van and went straight into the yellow building, which turned out to be a trailer propped on its hitch.

After waiting long enough to be convinced he wasn't coming out again, I hefted the bicycle onto my shoulder and approached the barn in a wide arc that kept a patch of mesquite trees and sagebrush between me and Cliff's trailer. The sun was higher now and toasted my back. By the time I reached the barn, my fancy black riding gear clung with sweat to my skin. I squirted the last of my water into my mouth, and wished I'd brought food.

I hid my bike halfheartedly behind a tall bush and crept toward the barn. The side of the white barn had been mended in several places and painted over with jagged brushstrokes. The planks were buckling, and through them I was assaulted by an awful smell, more repulsive and yet sweeter somehow than the smell I associated with cows and barnyards. Maybe it was goats, I thought, or maybe—and this made my insides bubble with nausea—Cliff allowed his animals to wallow in their filth.

On the other side of the barn a big door hung from tracks. It wasn't locked, so I gripped the splintered edge of the door and pulled. The wheels over the door squeaked loudly, and from inside the barn there erupted a strange cacophony of rattles, hisses and chirps. I imagined birds hanging in wire cages from the ceiling, weird sentries for the cows and goats. I took a deep breath and slid sideways through the dark crack between the door and wall.

By dim light from high windows on either end of the barn I could make out cages along each wall. I held my breath to avoid smelling and tasting the air, but it stung my eyes. The hissing and chirping and screech-ing got so loud that all I could think of was inmates in a prison (or a prison movie—I'd never been inside an actual prison). Gradually the din subsided, and I allowed myself a gulp of air. The smell was so total that I can't describe it as foul, any more than a man who steps into a burning building would describe the roomfuls of flame as hot. My eyes adjusted to the darkness and I saw that the cages, stacked two and three high, contained not birds but small, furry creatures. The barn had no stalls for goats or cows. For a moment I wondered if Cliff's dairy business was a front for a mink or ermine farm. Then I saw the harnesses.

In the center of the barn, on a table built around a thick central post like the mainmast of a ship, were little metal armatures shaped like spinal columns. Each was attached to the post, and from each hung tiny straps with shiny metal buckles. Here and there on the table were small, elaborately molded cuplike devices made of plastic. Each of these was connected by flexible hose to one of several translucent vats beneath the table, one of which was half full of viscous white liquid. When it occurred to me what this liquid was, I started gagging again and again, and the dense, putrid air overwhelmed me. I spun in search of the door—the tall sliver of light and fresh air through which I had entered—but the light was gone. The door had been closed. I ran to it, which caused the animals to screech and rattle their cages, and I tried to slide open the door again but couldn't. Then the door lit up orange around a silhouette of my body.

"Hello, sir."

I turned to see Cliff standing in the center of the barn beneath a hanging light bulb ensconced in wire. He was wearing a black t-shirt with a skull and the name of a rock band on it. "Welcome to my menagerie," he said.

Dizzy and nauseated, I couldn't think of anything to say, so I said I was sorry.

"For lots of reasons, I'm sure." Cliff glanced from side to side at his animals, who were calmed as though his eyes had mesmeric power. Now I saw that there were many different types: raccoons, squirrels, prairie dogs, and, in the furthest corners, the pink whipcord tails of a few dark rats. There were other animals too. Vermin I didn't recognize.

"I came for my book," I said, as if the book, unlike my person, were above reproach.

"Want a book? Here's a book." Cliff took something from a shelf by the cages and tossed it into the dirt at my feet. I knelt to see a notebook with a marbled black and white cover, the type found in schoolrooms. Without speaking, I lifted the notebook into the dim light and opened it. On the first page was written, in Cliff's unmistakable tiny cursive, "*But I had no money for food, let alone fine undergarments, and survived as it were on rabbits and other critters I shot and shucked on the cruel red hills, though even the animals were learning to avoid my demesne, as the hunters of Cornwall feared the forests of Morrois where Tristan lurked, bloodthirsty, waiting for his secret lover to emerge. I have not yet dined upon any of my milk animals but know it will come to that soon.*

Wasn't it the poet Mácha who wrote—"

I closed the book instinctively. The lowest part of my brain must have recognized the threat of madness in the desperate words.

"I've been translating it," Cliff said. A queer smile raised his sallow cheeks. "Josef's journal."

"Josef wrote this? I thought—"

"He was a mongoloid?"

I considered telling Cliff that *mongoloid* was not an acceptable term nowadays, but instead I kept silent. I was sick of my own voice, always explaining things, boiling things down to their simplest components. Why did I try so hard to cram Cliff and Josef into my book when they so clearly exceeded my understanding of human enterprise?

"I guess you don't want my milk anymore, huh?" Cliff asked.

"It's vermin milk," I said.

"Don't vermin feed their young?"

I admitted that yes, they probably did feed their young.

"And don't your kids like it better?"

I knew they did, but I hesitated to admit it.

"Do you even *know* what they like?" Cliff asked bitterly. "You write about service and how to manipulate people by smiling and doing what they want, but you don't even know what your own kids want. I'm doing you a favor. I'm giving you something to share with them. Something that's good."

I looked at the animals, who stared at us through shiny nighttime eyes. I wanted to say no. No way in hell. The thought that the milk my boys spooned into their mouths came from somewhere near the bases of long, pink rat tails revolted me. But I knew that my revulsion was irrational, even bourgeois. After all, were vermin any further from us biologically than cows and goats?

"Please?" Cliff asked softly, as if he'd taken my silence as a rejection of his earlier, more forceful approach. He was changing tactics. He was a salesman, I reminded myself.

"I don't have many kids on my route," he said. "Mostly it's retirees. They think it's cute to have a milkman." He crossed his tattooed forearms. "I know my milk is unconventional, but it's fine, fine milk. The taste changes because I tinker with it, I make it better. You'll thank me. I know you will."

I told him he'd already given me plenty to be thankful for, whether or not my book ever got finished, and that I'd continue to take his milk.

"That's not what I mean," he said. "You'll thank me for something else. Something better."

I had no idea what he was talking about. I decided I should go, in case he was coming unhinged.

Cliff gave me directions (it turned out I was less than ten miles from home), we shook hands, and I left. All of it was strangely cordial, as if each of us had tacitly admitted to the other that, despite his ideals, he was a low creature driven by vanity.

As I pedaled along the edge of the highway, filled now with cars on their way to Austin or San Antonio, I wondered if the people inside them were any different than Cliff and I, and if any of us, from my readers to my boys to my ex-wife in Dallas, were far removed from the vermin in Cliff's cages.

When I got home I leaned my bike against the wall in the garage, took a bottle of water from the beverage refrigerator, and walked into the cool, clean house.

Inside, I was startled to hear the clinking of spoons. I walked down the hallway to the kitchen, where I found my three sons hunched over cereal bowls, slurping and chomping. The breakfast table was crowded with cereal boxes, the wax paper bags poking raggedly from their open tops.

"What are you doing here?" I asked.

Dan, the oldest, pulled the spoon from his mouth. "I drove."

I was shocked. Dan had a learner's permit, but it was a three-hour drive. "Does your mother know?"

Dan shrugged and returned to his cereal.

Zach said, "Mom doesn't have good milk."

I admit it was with some satisfaction that I pictured their mother, my ex-wife, coming home from work to find her house empty, just as I came home nine months of the year to television and a blank computer screen and the mindless squawk of crows. But it was wrong. She'd be worried. I was about to say something when little Hunter glared at me from over his cereal bowl. The stern look on his face startled me. I wondered what thoughts in his six-year-old head could have hardened it so. I wanted to scold him, but for what?

Still peering at me, Hunter raised the bowl to his lips and slurped the last of his milk, sweetened irresistibly by sugary cereal.

THE MASK OF CAJOLO

Liz stared out the train window, trying to remain calm. It wouldn't help if she acted hostile toward Mick Herman. She just wanted an explanation, maybe some advice. She tried to concentrate on the dull scenery gliding past: the stations, the parking lots, the sprawling strip malls and apartment complexes. On a map there were all these distinct little cities, but in person they looked like puzzle pieces poured onto a table and spread around.

It was going to be a long day. After the train ride from Covina to Union Station, Liz would have to take a bus from Union Station to Studio City, and then, in Studio City, which was about as pedestrian-friendly as the surface of Venus, flag down cab after cab until she found a driver willing to venture ten miles into the Hollywood Hills with no promise of a return fare. Not that the driver would *need* a return fare. The one-way fare would be fifty or sixty dollars, Liz guessed. It was money she didn't have, and time she didn't have (the trip out would take two hours; the trip back, who knew how long), but Liz had no choice. She was desperate.

Mick Herman's notes on the fourth draft of their latest script, a splatter-horror feature called *Hex*, had taken Liz and her writing partner half a year to complete. But then, after reading draft five, Mick Herman dropped them without a word. Liz called him and left what she thought was an evenhanded voicemail, thanking him for his time and asking politely why he left the project, but Mick Herman didn't call her back. So in her next voicemail, Liz tried to sound available: "I sure would love a chance to meet you face to face. In person, I can be *very* convincing," etc. She'd heard that some of these Hollywood people were total sex zombies who would ask a near stranger, after a few minutes of conversation, "Wanna go home and fuck?" Plus, Mick Herman's movies featured so much sexual sadism that Mick Herman was more likely than most to be a sexual predator. But not enough of a predator to call her back, apparently, so in her third voicemail Liz really let him have it: "Hi, Mick, this is Liz. I can't force you to direct *Hex*, but I'd like to hear from you why you left the project. Your manager told our manager it's because you career can't take another failed splatter project. Well, why do you think *Hex* will fail? Because you know what? My career can't take another failed splatter project either. Oh, wait, I don't have a career. I'm thirty years old and work part-time as a sexy housekeeper. Recently, a man tried to pay extra so he could masturbate while watching me dust baseboards. Anyway, give me a call when you get a sec!"

Mick Herman didn't call.

What bothered Liz most was that Mick Herman had a reputation as the nicest guy in the business. Liz's writing partner, Bryan, who'd done lunch with Mick Herman to discuss Mick Herman's notes on draft four, confirmed that Mick Herman "seemed really nice." But Liz suspected he *wasn't* nice. In addition to his wordless Hollywood blow-off of her and Bryan, there was the issue of his movies. Not the dreck he made now but the ones he started off with, back when he was a mystery man down in Texas cranking out splatter on a shoe-string budget. Liz's favorite was *Cajolo*, in which a girl has a dream that she's seduced by a creature who's a man from the neck down, and kind of hunky, but has a face covered in hair, and also a tail, and thin pinkish fingers that feel cold as they tap tap tap along her body. A few months later, the girl, who's a virgin, finds out she's pregnant. Her parents disown her. She's living on the street when she gets taken in by homeless addicts, one of whom, the nicest, wears a balaclava because his face is burned. She's frightened by this nice man but tells herself it's only because she's grossed out by his burned face, like maybe she's prejudiced against burned-face people, so after some cajoling she lets him take care of her. Soon, she starts having pain. She worries about the baby. She wants to go to the hospital, but the man won't let her. He ends up chaining her to a radiator (classic) and feeding her weird sweet milk with a grainy mouth-feel. She starts having contractions, but just as she's about to give birth, hours later, a rat-faced baby rips through her stomach and starts eating her face (its own mother!) while laughing a high-pitched rat baby laugh. The milk turns out to have been vermin milk, milked from rats and squirrels kept by the freak, who turns out not to be burned but to have a rat face himself. He's the guy from the dream.

Cajolo was great, a real stomach-turner, but what kind of "nice guy" could make a movie like that? The same question might have been asked about Liz and her scripts, she knew, but she also knew, deep down, that she wasn't a very nice person. She was an angry person. A person who, in a different situation (growing up in a warzone, say, or even just with less supportive parents), might have been capable of violence. She suspected her writing somehow sublimated this, and she suspected the same of Mick Herman. At some level, she was going to Mick Herman's house not to confront him about dropping her script but to expose him for who he really was.

An hour later, Liz was in a cab on Mulholland Drive, winding past grand decrepit homes with floor-to-ceiling windows and mossy wooden decks cantilevered from the sides of hills. The driver turned off Mulholland onto a narrow street lined with cracked adobe walls. The street ended in a skinny cul-de-sac, at the end of which, facing Liz, was a house that looked to have been burned. The piebald roof had big black holes in it, and the glassless windows stared out provocatively, like an unspoken invitation to come inside and explore the wreckage. For a weird moment, Liz wondered if this was Mick Herman's house, and if he hadn't called her back because he'd burned alive inside it. But the driver stopped in front of the neighboring house, which had a blue Prius in front and wasn't burned.

Liz swiped her card to pay for the cab (what was another $44.73, on top of the thousands she already owed the credit card people?), then examined her dim reflection in the clear plastic that separated her from the driver. Her sand-colored hair was in a ponytail, which she re-tied in a deliberately casual way, leaving a few strands loose and pulling them behind her ears. The shirt she was wearing was tight but tasteful, with a skirt that showed off her shaved legs.

Liz got out of the cab, was bid farewell by the driver, then walked up to the oversized front door and rang the doorbell. Inside the house, a bell chimed. She waited. She knew from Mick Herman's agent's assistant, whom she'd tricked into giving her the address by pretending to be a courier, that Mick Herman was "pretty much always home." If he wasn't home, she planned to wait as long as it took, but the heavy door opened almost immediately, revealing a small, slightly chubby man in a paisley bathrobe and slippers. He had a closely cropped beard and thinning hair, which was short except for a dark wisp that curled up in front. When he smiled, he looked like the happy statue on a Big Boy hamburger restaurant.

At first, Liz thought this couldn't be Mick Herman. He didn't look serious enough, or bloodthirsty, or whatever it was she expected based on his movies. But when he said "Can I help you?" she recognized his peppy voice from their sessions on the phone.

"Yes," Liz said. She didn't say her name, though. She wanted him to recognize *her* voice. "I'm here about *Hex*," she said, to give him more of her voice.

Mick Herman's face took on a forced thoughtful expression, like a person at a funeral for someone he didn't know very well.

Finally Liz just said it: "I'm Liz."

He squinted and cocked his head.

Unbelievable. "Liz Durden," Liz said. "I wrote *Hex*. With Bryan. You met Bryan."

"Of course!" he said, smiling again. He reached out his hand and Liz found herself shaking it. He held onto her hand when the shake was over, which was weird, and Liz wondered if now was the time to do something sexy, like sweep her hair back, but it was too late; he was pulling her through the door saying, "It's so nice to finally meet you. Sit down, sit down."

Inside the house, a big white sectional sofa was angled toward a wall of windows facing Laurel Canyon and, beyond it, the city. Skyscrapers stood in the hazy distance. Mick Herman waved Liz toward the sectional. It was the only place to sit, but Liz defiantly sat on the single cushion that faced *away* from the windows. She hoped her meaning was clear: *I'm not here to look out your fucking windows.*

"Want a drink?" Mick Herman asked, then made a joke about how early a person was allowed to start drinking.

"No thank you," Liz said.

"Coffee?"

"No thanks."

"Bottled water?"

"No."

Mick Herman stood there with his brow furrowed, as though trying to come up with another beverage to offer, but Liz was determined to deny him the position of gracious host. Whether he wanted to or not, they were going to discuss *Hex*. He was going to tell her why he quit on her and Bryan.

"Be right back," he chirped, then disappeared through a swinging door.

Mick Herman was avoiding her, Liz decided. He was afraid of women. She was powerful. He felt guilty. Then he poked his head through the door and said, "Put your feet up!"

Liz didn't want to put her feet up but felt compelled. There wasn't a coffee table, so she wondered if she was supposed to put her feet on another part of the sectional, and, in that case, if she needed to take off her shoes first. Then she noticed a row of shoes by the door and realized she was supposed to have taken hers off when she came inside. But she couldn't get up now and take them off, because what if he came back and she was standing by the door? In a script, that would have given him the power, subtextually, and the whole shoe thing was an obvious power game anyway. What kind of poseur made guests take off their shoes?

Liz slipped off her shoes and scooted them under the sectional. While she waited, she tried to come up with an opening, something she could say that would put Mick Herman on his heels while at the same time convincing him of her wit and forceful personality ("It must be easy to blow off a person you haven't even met, huh?" or "We addressed your notes on draft four, so what's the problem? Were the notes *wrong*?"), but soon she was thinking about how long Mick Herman had been gone. She thought she heard voices, but maybe it was a TV in another room. Maybe he was watching TV while he brewed coffee or pumped well water or whatever the hell he was doing.

There were framed photos everywhere, hung floor to ceiling like in a British gallery. Most of the photos showed Mick Herman smiling with his arms around other smiling people. Liz wondered if the other people were famous. A big panoramic photo above the fireplace showed what looked like an African desert. Everyone in the photo was wearing sunglasses. One of them, an old guy, looked like Rick Zorn.

Liz was about to get up and check if it was really Rick Zorn when

Mick Herman walked back into the room, holding an oversized bottle of water. His face had changed. It was more thoughtful, less eager, as if he had composed the proper face while in the kitchen. He sat down on the sectional and leaned forward with his elbows on his knees. "I know you're here about *Hex*," he said.

"Yeah," Liz said, thinking of course she was there about *Hex*. She'd said she was there about *Hex*, and why else would she be there?

Mick Herman nodded. He raised the big bottle of water to his mouth with both hands like a baby. After three long gulps he said, "How old are you? Twenty-three, twenty-four?"

"Thirty," Liz said.

He eyed her, squinting. "You look great!"

"Thanks," Liz said, embarrassed. She reminded herself to be sexy and powerful and crossed her legs. Then a tall man pushed through the swinging door with his head slumped forward and walked across the room without glancing at them. He looked familiar.

"That's my boyfriend," Mick Herman said.

"I'm not your boyfriend," the man said, then disappeared through another door.

So Mick Herman was gay. Of course he was gay. He was gay because Liz had dressed up, assuming he *wasn't* gay, and this was her lot in life. She imagined Mick, later, telling this boyfriend or non-boyfriend, 'My God, what was she wearing?' She felt the power escaping her, felt that somehow, without moving at all, she had begun to slouch.

"His name's Brandon," Mick said. "Do you recognize him?"

"No," Liz said.

"He's an actor."

"Really?" Liz hadn't met many actors, living in Covina. "Is he in movies?"

"Commercials," Mick said, "like Reformulon, the antidepressant for athletes? Brandon's the tennis player. At the end he says, 'I wanna focus on my serve, not my suicidal ideation.'"

"Oh yeah," Liz said, not even disguising her disappointment.

"There's good money in commercials."

"You don't say."

"Better money than in daytime TV, anyway." Mick sighed. "Brandon thinks I should try directing commercials."

Liz said nothing.

"I know what you're thinking," Mick said, "but the way movies get tuned up with marketing research, there isn't much difference anymore."

"I wouldn't know," Liz said.

"Look," Mick said, "if you hang around this town long enough, you'll realize I'm one of the nicest guys in the business."

"One of the nicest," Liz said bitterly.

"That's right," he said, but a little tentatively, as if he wanted affirmation of this. He looked over Liz's shoulder at the window, at the vista his career had afforded him. "I'm in the middle of a formal letter to you and your partner."

Liz snorted. "You don't even remember his name, do you?"

"Of course I remember. We did lunch."

"Then what is it?"

"What's what?"

"His name!"

Mick paused. Liz almost said she was sorry for raising her voice, but Mick's eyes had slid sideways in a way that suggested he was thinking hard. The eyes were bloodshot.

"Chumholtz," Mick said.

"What?"

"Snarfbarn."

"Are you fucking with me?"

Mick laughed. His laughter had a florid quality, like the recitative of an opera. "His name's Bryan," Mick said. "I knew that the whole time. I was just joking."

"Great joke."

"Thank you! You could use a joke or two, seems to me."

"Maybe you're right. Sorry."

"It's okay. You're disappointed. The letter explains everything, but since you're here, let me tell you where I'm coming from."

Liz almost said no, wait, send the letter, but he spoke too fast.

"I can't have my name attached to another big splatter project that goes out and doesn't get financed," he said. "It would be my third this year." He looked at Liz as if it were hard to say it, but there, he'd said it. It was exactly what his manager had said to *her* manager.

"Why won't it get financed?" Liz asked.

"Maybe it will. And you guys are gonna make it. You're young, *Hex* is crazy and cool, and one day you'll get it done. But I'm old and can't wait around, especially now that I've got some momentum from *The Old Neighborhood.*"

This was a reasonable explanation, but Liz wasn't satisfied. First of all, *The Old Neighborhood* was dreck. It was a made-for-TV movie about elderly Italian men who sit around a sandlot reminiscing (in soft-focus flashback) about childhood memories there until, at the end, they team up with business school students to keep it from getting paved over. The whole thing looked like it was shot in Atlanta for two thousand bucks.

Mick raised the bottle of water again. Bubbles of air glugged from his mouth up the length of the bottle to the base, which was lanced by sunlight from the tall windows. He noticed Liz looking at him and put down the bottle. He made a feeble smile, as if to test whether or not his explanation was enough, and was everything okay between them?

"You know," Liz said in a reasonable voice, "I've never seen *The Old Neighborhood.* What kind of splatter does it have?"

Mick laughed awkwardly.

"Stabbings?" Liz asked.

"Afraid not."

"What about torture?"

Mick shook his head.

"Dismemberment?"

Mick took a deep breath. Liz could tell she was pushing him, and it felt good.

"You know I'm a nice guy," he said, "right?"

"The nicest in the business."

"So I say this in the interest of honesty, because, in the end, maybe it's better to be honest even if it's hard, you know?" He waited for Liz to affirm this, but she didn't. He picked up the water bottle and turned it in his hands. "Splatter is dead. It's been a great run. Over fifty years if you count the Australian stuff, which was my own inspiration. People just don't want sadism anymore, let alone bloodsport, cannibalism, or creatures being born from human women."

Liz recoiled almost physically, unwilling, or unable, to hear such a thing from someone she admired.

"Honestly," Mick said, "the last few I did, my heart wasn't in it. I did it for the money. Look at this place." He twirled his water bottle over his head to indicate the giant room. "I can barely pay the bills. Brandon has to chip in."

Liz had heard the death of splatter foretold by many people, even Bryan, but she didn't expect it from Mick Herman.

"When we met," Mick was saying, "I was like his sugar daddy, this bigtime director. The house is paid off, but the property tax is fifty thou a year."

Liz didn't care about Mick Herman's finances, but fifty thousand was a lot of money, and she said as much.

"I know, right? Forget about vacations, kids, a second home in Utah." Mick shook his head and drank more water. "Brandon just paid it yesterday. That's why he's grumpy, why he brought up the thing about directing commercials. I'm going to, but I gotta do it my way. I'm taking meetings about something very big."

"A new project?"

"Not yet. More like a new area. A niche. Very promising."

Liz nodded. The way Mick Herman was talking made the "new area" sound sketchy and desperate. She felt badly for him. He could have sold his house, of course, but he was getting old, and old people seemed to have a hard time moving.

Liz's feelings must have shown on her face, because Mick Herman said, "Don't worry about me. This thing, it's gonna be huge."

"That's great, Mick," she said.

He stared dreamily at the tall windows.

Liz wondered if she should leave. As much as she wanted to think that Mick Herman was screwing her over, that he secretly *wasn't* nice, he really did seem nice. And his career wasn't what it used to be, clearly. Liz tried to come up with a polite way to make her exit, but then the tall man, Brandon, returned abruptly through the swinging door. His head was still down, as if he didn't want to draw their attention, but Mick noticed him and smiled. Brandon started putting on a pair of topsiders by the door, and Mick dashed toward him with surprising quickness. "Brandon!" he said in a high voice.

Brandon had put on his topsiders and was poking through an umbrella holder for something else.

"Brandon," Mick said, "where are you going?"

Brandon said nothing.

Standing so close to the taller man, Mick looked childish, but his face bore a complicated expression that combined panic with the pathetic expectancy of a person who'd just made a joke.

Liz had to go. The two men needed to have a serious conversation, and what did she stand to gain at this point? Really, there was more to lose. All Mick Herman's talk of commercials and property taxes was sapping her energy, and he seemed to be trying to convince her that splatter was a waste of time. She wasn't ready for that. But how could she escape? She didn't dare approach the door, where Mick was circling Brandon in what looked like a supplication dance.

Having located a brightly colored scarf, Brandon turned to the door. Mick grabbed his arm and pulled himself into Brandon's body. "Brandon?" he said, as if Brandon were a parent taking a nap. "We were gonna go to Foot Locker, remember? Because of your shin splints?"

"Are you high right now?" Brandon whispered.

"Aren't you?" Mick said.

Liz scanned the room for a bathroom, a closet, any place where she could wait for Brandon to leave, then slip out. Seeing none, she rose quietly, walked to the swinging door and pushed through it into the kitchen, which was white and dominated by a granite island the size of a luxury sedan. On the island was a big red plastic bowl and a limp sack of pancake mix. Behind her Mick was saying, "I'll be done in a minute. I swear, Brandon. It's just, I did something not very nice to this kid." Brandon's voice was muffled, then Mick said, "But you haven't eaten. What about Mick's famous pancakes?" Brandon yelled about not being mollified by pancakes.

Liz sped across the kitchen into a hallway. She could still hear them arguing, so she walked to the end of the long hallway and opened a door there, expecting it to open onto a guest bedroom or study, but what she saw was a sort of sitting room.

The windowless sitting room didn't have a TV or stereo, weirdly, just a couch facing a wall of framed photos and plaques and other miscellany. The greenish couch looked to have spent time outdoors.

Unlike the photos in the living room, the photos in this room showed a younger Mick Herman who bore little resemblance to the man Liz had met. No beard, no chubby body, but the cheerful smile was unmistakable. In one photo, a group of teenage boys in matching polo shirts and acid-washed jeans were standing with their arms draped over each other's shoulders. It took Liz a moment to recognize Mick

Herman, who had spiky blond hair. Had he been a child actor?

The room had other, more peculiar features, like a rusty radiator in one corner that didn't seem to be attached to the wall or floor. At the base of the radiator was a pair of handcuffs. Liz approached the radiator and toed the handcuffs. They were heavy, like real handcuffs, not the cheap plastic costume kind.

Confused, Liz turned around, and in doing so saw that the couch, facing her now, had dark stains all over its cushions. *Blood stains?*

With a rush of fright, Liz pictured Mick Herman in the doorway brandishing a knife. Or maybe it would be Brandon, and then Mick, wretched Mick, would come in later to clean up the mess made by his beautiful psychotic boyfriend. Liz allowed her mind to wander, but the feeling of fright diminished quickly. She could still hear the two men arguing. And the longer she stared at the soiled couch, the more familiar it looked. There was a scene in *Master of Scaremonies*, Liz remembered, in which a vacationing family was chained together on a couch inside a madman's trailer. The family had been on a cross-country trip, she remembered. The father had knocked on the trailer door for help with a flat tire, then been invited inside and served a mug of laced coffee. The madman asked the chained-up family a series of questions about Bible passages and Civil War arcana, and after each wrong answer he demanded the family negotiate among themselves to choose the limb of one family member to be amputated.

Liz inspected the crowded wall for other memorabilia. There were photos of obscure actors she remembered from Mick Herman's early movies. There was a key to the city of Eloy, Arizona, thanking Mick for shooting *Satan's Womb* there. The single weirdest item, though, was what looked like the poorly preserved head of a javelina hog. Up close, Liz saw that the head was hollow. Actually, it wasn't a head at all; it was a mask, and it looked more like a big brown rat than a javelina. Was it a *rat* mask? Or no, could it be…?

Liz ran the backs of her fingers along the dark hairs on one cheek of the mask, and she was surprised by how soft they felt. She stuck a finger through an eye hole, felt nothing. The mask had some give to it.

Liz went across the room to the bloodstained couch, where she sat down and considered the eyeless mask staring back at her. She'd been a kid when *Cajolo* came out, so she'd watched it in secret, after her parents went to sleep. She was so scared afterward that she almost crept into their bedroom to admit what she'd done so she could sleep with them in their bed, but instead, for reasons that weren't clear to her at the time, she had taken the more difficult path of trying to sleep alone in the dark of her own tiny bedroom, of trying not to think about the rat-faced man who, she was certain, would assault her in her dreams.

From a distance, the *Cajolo* mask was still a little scary, she assured herself.

To kill time, Liz took out her phone and checked her e-mail (nothing), then watched the second half of an episode of *Meth Masters* she'd started on the train. Finishing the show took only fifteen minutes, so she considered calling Bryan. But Bryan always acted awkward at work, worried about getting caught taking personal calls. And Bryan wouldn't have approved of what she was doing. He wanted to wipe his hands of Mick Herman, and Liz feared he was almost ready to wipe his hands of screenwriting altogether. So instead of calling Bryan, Liz read an article on her phone about a man in Cleveland who'd kept two women in a boarded-up spare bedroom for six years.

By the time Liz left the sitting room, an hour or so later, the house was quiet. She made her way to the kitchen and put her ear against the swinging door to the living room, heard nothing. Had Mick and Brandon left? Gone to Foot Locker? She nudged open the door and peeped through the crack. There, face down on the sectional sofa, lay Mick. His robe was bunched up beneath him, exposing the hairy backs of his thighs and the bottom of one pale butt cheek. On the wall, in front of the framed photos, a retractable screen had been lowered from the ceiling. On the screen, some longhaired people by a campfire were watching a bare-breasted woman smearing blood on her face.

Liz didn't want to wake Mick and alert him to the creepy fact that she'd been hiding in his house for an hour, so she snuck through the living room to the front door, where she saw the shoes lined up and re-membered she was barefoot. Her shoes were under the sectional. And so, at the risk of waking Mick, she crept back through the living room, careful to step on the oriental rugs that covered most of the parquet floor. As she came around the sectional, she could hear Mick's heavy breathing. She figured he was in a deep sleep until she saw his face.

His eyes were open.

In a startled voice he said, "Brandon?"

Liz took a step back, just as startled. She began a nervous explanation of how she'd wanted to give him and Brandon some privacy, but Mick Herman wasn't paying attention; he was staring at a water bottle that had fallen from the couch and was glugging water onto the rug. He leaned forward and fumbled with the bottle until it was righted.

"Sorry," Liz said, "I guess I should—"

"Stay," Mick said, looking up at her, "won't you?"

Mick's expression, though fuzzy, had an openness that made him look vulnerable. Liz remembered the pathetic fight, the way Mick had circled Brandon as he pleaded with the younger man not to leave. "Well," she said, "I guess I'll have to wait for a cab anyway."

"I'll drive you," Mick said. "It's the least I can do. Just stay a while longer."

"Only if you direct *Hex*," Liz said. She meant it as a joke, but Mick said, "Fine."

"Really?"

Mick nodded. "What's *Hex*?"

"Mick, are you okay?"

Mick thought for a moment. "Brandon and I were fighting, weren't we?"

"Yeah. He seemed pretty mad."

Mick stood up and went unsteadily to the window. He leaned with his palms pressed against it. For a moment, Liz thought he was going to vomit, but then he said, "Want some food? I was planning a pancake brunch, but I can make sandwiches since it's gotten later."

"No thanks," Liz said, even though she did want a sandwich. She hadn't eaten since leaving Covina. But she didn't want to put Mick out. He seemed troubled.

"I have turkey and ham," Mick said in his flat voice, "and also peanut butter and jelly. Or banana. Brandon likes peanut butter and banana." He sighed. The way his eyes looked, Liz thought he might tip over and fall asleep again, but then he said, "You know what? I've got roast beef, too. I forgot about that. Pretty nice roast beef. How about a roast beef sandwich with horseradish?"

"Sure," Liz said, trying to disguise her excitement. She hadn't eaten roast beef in years. It was too expensive to buy for home use, and too uncouth to order at restaurants, where it always seemed like half the people she was with were vegetarian.

In the kitchen, Liz sat on a stool at the big granite island and watched Mick take out all the ingredients for roast beef sandwiches, including delicious-smelling rye bread that came out of a paper sack.

"Brandon thinks I should direct commercials," Mick said absently, slicing the bread.

"You mentioned that," Liz said.

"I don't know, though. I've got this other thing."

Liz said nothing. She would eat her sandwich, then leave.

Mick began arranging the sandwiches: Swiss cheese, roast beef, and a thick horseradish sauce he spread with a butter-knife. "Can you keep a secret?" he asked.

"Sure," Liz said.

"Commercial shows."

"Pardon?"

"That's the secret."

"What's a commercial show?"

"A TV show that's also a commercial. You've probably seen some and didn't know it."

"I doubt that."

"Remember *Planet Grandpa*?"

"Sure." *Planet Grandpa* was an animated show about a group of disgruntled old men who take over the town where they live, kick out all the young people and immigrants, and start imposing a Sharia-like code based on homey morals until the President has them arrested and sent on a trash rocket to the moon. There, the old men confound the President by terraforming the moon and brokering trade deals with China.

"*Planet Grandpa* was paid for by a Chinese retail conglomerate," Mick Herman said. "Ever notice how the grandpas get so many timely packages with undamaged contents?"

"Huh. Now that you mention it."

"There's good money in commercial shows. Better money than most regular shows." Mick placed the two sandwiches inside a toaster oven, then stared at the closed door of the toaster oven while chewing his fingernails.

Liz was disappointed, and a little depressed, honestly. Whether or not Mick Herman was the person she thought he was, she admired his early movies, so it was sad to imagine him redirecting what remained of his talent in such a mercenary way. But she wondered if she was any different. When that client offered to pay extra to masturbate while watching her dust baseboards, she'd actually considered it for a moment before composing the proper outrage.

Mick removed the sandwiches from the toaster oven, filling the kitchen with the delicious smell of melted cheese and warm roast beef. He put the sandwiches on plates and set one plate in front of Liz, along with a little napkin and a fork, in case the sandwich was too sloppy to eat barehanded. He sprinkled a crushed-up pill on his own sandwich, then sat down across the island from her.

The sandwich was very sloppy, but Liz shoved it into her mouth and held it there, letting the juices dribble through her fingers onto the plate below. She would have felt self-conscious about the display if Mick weren't eating even more ferociously, taking bites the size of small fists and wiping his mouth with the hairy backs of his hands.

When they finished, they remained hunched over their plates as though stunned.

"Thank you," Liz said.

"That was a fucking good sandwich," Mick said, "if I may say so myself."

"It was," Liz said. "Thanks again." She hoped her words sounded genuine, because she really was thankful for the sandwich, if nothing else.

Mick checked his watch, and Liz rose to carry her empty plate to the sink, but Mick intercepted her and carried both plates to the sink himself. Liz was left standing near the swinging door.

"I guess I should go," Liz said.

Mick nodded. "Come on, I'll walk you out."

Together they walked to the door, and Liz followed Mick onto the driveway. The sun had sunk low enough that the houses had a slightly bluish tinge, and the tangled vegetation appeared black.

Liz hadn't called a cab, and she didn't want to stand there awkwardly chatting for half an hour, so she decided to tell Mick her car was down the hill. She would walk out to Mulholland Drive and wait on the corner alone, which was fine. She was in no rush to get home, where no one was waiting for her.

"Well…" she said.

"You and Bryan are so talented," Mick said, looking past her at something. "You have that *thirst*. I wish I could bottle it up and steal it.

I'm serious when I say be in touch. Think of me as, like, your mentor. The mentor-mentee relationship is important in Hollywood." He grasped her shoulders and did an awkward double-cheek kiss.

"Thank you," Liz said, embarrassed, "I'll take all the advice I can get," but she wondered what kind of advice Mick could offer.

"And if you're ever in trouble," Mick said, "you can stay in my guesthouse."

"Thank you," Liz repeated, but she was confused. Though Mick's house was big, with plenty of room for guests, it didn't have a guest-house that she could see.

But Mick was looking at the burned-out house next door. He'd been looking there the whole time, Liz realized. In the dwindling daylight, the house looked more normal, but also scarier, because the closeness to normalcy made it uncanny.

"How long has it been like that?" Liz asked.

"Years," Mick said, "but it's important to me that it stay empty. The realtor hates me. Wanna know what I do?"

Some of the peppiness returned to Mick's voice as he explained how the house went back on the market from time to time, and when it did, how he and Brandon sabotaged potential sales by playing pranks that made the house seem haunted, or by spreading rumors about neighbors, like this little old Southern lady across the street who was always puttering in her yard where buyers could see her. "She has this fabulous, sculptural hair," Mick said, "but she's deaf as a post, bless her, so we make up these awful stories. There was this one buyer, a slick finance type, and I get real close to the guy and say, *Hear that?* The guy says no, and of course he doesn't; there's nothing to hear. *Anything unusual?* I ask. He says it's pretty quiet. *That's because the animals are gone.* He asks what animals. *The pets. She poisons them.* Just then, I wave at the old lady and she smiles at us." Mick chuckled. "The guy was horrified. An animal lover, clearly. He asked how she could do such a thing, why we didn't call the police. I said the police have *people* to worry about. Forget animals. If we weren't so lazy, I said, we'd move. That lady fucking *scares* us."

Mick glanced mischievously at Liz, who smiled. To keep him going, Liz asked why it was important to him that the house stay empty. She expected a joke about the charm of having a creepy burned out house at the end of the street, or maybe about the quiet afforded by the lack of neighbors, but Mick didn't reply. He was looking at the house, or rather glaring at it.

"I like it the way it is," Mick said at length, and then added, almost as an afterthought, "because I used to know the people who lived there. The ones who burned."

Liz was startled. There'd been *people* inside the house when it burned? Had they burned alive? She didn't dare ask Mick these questions, but he seemed to sense she was thinking them.

"It was easy," Mick said in a husky voice.

"What was easy?" Liz asked, still staring at the house, imagining the deadly fire.

"To light the match."

Liz's throat caught.

"When someone burns," Mick said, "before their skin peels off, it has these beads of moisture all over it, like a sweaty can of soda. Do you know what the beads are?"

Liz shook her head.

"Boiling fat."

Liz thought about the roast beef in her stomach, and the mixture of fear and mild nausea made it hard to take stock of her situation. If Mick attacked her, would anyone hear her scream? She could outrun him, she was pretty sure, but not Brandon, and the Prius was still in the driveway, which meant Brandon might be lurking nearby. Brandon would do Mick's bidding, she was sure, and help him dispose of her body, or maybe incorporate it into one of their kitschy exhibits, like the bloody couch. How perfect. She braced herself, preparing to turn toward Mick Herman. His expression would be placid, as it had been before, but with a slight fervor about the eyes. A moment would pass before he struck.

But when she turned to him, Mick was smiling.

"You know I'm joking," he said, "right?"

"Sure," Liz said. Of course he was joking, but she'd hoped there'd be more to the joke. A joke could linger in the space between belief and disbelief, and if it stayed there long enough, wasn't it something like art? The difference was a matter of scale. Of commitment. Liz had wanted Mick to hang on longer, to be fiercer. To summon some kind of creature (Brandon in disguise?) and supervise a grimy torture in the kitchen or rec room of the burned-out house. Maybe even to exsanguinate her, just a little, and save her blood for his next splatter movie. But there wouldn't be another splatter movie, for him or her either. She had to change course, do something more practical. She would call Bryan.

Mick waved at the house. "It's wrapped up in some kind of legal deal. Arson, I guess. What people won't do for money, huh?" He laughed his bright laugh.

"What people won't do," Liz repeated.

YOUNG SHACKLETON

I sit at a sticky kitchen table over a bowl of what looks like tomato soup but smells like syrup. My hand, wrapped around a dull pewter spoon, is smooth and hairless. I'm wearing what they call a newsboy outfit: short pants, suspenders, and a stained white shirt that's much too big. I feel the weight of a hat on my head. Later, I'll see the hat—a brown riding cap tilted at a jaunty angle—reflected by a window overlooking a model of Dublin, and beneath the hat, my pale and malleable face.

"Where are you, you rascal?" comes the snarling voice of an old man.

I stand quickly, knocking over a wooden chair that's hinged to the floor so it will fall the same way each time, without sliding. I turn from the hips, creating a snapping effect, and then, careful to leave one hand on the bowl of soup, I watch the old man, my grandfather, stagger through the doorway pulling off his belt. His wrinkled eyes are squinting. An uncombed gray mustache hangs over his lip. After freeing the belt from his pants, he loops it once around his fist and whips it against the wall.

"Grandpa!" I say. "Grandpa, no..."

My grandfather's face contorts with rage. He whips the belt at me but misses badly, and though the belt hits only air, a loud *crack* sounds through the kitchen. I raise the bowl of viscous, sweet-smelling soup and fling it as hard as I can toward an empty wall several feet from him. Suddenly his chest is splattered bright red and he's clutching a second, identical bowl.

"Damn you!" he says. "Where's your newspaper money?"

"I gave it to Mom," I say.

"Don't mention that tramp in this house."

"She isn't a tramp!" I turn away from him and cover my face, as though crying, and when I turn back I feel damp trails on my cheeks. "One day," I say, pausing to suck air once, twice, "one day I'm gonna be a famous explorer and go far away from here, to a place where there aren't any grandpas."

"You fool," he says, "grandpas are everywhere."

"Not in the Arctic."

"The Arctic?" He laughs and clears his throat. "There's nothing in the Arctic but scurvy and polar bears and getting your throat cut in the night by vicious scheming Eskimos. By the time those Eskies are done, you'll be cryin' for dear old Grandpa!"

My grandfather stares at me, and in his stillness is a challenge. I try not to breathe. I ball my fists. His gaze shifts expertly from my right eye to my left and back again—active staring, the technique is called—but despite the stare and the stillness of his body, I sense that my grandfather's mind has wandered to other scenes, and perhaps, I think, he's weeping at the grave of Myrna, my grandmother, or slapping the face of my mother when she brings home her latest boyfriend, a tall and striking merchant seaman. Or perhaps, I think, feeling a twinge of jealousy, he's fighting thugs in an alley, or making love to his best friend and legal partner's beautiful wife, or skiing across the Alps in search of the nefarious Klaus Würfel, biathlete turned assassin, who will meet his end when he underestimates our hero's doggedness.

They say an actor's mind is a landscape of every scene in every role, and that the greats wander endlessly.

I watch a delicate Chinese junk unload her crates and colorful crew. I run from policemen who caught me stealing medicine. I lay in a cargo hold making snow angels in sawdust and listening to the snaps and clanks of the rigging high above. I circle the kitchen, chased and whipped again by my grandfather, only this time my mother's kindly doctor enters the room, takes off his stovepipe hat and says, "Leave that boy be."

My grandfather looks up and smiles, recognizing Dr. Douglas.

"If it ain't the negro doctor," he says, "condescending to call on us."

"Just making my rounds," Dr. Douglas says warily.

"She ain't here, Doc. She's dead, remember?"

Dr. Douglas eyes my grandfather, who has begun putting his belt back on. In a different scene, outside my mother's sickroom, Dr. Douglas tells me the Navy made him appreciate his talents and what a joy it is to serve his fellow man. Now I want to scream at him to run, run while he still can, but I don't scream, and I hope the unvoiced scream shows in my face.

"Go to your room, Ernie," Dr. Douglas says. "Git now, hear me?"

As Dr. Douglas motions to the hallway, Grandpa reaches into his drooping pants and pulls out a gun. The small, nickel-plated revolver gleams in his palm for a moment before he snatches it up and takes aim.

"Grandpa, no!" I cry.

He shoots five times.

Clutching his bloody chest, Dr. Douglas trudges to the window and wheezes, "Myrna, finally I come to you," and while he makes a lengthy death-speech about Myrna, his former lover, who was also, I think, my grandmother, I wonder what to do with my hands. Then my grandfather comes up behind me and I wonder if I'm supposed to hit him or cry into his shirt, but he lays a familiar forearm on my shoulder and says, "Great, isn't he?"

"Yeah," I say, thinking he means Dr. Douglas is a great doctor.

"He's been prepping in his trailer since daybreak. What a waste of talent."

"For sure."

My grandfather looks at me, and I'm reminded by his bemused expression that he's Rick Zorn. I feel embarrassed.

"Relax," Rick says, "the camera's on Marv. I'll break down sobbing over his body here in a minute. That's when you run off."

"I know," I say, "I was just staying in character."

Rick takes his forearm off my shoulder and pats my back. Then he steps away to shake out his hands and feet, prepping.

Dr. Douglas's hand slides down the window, smearing blood,

and I know from licking the window once in secret that the gooey blood tastes sweet, like tomato soup. This is the taste I think of as *red*. The *feeling* I think of as red is the feeling of watching the lines around Dr. Douglas's dark eyes clench and unclench as his breathing slows and his body relaxes until, with a tiny hiccup, his death is complete.

Dr. Douglas and I are standing with cups of water when he asks if they have me going to school. I say no, trying to sound regretful, as though it's not something I'm proud of, but I don't really think about school. I don't think about home. The past, to me, is my father's mustache and a wood-paneled television. Shag carpet and legs folded Indian-style.

"I was gonna make a joke," Dr. Douglas says, "about Ireland."

"Where's Ireland?" I ask.

"Here, boy." He flips a hand toward the set, a cityscape, then down at our feet, where the black and shiny pavement makes a hollow sound like cardboard. "Ain't you heard? This is Dublin, Ireland, right here. Eighteen-ninety or thereabouts."

I nod, confused. "Is that the joke?"

He shakes his head, takes a sip of water. "Joke is," he says, "what's a black doctor doing in Dublin, Ireland, in eighteen-fuck-ing-ninety?"

Some actors laugh from a nearby ring of folding chairs. One of them says, "And what's an actor like Marvin Chalmers doing on the set of a fleabag like this?"

"That's my agent's best joke," Dr. Douglas says, and when he turns to them, smiling, I try to think of a joke I could make, but then they're speaking in a murmur and I don't understand.

I prep until the voice calls, "Places!"

I sell newspapers to charmed passersby.

Shouting headlines, I think of the carpet in front of the TV, like thick little ropes mowed by a lawnmower, ropes I can grab by the handful during scary parts. The screen is so shiny, the color so bright, that an actor could reach out and grab hold of your neck or kiss your lips.

*

I'm belowdecks on a ship bound for Singapore, in a narrow space between a wooden crate and the curving hull. There's sawdust on the floor where I lay, and in the darkness I sometimes hold my breath. If I hold it long enough, colors emerge. Time slows. My mind wanders and my world gets bigger, but my heart gets so quiet that I wonder if I'm dead.

But I can hear them speaking. The merchant marines.

The actors who play the merchant marines.

"There was alcohol," one says.

"And drugs," says another.

"No doubt, but it's endemic to the profession. Look at Zorn."

Murmured assent.

"That sportscaster woman…"

"A beautiful woman." I recognize the voice of Frank Mesplede, who's older than the rest and speaks with an accent. "But he's a good boy at heart."

"He cut her, is what I heard."

"Zorn?"

"No, the kid. Are you drunk?"

Laughter.

"A good boy who hits his marks," Mesplede is saying. In another scene, when the merchant marines are waylaid by Spaniards, he draws his sword to fight, and in the shadows Rick Zorn grabs my arm and tells me to watch, watch the sword, and I watch the tip droop lazily to the floor before it stiffens, as though electrified, and my eyes run the length of the sword and the length of Mesplede's long arm to the face of the man himself, whose pinprick black eyes peer at a doomed Spaniard.

"Boys like that," Mesplede is saying, "they never have a chance."

Boys like what, I wonder, thinking of a boy I've seen. A young man, really. He acts in the London scenes and on the first expedition, before the bloody climax on the Welsh tramp steamer. They call him Ernie.

They call *me* Ernie.

I find the merchant marines in their folding chairs with their cups of water. They tease me as they always do, and I charm them with my rascally antics. I expect one to say, "Be careful, young

fellow, or you'll end up six months at sea with the likes of us!"
But the one who says that doesn't say it. He looks at Mesplede.
Mesplede looks at me.

"Can we help you, my young friend?" Mesplede asks.

I hesitate. It's so hard to go off-script.

"Yes, hello?" Mesplede says, smiling the yellow-toothed smile
that Rick tells me is why Mesplede will never get speaking roles in
this country.

I swallow and say, "Was it me who cut the girl?"

The others laugh quietly, embarrassedly, but Mesplede only
watches me. "Tell me," he says, "Young Mr.—what's your name
again?"

I look around, as though my name might be hanging from the
rigging with the lamp heads and softboxes, as though the contents
of my mind are spread around me like a set to be wandered.
Somewhere on that set, Rick Zorn is looking for his lucky mug, or
reaching for me from inside a TV. Somewhere there's a woman, a
mother, who calls from the darkness to say, "Prompt him already.
Can't you see he's struggling?" But she doesn't say my name.
Neither do the actors, who call me Ernie, Shack. Shackie. Most
look askance and start up muttered conversations. Only Mesplede
keeps his eyes on me, and I'm thankful. He's going to pull me
through the scene, I think, cigarette break be damned. An old pro,
as Rick would say.

"Say it again?" Mesplede turns an ear to me. "I didn't hear."

I approach with nothing, hoping he'll give me my line. "I'm
sorry," I say, "but I—I guess I don't remember right now."

He nods, as though this is a common occurrence, and maybe
it is. "Ah yes," he says, lowering his voice, "but I believe I've heard
it on set."

"What is it?" I whisper, hoping the others won't hear. I lean
in, closing the distance between our faces until I can see that Mesplede's long gray hair, pulled behind his ears, is really a mixture of
black and white hair.

"Hmm, yes..." His eyes are closed, his arms limp at his sides.
On the floor, near one dangling hand, is a plastic cup half-filled
with whiskey. "It was..."

The voice calls, "Places!"

I start to turn but Mesplede grabs my hand and opens his eyes as if stabbed.

"Your house," he says, and though his breath smells like wet newspaper, though his grip feels cold and damp, the mention of a house excites me. I imagine a large overturned ship (wood-paneled television, carpet) where parents (father with mustache) call me by my name. A kitchen like the one where my grandfather chases me but bigger. Chairs with padded seats like the good folding chairs the older actors always claim for themselves. Like the one Frank Mesplede is sitting in right now.

"Places!"

"In your house," Mesplede whispers, holding tightly to my hand, "they called you…"

"Yes?" I've never missed a cue, but this is too important.

"They called you"—he rubs his temple, as though working loose the name from his own vast mind—"meal ticket."

The others laugh.

I hold my breath until I feel the tight thick fibers between my fingers and see the wood-paneled television. On the curved glass, a man is being led through a slimy dark corridor, naked and chained, and yet his hips sway as he walks. His wide shoulders swivel. Suddenly, he wrenches his cuffed hands from his captor and slams the captor's forehead into a wall. The captor slumps to the floor, and the fierce man turns to me.

Rick Zorn's shoulder-length brown hair is feathered on the sides, and his forehead is smeared with the captor's blood.

"Frank's a dick," Rick Zorn says.

I look around the empty living room. Is Rick Zorn talking to me?

"He was fucking with you," Rick Zorn says. He wipes his forehead with the back of his hand, and then, in one of the gestures that make his work unmistakable, sniffs the sweet-smelling blood on the backs of two fingers before wiping them on his freshly waxed chest. He looks around at the dark corridor, the slumped captor, the concrete floor dappled with water that catches the light.

"Which one is this?" he asks me.

"Which what?" I reply, but before he can answer I remember the name of the movie. His character, Dan Steel, is a renegade cop who gets framed by a DA on the take from a notorious drug kingpin. "You just got to prison," I say, "and they're leading you to your cell. You're about to escape, though."

"*Lockdown?*"

"*Lockdown Two*. The one where you go to jail on purpose, to rescue your 'Nam buddy."

Rick Zorn nods. "Johnny Tran, an upstanding member of LA's Vietnamese business community who got framed by the same crooked DA, played by the inestimable Jerry Curnow."

I hear my mother in the kitchen but I don't turn to see her. When Rick Zorn was in the news because he hit his girlfriend, a sideline reporter at football games, Mom said he was slime. Dad said those reporters were bimbos. I didn't know the word *bimbo*.

"Will I be an actor?" I ask.

"That's up to you," Rick Zorn says, "but whether you're the greatest actor of all time or just land a few commercials, the money will be a big help to your family. Take it from me. Mine is a true American rags-to-riches story, so when people criticize me for doing cheapies, I'm like, walk a mile in my shoes, you know?"

I nod.

He reaches for me.

"There's nothing to be afraid of," he says, but his big hairy hand is filthy with blood and dirt, and I'm afraid. I know so little. I don't even know the technique of active staring, let alone that an actor's mind is a landscape of every scene in every role, and that the greats wander endlessly, and what happens if there's only one role?

Five scenes?

"I'm a cagey fighter who never lets down his wingman."

I know from his movies that this is true, so I reach toward the light, toward the sounds of gunshots and speeding motorcycles, toward the smells of sweat and blood and the glossy faces of men who act.

*

A harbor where he watches the loading and unloading of ships.

A schoolyard where he leads chums on an imagery adventure involving frogs.

A city street where he sells newspapers to charmed passersby.

A hospital room with a dying mother where he is comforted by a kindly doctor.

A kitchen where he eats soup and his grandfather says, "The Arctic? There's nothing in the Arctic but scurvy and polar bears and getting your throat cut in the night by vicious scheming Eskimos. By the time those Eskies are done, you'll be cryin' for dear old Grandpa!"

The soup has been thrown.

The belt is out.

Dr. Douglas comes in with his stovepipe hat.

Once, for a joke, I snatched the nickel-plated gun from Rick's palm and pressed it to his temple. I expected him to laugh and raise his hands, but instead he closed his eyes and said, "Pull the fucking trigger."

They say not to look into another actor's eyes and instead to look at the center of his forehead. The eyes of trained actors are like guns that shoot laughter and tears, they say, but I can't help looking, and when I look I see acres of snow where the actors ski on and on, forever overtaking their cackling nemeses. I see courtrooms where they argue with equal parts bombast and tenderness for long-suffering clients, all the while battling personal demons and perhaps winning back loved ones. I see dank corridors where they couple and uncouple in luxuriously choreographed fights, each flaunting his eternally glistening body. And I wake up, gasping, in the darkened hold of a ship, in a dreary kitchen, spare and clean, on the unlit side of a set, on the street in a cordoned off section of downtown Dublin, near the docklands. I've got a stack of newspapers by my feet and a few in my hand. The headline says, GENERAL GORDON DEPARTS FOR KHARTOUM. I wave the papers until a man with a mustache gives me a nickel for one. Do I recognize the man? Does he double as a merchant marine?

He tells me that with my positive attitude I'll surely go far.

I say, "Gosh, Mister, I sure hope so. My dream is to one day find a place where no one's been and draw a map about it."

"Sounds like an adventure," he says, and I search my mind for where I've seen him before, but my mind is so small.

A few seagulls caw raucously and the voice calls, "Cut!"

The man winks, and his rising cheek pulls one end of his stiff mustache off his lip.

"Fucking birds," the voice says. "One more time from the top."

LEGENDARY AMERICANS ON WHEELS

1.

In my side mirror I can see the man, the thing, shambling towards the front door of the little house. He looks good, considering the miles on him. The gold buckles on his shoes are polished and shining. His socks are stretched tight all the way up to his knickers. His jacket has been mended where the tails were frayed, and the satiny black fabric almost shimmers in the sunlight. But the jacket is too small. It won't close anymore around his big belly, which leads the way like a divining rod. And half the jacket is hidden by his long gray hair, which lies in greasy tentacles across his back. There used to be a ribbon to tie the hair, but the ribbon got ragged so the handlers let the hair go natural. It's frizzy near the top where he's bald. He used to have a hat, a sort of three-cornered hat like a captain's hat but smaller. Those were the old days. The ribbon-and-hat days. The days when I didn't hold my breath while he walked from the truck to the house or school or wherever else he was scheduled to make an appearance. Churches, Elks lodges. Convention hotels. Onetime we went to a concert where some punk kids wearing waistcoats played antique instruments. He was the opener. He sang a song. People didn't clap or boo, they just listened. A girl in the back, next to where I was standing, started to cry.

Now he's at the front step. His foot comes up off the pavement a few inches and freezes midair. I wonder if this is how it ends: if one day, today, he just can't get his damned feet up the steps. The two handlers, standing behind him in colonial dress, don't help him. They never help him. They don't want him to appear infirm.

The foot is shaking now. I try to convince myself the knee is slowly rising. He's getting there, I think. The old guy's gonna make it one more time.

Sure enough, the foot falls into place and his body lurches upwards one more step. Now he's standing at the front door. He rings the doorbell and waits.

I wait.

The door creaks open but the screen stays shut. There's a nightgown and a black face. A woman. I can't quite make her out. Long hair. Yellowish eyes.

His hands go up to his head, to where his hat used to be, then he removes an invisible hat and lowers it to his chest, above his big belly. He makes a little bow.

The woman backs away from the screen when he starts clearing his throat, which is awful to hear, like an old lawnmower that won't start anymore but whirs a few cycles each time you crank it, except there's stuff rattling around inside the lawnmower, like pebbles or tiny animal bones. He's talking now, still holding the invisible hat. I can't hear him but I know what he's saying: "Good day to you, m'lady. Permit me to introduce myself."

The woman says something behind the screen. He flips his hand and says something inaudible, probably a witticism. He has hundreds, if not thousands, of witticisms.

She shakes her head. She doesn't understand.

He flips his hand again and it bangs into a porch light caged in metal. The light comes off the wall and dangles from wires. He doesn't notice. One of the handlers, Artemio, rushes up next to him and tries to stick the porch light back in. Artemio uses his thumbnail to twist the screws into the siding. He hasn't noticed yet that the door is closed. The woman is gone. The other handler, Mike, makes a joke. Artemio drops the porch light with a heavy sigh.

Mike and Artemio help the man down the stairs and back to the truck, which is a modified ten-foot moving truck with an extended cab. Moments later, the two handlers are climbing up into the cab with me.

"Step on it," Mike says from the back seat, pulling off his powdered wig.

I put the idling truck in drive and begin weaving through the junkers parked on either side of the crumbling street, watching for kids out of habit. They used to spring out from behind cars, after balls and skinny dogs. But there aren't any kids this time. Not here.

The houses are all alike, dingy vinyl-sided shoeboxes with flaky shingled roofs. Some are burned out. Some are gone entirely, just empty lots with a couple charred beams or a concrete slab. We're in Oklahoma City.

"Bitch is probably calling nine-one-one," Mike says.

Artemio shakes his head. "She didn't even give him a chance."

"Why would she? Some big white asshole rings her doorbell, greets her in what might as well be Middle English, breaks her porch light."

Artemio doesn't speak for a moment. "Maybe she was getting her kids."

"Yeah, right."

"Never know."

"Her kids wouldn't even know who he is. Ben goddamn Franklin, right on their front porch, and he might as well be a smelly old hobo."

That night, Mike is stretched out asleep in back and Artemio is in the passenger seat staring out the window. This is my preferred arrangement. Mike is one of those techie types who's always trying to say something smart or funny. He doesn't understand the easy back-and-forth of pleasant conversation. Artemio is more thoughtful. He's a scientist. A biologist. He used to teach college.

We're heading west towards Amarillo for our next gig. No one uses this stretch of highway anymore so the streetlamps are dark. The flat earth goes for miles. It's cropless, almost treeless, and the moon makes it look like crinkled up tinfoil.

After a while I say, "Can I ask you a question?"

"Sure," Artemio says.

"Why did we even visit that lady's house? Seems like an awful lot of trouble for just one lady, even if she was some kind of Franklin enthusiast, which she didn't seem to be."

"Her husband died in a fracking accident. She has five kids."

"But what was Franklin supposed to do?"

"Talk to the kids, I guess. Inspire them."

I picture five little kids lined up on the porch while Franklin tells them "a penny saved is a penny earned," or "a good conscience is a continual Christmas," or "a countryman between two lawyers is like a fish between two cats." The lessons would be cryptic even if the kids understood him, but these days his flabby mouth makes a gobbling sound when he talks so he's pretty hard to follow.

"Isn't he a little scary," I say, "you know, for kids?"

"He's a great man."

I nod.

A moment later Artemio says, "Sorry. I get defensive sometimes, thinking about how it used to be. I put a lot of work into it, you know?"

"Of course," I say, even though I don't understand the nature of the work he did, or the nature of the body in the back of the truck, really. Theories abound—animatronics, cybernetics, genetic engineering—but the handlers seem to make a point of avoiding technical matters when I'm within earshot.

"What would you do if this whole thing was over?" Artemio asks.

"Legendary Americans?"

"Yeah."

I think about it. I used to be a realtor, back when there were realtors. Then I worked for a leasing agency, where my job was to kick out people who stopped paying rent. But pretty soon nobody cared about rent. Money just stopped changing hands. I got the Legendary Americans job because I had driven for a ride-sharing service in college. Maybe I could get another driving job? It's hard to imagine. No one has enough money for gas, let alone drivers. In the end I tell Artemio I don't know, which is true. "What about you?" I ask.

"I'll move to China," he says, "maybe tech in a lab there. I should have done that years ago. I just thought things would get better here."

I nod, thinking I'm lucky. It's probably even harder to get work as a scientist than as a driver. "Why do you ask?"

Artemio shrugs. He stares out the window for a while. "When you were in school," he says, "did they make you watch that video where Franklin helps the kid save money?"

"Sounds familiar."

"It was black and white, from the fifties, I guess. This kid wants to go to a dance but it costs two dollars and he doesn't have the money. He spits on a coin and Franklin appears. But it's just Franklin's shadow, in a doorway, like a silhouette or whatever. Turns out the kid gets two dollars a week from his dad and three from making deliveries at the pharmacy, so Franklin's shadow tells the kid he's got plenty of money already. He just has to spend it right. Franklin helps the kid make a budget. Then the dad's so impressed by the budget that he gives the kid an advance on his allowance and he goes to the dance."

"Sounds like a valuable lesson," I say.

Artemio nods.

"Is that what got you into Franklin?"

Artemio laughs. "Nah, man, that video was ridiculous. Just another cheap-ass video they showed us to kill time. And I didn't know anybody who looked or talked like the people in the video, so it might as well have been about Martians." He pauses, as though replaying the video in his mind. "You know, the biggest problem with it wasn't the dumb kid or the ridiculous premise; it was the guy who played Franklin. The shadow. He had no charisma. Even as a kid I understood that Franklin, the real Franklin, had to have been a genius."

"I bet you're right. All those inventions…"

We drive for a while in silence, and I worry I've said something stupid. Honestly, I don't know too much about Benjamin Franklin. But eventually Artemio says, "Confronted with the way we live now, Ben Franklin wouldn't say the same crap he said before. The same old homilies about a penny saved and whatever. He would say something new. You know?"

"I bet you're right," I say again, almost automatically, but then I wonder if there's anything new to be said. It seems to me everything is recycled or repurposed. I say something to that effect and Artemio nods. "Even people are being repurposed," he says.

"That's right," I say. "Like you and me, with Works Progress."

"So why not historical people? Why not history itself?"

"There you go," I say, smiling uncertainly.

Artemio stares out the window. The landscape is almost black now. The moon must be behind some clouds.

The gig in Amarillo is at a derelict YMCA. Some of the windows are broken, and one side of the building is painted white for some reason. In the midday sun, it's almost too bright to look at. We're half an hour early so I park across the street at a church. We wait inside the truck, sipping coffee we brewed in a contraption Mike made that boils water using the truck's phone charger. No one speaks.

Soon a few pickup trucks lumber into the YMCA parking lot, and men in camouflage clothes and trucker caps get out of the trucks and greet each other. One of the men has a boy with him, maybe twelve or thirteen. The boy hefts a big olive drab bag out of the back of a truck and follows the men through a gap in a chain-link fence, then along the bright white side of the YMCA. They disappear behind the building.

"Interesting crowd," Artemio says.

"Guys like that are patriotic," Mike says.

For the next half hour we watch more trucks and big sedans pull into the parking lot, unloading a mixture of men and boys. Some of the boys are young, maybe seven or eight. Last to come, right at twelve-thirty, are a few older boys on dirt bikes.

"Maybe we should bring Daniel this time," Artemio says.

I'm Daniel.

"Why?" Mike asks.

"Three is better than two," Artemio says.

"But he doesn't have a costume. It'll ruin the effect."

"He can stand in back."

"Like a pimp?"

Eventually it's decided I'll follow at a distance, so as not to ruin the procession, then discreetly position myself near the door.

I drive across the street to the YMCA parking lot and get out with Artemio and Mike, careful to lock the cab of the truck. We go around back and Mike lifts the gate.

Franklin is sitting in what looks like a lounge chair, staring forward unblinking. An eerie moment passes before his oily eyes slide to look at Mike, then Artemio, then me. "Good afternoon, Daniel," he says. Then he says something that sounds like "bilf mork today." I have no idea how to reply.

"Daniel's helping us today," Mike says, and the two handlers climb into the back. Mike goes over the front of Franklin's waistcoat with a lint brush while Artemio smooths down Franklin's hair, which sticks up in places like broken shafts of wheat. Then the handlers put on their own outfits, which consist of knickers, blousy looking dress shirts, and powdered wigs. I extend the ramp and they lead Franklin down to the asphalt. He sniffs the air, standing perfectly still, then lowers his chin to examine the YMCA through the tops of his bifocals.

"Young Men's Christian Association," he says, "founded in eigh-teen-forty-four by George Williams, the manager of a London draper's shop, who, appalled at the terrible conditions in which young working men toiled, raised funds to create a place of refuge that wouldn't tempt them into sin."

"Sounds like he's ready to roll," Mike tells Artemio, who nods. They retract the ramp, close and lock the back of the truck, and flank Franklin as he trudges towards the metal front door of the YMCA. I follow about ten paces behind. Franklin knocks. We wait.

"Hello?" Franklin says.

We wait some more.

"Young Christians, will you offer us a welcome that does honor to your founder, George Williams, who in eighteen-forty-four—"

"Let's go around back," Mike says.

Artemio sighs.

We walk to the gap in the fence that the men and boys went through and follow their path into a small field. The grass is tall and full of shaggy weeds, some with yellow and purple flowers. Franklin raises a handkerchief and blazes ahead, waving the handkerchief like a signal flag. "March of my officers!" he declares.

"Around back," comes a high-pitched voice with a needling twang.

Franklin marches towards the voice, followed by Mike and Artemio. When Franklin clears the back of the building, he smiles and waves as he continues walking. Artemio and Mike hesitate. I can't yet see what they're seeing. Artemio looks back at me; there's panic in his eyes. Franklin starts talking: "Greetings, countrymen…"

I stick close to the wall and walk just far enough to see the assembly: about two dozen people, men and boys, standing and sitting in a half circle, facing us. The youngest boys sit cross-legged in front, some with their chins on their fists, looking exhausted. The long olive drab bag has been emptied, and the rifles it contained lie across men's laps or lean against their chairs. The men themselves stare almost expressionlessly at Franklin, as though they're posing for an ancient photograph, back when exposure took so long that no one was encouraged to smile.

"A house is not a home unless it contains food," Franklin is saying, "and fire for the mind as well as the body. Do you know that fire?" He splays his hands and looks around. No one responds. He turns his attention to a cross-legged boy in a Davy Crockett cap. "I admire that cap, young man," he says, "as well as the clever creature from which it derives, whose tiny, finger-like claws have caused all manner of trouble for farmer and burgher alike."

The boy tilts his head, causing the tail of the cap to curl on his shoulder like the tail of a living animal.

"During my time in France I wore a similar cap," Franklin says, "to give those lugubrious Frenchmen what they expected, which was a rustic American in desperate need of support from sophisticates like themselves. I wore a threadbare coat and horsehair breeches as well. John Adams was very embarrassed for me! It was shortly thereafter that King Louis the Sixteenth appointed me to his special commission to investigate the legitimacy of Franz Mesmer's controversial theory of animal magnetism, viz-a-viz the interpersonal and general effects of reciprocal influence among bodies and their so-called ethereal fluids."

The men stare. They're beginning to remind me of sated wolves. One, an old timer whose hat looks too big for his head, seems to have fallen asleep.

"Ethereal fluids," Franklin repeats like it's the punch line of a joke.

"What the hell are you talking about?" a bearded man asks.

Others second the bearded man.

"Franz Mesmer's controversial theory of animal magnetism," Franklin says affably, "viz-a-viz the interpersonal and general effects of reciprocal—"

"We don't wanna hear about that."

"What do you want to hear about?"

The bearded man says nothing.

Franklin says something that sounds like "groble mirmor."

"Huh?" the bearded man says.

"A life of leisure and life of laziness are two things," Franklin says, and then, when that gets no response, "there will be sleeping enough in the grave. Admiration is the daughter of ignorance. A place for everything, everything in its place."

Men start whispering. Artemio clears his throat.

"In seventeen-sixty-one I invented a glass harmonica for which both Mozart and Beethoven composed," Franklin says. "Have any of you young rapscallions tried your hands at music?"

The children say nothing.

"My harmonica consists of thirty-seven glass bowls mounted horizontally on an iron spindle, which is turned by means of a foot petal. The layered design makes it possible to play ten glasses simultaneously, whereas the traditional so-called 'upright goblet' arrangement precludes—"

"Didn't know Ben Franklin had long hair," the bearded man says. The children laugh.

"Didn't know he had faggot slaves," another man says.

I glance at Mike and Artemio. Mike is standing perfectly still, hands clasped behind his back, but Artemio seems to have turned slightly, as though preparing to run.

"Aw, they ain't faggots," the bearded man says, "just ugly women."

The men laugh.

The bearded man looks directly at Mike. "How about it, ladies? Which is it?"

"Pardon?" Mike says.

"Faggots or ugly women?"

Mike chuckles nervously. I'm waiting for Artemio to give me a sign, but I'm not sure what I'll do if he does. I haven't been in a fight since college, and I don't remember anything about the fight except that it ended quickly, in the arms of a bouncer who used my head to open a swinging door.

"A gentleman never tells," Franklin blurts.

The man who asked the question looks confused. "Didn't ask them if they fucked each other," he says, "just if they was wearing wigs."

This time, no one laughs.

Franklin doesn't say anything. Instead, he removes his reading glasses and begins to wipe them with his handkerchief.

The men are waiting.

Mike glances at Artemio, who's staring at the ground. "Wigs," Mike says, in delayed response to the man's question. "In the eighteenth century it was common for men to wear wigs on formal occasions. You'll notice on the dollar bill that—"

Franklin claps three times and starts doing his hornpipe dance. The children laugh. The men try to shush them but the laughter can't be stopped. One little boy hops to his feet. I think he's going to start dancing, but instead he sort of crouches with his fists balled up at his chest like he's about to burst into the air. Franklin moves towards him with his hand out, as if to request the favor of a dance. A rifle cocks.

I look at the bearded man, but it isn't him. It's the old man who looked like he was dozing. Now he stares darkly from beneath the brim of his oversized hat. The butt of his rifle is propped in the crook of his thigh. Franklin's hand freezes midair, as though the offer of a dance still stands, but the boy is slinking backwards like a wary animal.

I wonder if I should run for the truck and crash through the fence, to cause momentary confusion while Mike and Artemio climb in and we escape, but what about Franklin? Are we willing to leave him? I think I might be, but before I can do anything, a man notices me and lets his rifle stock fall lazily into his hand, such that the weapon is pointed more or less in my direction. He eyes me coolly.

"Well?" the bearded man says.

"Will you repeat the question?" Franklin asks. His outstretched hand has been still for so long that he's begun to seem less human, and to me, at least, a little menacing. A few flies buzz around his head. The children have backed away from him and are standing at the feet of their fathers and brothers. Because of his size and the radius that has formed around him, Franklin looks like a bull in the middle of a ring.

"Didn't ask no question," the man says.

"Then shall I tell you about my diplomacy in France? My adventures as the first Postmaster General in Philadelphia? My apprenticeship to my half-brother, who worked me like a dray horse, lashed me, and made me watch while he assaulted filthy street girls my own age whom he forced, afterwards, to clean his printing press?"

The men stare.

"Get outta here," one of them says.

Artemio turns quickly and heads straight through the weeds, not even bothering to find the trodden path by which we came.

Mike hesitates, glances at Franklin. "Mister Franklin?" he says.

Franklin straightens, makes a florid bow, and walks with Mike back to the fence.

I follow.

Fifteen minutes later we're sitting in a booth at a gas station diner outside of Amarillo. Through the window, I can see a woman with three small children filling a battered car with gasoline. The bright blue sky yawns above her. Mike is saying, "Don't be so dramatic. They were just having a laugh."

"They had *guns*," Artemio says.

"Guys like that take their guns everywhere. They're just bored."

"Bored, sure, so why not lynch some guys. Some *faggots*."

Mike smiles. "Come on, give 'em a break. Can you imagine life in a place like this?"

"I don't want to."

"Well, these people don't have a choice."

"I do."

"You're being petulant."

Artemio squints at Mike. "We're on the road every day, away from our homes, and for what? For some fucking degenerates with guns? Assholes who haven't learned *anything*?"

An old man, the only other customer in the diner, glances up from his coffee.

"At least the kids seemed to enjoy themselves," Mike says, "for a while."

"Ah yes," Artemio says, leaning back in his seat, "and so the union of engaged citizenry is affirmed for one more generation. Thank goodness."

Mike laughs. He's trying to be cool, but I can tell he's rattled. My guess is he shares some of Artemio's misgivings but feels self-conscious admitting as much in front of me. I get up and go to the bathroom, to give them some privacy.

While I use the toilet and wash my hands, I think about the men and their rifles, about their slouched bodies and lazy stares. I wonder if the crowds are getting worse as time goes on, or if it's Franklin. Or maybe it's just a matter of venturing further afield. Maybe the kids out here don't even know they're U.S. citizens.

When I come back, both handlers are sitting in silence, their hands wrapped around their mugs of coffee. It's as though something has been decided. I sit down.

"Bad news," Mike says.

"Oh yeah?" I say, glancing at Artemio. He doesn't look at me, just stares into his coffee.

"The hotel in Lubbock closed," Mike says.

"Shit," I say, but I'm not surprised. We book the cheapest hotels. "Want me to call around?"

"DC already did. Looks like we're roughing it."

He means camping, which doesn't bother me, except I've never been to Lubbock and if it's anything like Amarillo we might be in trouble. I picture rattlesnakes slithering into our sleeping bags, coyotes howling in the distance.

On the way to Lubbock, Mike talks nonstop. He tells me the farms in the area used to grow cotton, but then the government subsidies ran out, along with something called the Ogallala Aquifer. Now the arid landscape has reasserted itself. The ground is flat and cracked. The white and gray towers of downtown Lubbock stand like tombstones in the hazy distance.

The campground is empty, indistinguishable from the rest of the flat landscape except for a small hill covered in desert scrub.

I drive towards the base of the hill, even though it means trundling half a mile on a rocky dirt road. Maybe some primitive part of my brain understands that this hill will provide shelter from wind, or high ground in case of attack. Neither Mike nor Artemio complains about the bumpy ride.

We set up the canopy on the side of the truck and lay the ground tarp. Each of us blows up his air mattress. The sun is low now, screaming orange and pink through the western sky. Mike, who was a Boy Scout, says we should gather a mixture of twigs and sticks about the thickness of our fingers.

By the time we're done gathering wood, the sun is gone except for a rim of purple beyond some far-off mountains. Mike constructs a little teepee of twigs and sparks a fire. We sit around the fire sipping water mixed with the last of Artemio's gin. We don't drink much anymore, so the liquor has a strong effect. I find myself musing aloud about the liquor laws of various states. Texas, I'm sure, has a strict one. "Maybe we can buy more gin in New Mexico," I say, "or whiskey. I don't really like gin. My grandmother used to say it was slightly narcotic. We go to New Mexico when? Monday?"

"Tuesday," Mike says. "Clovis. First we hit Midland. Isn't that right, Art?"

"Yeah," Artemio says.

It's surprisingly cold, and I'm thankful for the fire. For a moment I think about Franklin sitting in the back of the truck. I wonder if he's cold, and if he's conscious of things like cold, or wet, or lonely.

Mike pokes the fire with a stick and tosses the stick onto the fire.

I find myself wishing Franklin was sitting with us. When I first started driving, we used to ask him questions just to hear what kind of crazy answers he came up with, or to get him to launch into one of his ribald stories about the women of France. But by now we've heard all his stories, too many times.

We talk about baseball for a while, since we read the standings and some box scores in a newspaper at the diner in Amarillo. Artemio likes the Angels. He grew up in Riverside. I don't care about baseball but I used to go to minor league games with my dad. I tell Mike and Artemio about the glorious Batavia Muckdogs. Mike says he takes his twin girls to Orioles games even though they're too young to understand what's going on. Artemio says his husband's father, who used to live with them, watched every single Cubs game start to finish. Then a silence settles over us. It was decided long ago that we wouldn't talk too much about home.

Mike tosses five or six big sticks into the fire and we climb into our sleeping bags. I shut my eyes and do a thing I do to fall asleep, which is to imagine my body spreading thinner and thinner, like a puddle, until it disappears. But I'm still awake. My mind is tingling. Sometimes I envy Mike and Artemio, with their home-lives, but then I think about how hard it must be to be away from all that. I had a girlfriend back home, but we had a fight when I left. We broke up. It wasn't a big deal, I guess. I never imagined us getting married. But sometimes I think about all the things we did together. Now I do everything with Mike and Artemio. And Franklin.

I'm still thinking about my girlfriend, the way her long dark hair fell around her neck and over her pale chest, when I start hearing the nighttime noises: coyotes, probably, but I imagine a large wolf circling our campsite at a distance. My thoughts have begun to bend towards dreaming. The wolf trails a wide and inky swath of night. He tells me he's been following me for a long time.

2.

Half dreaming, I think I've overslept. I think Mike and Artemio have taken Franklin to Lubbock without me. But the gig isn't until ten, I remember, and the sun hasn't risen yet. There are tire tracks where the truck was parked. My clothes are in a pile on top of my shoes. The only other remnants of our campsite are the ground tarp, my bedding, and a circle of ashes and charred sticks where the fire used to be. I scan the flat horizon for the truck, but everything is still dark blue and hard to see.

When I start putting on my clothes, I find a wad of cash in my shoe: three hundred and forty-six dollars. In my other shoe is a roadmap of

Texas. I feel around inside my shoes for a note, find nothing. I search the pockets of my pants. Nothing. My phone is missing too.

Confusion gives way to anger. If they wanted to quit, why didn't they tell me? Were they worried I would call DC? I wouldn't have. And I wouldn't have quarreled with them. It's their project. They make the decisions. Eighteen months together on the road, and they didn't even know me.

I put on my shoes and start walking up the hill to get a better look at my surroundings. The hill is bigger than it looks. At the top, I'm winded and realize I didn't bring water. But there wasn't any water to bring, was there? For a bewildering moment I think Mike and Artemio are trying to kill me, but then I remember the cash. They wouldn't have left so much cash if they expected me to die. And Lubbock doesn't look very far away. Five, maybe ten miles. A few tall buildings stand in the distance.

I descend slowly, conserving my energy. I keep my mouth closed and swish saliva through my teeth. The spit feels gummy.

Coming down the hill, I see a mound of dirt a little ways from where the truck was parked. I can tell it's fresh because the soil is dark and there aren't any weeds on it. In a flash I picture Artemio murdering Mike, or Mike murdering Artemio, like something out of the Bible, but the grave looks too big. Or maybe *grave* isn't the right word, considering what's almost certainly inside it. I can't believe I slept through the digging. It must have taken hours. Or maybe they made him—it—dig its own grave?

I stuff my sleeping bag into the sack, find room for the air mattress too, then I sling the sack over my shoulder and start walking.

The ground is so flat and free of vegetation that the best thing to do, I decide, is head straight for Lubbock. A person walks about three miles per hour, so if Lubbock is five miles away then I'll be there in less than two hours. The sun is directly in front of me but still red with distance. It isn't hot yet.

After maybe half an hour I reach a two-lane highway. I stand for a moment on the shoulder. Yellow grass twists up through the gravel at my feet. I unfold the part of the roadmap that shows West Texas and see several Farm-to-Market roads that run north and south. The question is whether this road is FM 179, on the outskirts of Lubbock proper, or FM 2378, about six miles away. Though I suppose it could also be FM 230, which is halfway to someplace called Levelland.

While I'm puzzling over the map I hear something rustle. I look up, expecting to see a jackrabbit or maybe a lizard, whatever can survive out here, but I see nothing.

I keep walking.

Downtown Lubbock doesn't look any closer. I tell myself to stop looking at the buildings so maybe next time I look they'll seem bigger. But without looking, there isn't anything to do except think. I think about those runners from Kenya, about their big powerful hearts and lightweight bodies. My own heart must be tiny. A flabby little rabbit heart sort of wafting blood through my big ungainly body. And Franklin, did he even *have* a heart? If so, is it still pumping? I picture him with his eyes open, his eyeballs smeared with wet dirt, staring into darkness as he did in the back of the truck for so many months. Fucking Mike, I think. Fucking Artemio. What harm was he doing, sitting in the back? Was he really such a burden? Was *I*?

It's getting hotter. My skin feels chalky. My girlfriend, ex-girlfriend, told me it was dangerous away from cities. That's where people die, she said. I told her she was being a snob. But maybe *this* was what she meant. This emptiness. This heat. I wonder if I should rig up some kind of hat. I could use the extra fabric from the tails of my shirt to make a sort of headdress like Arabians wear.

I reach another highway—FM 2378?—but downtown Lubbock still doesn't look any closer. The sun is high now and seems to be focusing all its rays right on my forehead, which is hot and oily as a frying pan. I have to take shelter, at least until the hottest part of the day is over. I see a few ragged wooden buildings up the highway and head towards them along the shoulder, though I might as well walk down the center of the road. I haven't seen a car since yesterday.

The buildings turn out to be what's left of a barn and a shed. They used to be white but the white paint has peeled so badly that it looks like ashes. The shed is full of cobwebs and rusty metal barrels. The barn is empty. I circle once around the property, looking for a water spigot, but I find only a few empty wooden spools and a broken-down cart of some sort, maybe for cotton. I go into the barn and lay out my air mattress, but I don't have the energy to inflate it. I unroll my sleeping bag and lie down.

The vaulted ceiling of the barn is full of bright blue holes, but

the rafters are straight and look solid. One massive beam traverses the
entire barn and has hooks hanging from it. It's a very well made barn,
I decide, and for a moment I imagine re-shingling the roof and drilling
a new well and staying forever. Then I remember what Mike said about
the Ogallala Aquifer drying up. I close my eyes.

When I started the job, all I knew was that I drove three guys
around in a truck, and that one of the guys was old and fat and
stayed in the back of the truck. At first we just went to places in DC,
Baltimore, Philadelphia, small towns in and around there. It wasn't
until we did a Fourth of July parade in Columbia, Maryland, and I had
to help Mike and Artemio lift the old guy onto a parade float, that I
realized he looked familiar. Another guy, watching us, was dressed up
as George Washington, or maybe Thomas Jefferson, so clearly our guy
was a founding father. I wondered why we were chauffeuring a guy
dressed up as a founding father. Didn't other cities have their own guys
who dressed up as founding fathers? I decided this was one of the
jobs Works Progress slapped together just to get people off the street,
and I was fine with that. Most of those jobs were building highways,
fixing up schools, but some of the jobs were pretty queer, I knew. My
brother-in-law was part of a crew that dug a ten-thousand-acre pond
in Georgia and planted algae in it.

I hear scratching, or dream I hear scratching. Claws dragging slowly
down the walls of the barn, or is it my apartment? I tell my girlfriend to
lock the doors because the wolf is coming, but she just sits there on the
couch with her arms crossed, saying it's no use, the wolf knows all our
passwords. I run into the kitchen, where the clawing is louder. I want
to tell my girlfriend to hide in the bathroom, the only room without
windows, but I know in my heart that the wolf already has her. I'm
trying to cram myself into a cabinet under the sink when I wake up. My
heart is racing. For a panicked moment I think I've been buried alive. I
can almost feel the wet dirt on my eyes and in my mouth, but then I see
the bluish spots in the ceiling. They're darker now. It must be evening.
My throat is burning with thirst. My mouth, which hangs open when I
sleep, is numb and cracked on the inside.

The scratching persists.

The wide barn door rattles with each feeble scratch. I picture the
wolf, but there aren't any wolves anymore, I tell myself, and anyway

that was a dream. At worst it's an emaciated coyote, or maybe a dog. One of the thousands left behind to wander the streets of abandoned suburbs and towns.

There's a shuffling sound, as though the animal has exhausted itself and is slinking off somewhere to sleep, or maybe die. Quietly I roll up my sleeping bag and air mattress, slide them into the stuff sack, and creep towards the far side of the barn, opposite the door. I knock the few remaining shards out of a windowsill, drop my sack out the window, and climb through.

Back on the road, the sun is low and the buildings of downtown Lubbock show their full colors: deep oranges, chalky grays, a single white tower that looks like alabaster.

Sleep has done nothing to rejuvenate me. Still, it's better to be walking at night. Less chance of sunburn, dehydration. I make a game out of choosing a little evergreen bush and heading towards it for a while and then, when I get to that bush, choosing another. Then another. I convince myself that the buildings are getting bigger. Light from the setting sun bounces off the windows of one tower in a shimmering burst of orange that makes me think of a broken mirror and then, later, as my exhaustion mounts, of a second sun in a distant galaxy not unlike our own. An exploding sun that's engulfing the planets all around it.

I'm approaching my seventeenth bush when I hear the shuffling again. I try to keep a steady pace, to pretend I don't hear anything, but I can't escape thoughts of the wolf. In my mind, my girlfriend is hanging from its giant mouth. Mike and Artemio too. Slobber drips from the loose flesh of its lips. *Groble mirmor. Bilf mork today.*

The sky is dark now, full of stars. I cross a road. FM179? I wish I'd counted the roads. I think I see a building in the distance. Dim lights. Cars. A gas station? I turn to head towards the gas station, and when I do I hear a sound like a car skidding on rocks. A big bush I passed earlier is shaking gelatinously. I can't decide if I'm hallucinating or if there's something behind the bush. A coyote? A dog? A man? I turn around and keep walking. Fuck the gas station. I'm almost to Lubbock.

As I walk I try to listen for whoever, or whatever, is following me, but the shuffling of my own heavy feet makes that impossible. I trip over a root and stumble a few paces. I throw down my sleeping bag in frustration.

In the silence, I can hear the same sound as before. The skidding. I turn around, see nothing.

"Who's there?" I ask.

Still I see nothing.

"What do you want? Why are you following me?"

In the darkness, the silence is menacing. I think of the hill where I was abandoned. I think of the grave. I think of the crouching boy at the YMCA with his hands cocked at his sides, ready to explode into the air. I keep walking, but the sliver of moon does nothing to light my way, and my game of following bushes is ended. I keep stumbling. My feet hurt. My mouth too, like there are cuts inside it. I have no choice but to stop, to sleep under the stars with no fire, no food, and no water, but where can I lie so I'll feel some semblance of security? There aren't any hills or buildings I can see, so I head for a dark spot that turns out to be a cluster of prickly bushes. There's a space among the bushes for my prone body. I unroll my air mattress and start to inflate it, but blowing hurts the inside of my cracked mouth so I give up. I lay out the sleeping bag and climb inside. It's hot in there, but the bag makes me feel secure. I cinch the cord until the only parts of me exposed to the night are my nose and eyes. Above me, the stars are so bright I can see the Milky Way, which looks like ghosts marching away from the Earth.

The noises come as if on cue, but I don't have the energy to sit up or even call out. I don't care anymore if it's a wolf or a highwayman or Franklin himself. I almost laugh, imagining the weird oaf shambling after me all those miles.

Franklin.

My first theory, after that Fourth of July parade in Columbia, was that our Franklin impersonator was just a really good actor. A national treasure who fell on hard times. At the end of the parade, he gave a funny self-deprecating speech about his own vanity, and I thought it was just for a laugh until he started talking about the role of pageantry and tradition in keeping up spirits. It was a great speech. Way better than the George Washington guy's speech, which didn't surprise me; our guy was a professional. Or so I thought. Another driver told me that they captured Franklin's DNA from inside a tooth of his corpse, and that they used hormones to make him grow at an accelerated pace, and that the rapid, hormone-fueled growth was why his skin sagged so unnaturally and had a flaky, pastry-like quality that made the driver think of Bible lepers. For my own part the awful skin made me think of a fish belly-up on a scummy lakeshore, or of an old leather football left in a damp field. But the fact that Mike was a computer programmer made me wonder if Franklin's brain was a computer of some sort, which would have explained how heavy he was and why he repeated himself sometimes, like a glitch. Now, knowing how they abandoned him, I wonder if Mike and Artemio weren't a little afraid of Franklin. If there wasn't something nefarious about the whole project. Something unknown even to them. Necromancy. Grave robbing. Bodies aren't hard to come by these days, and cosmetic surgeons need work too. Worse, the body may have had to be fresh. I can imagine Artemio watching DC homeless through binoculars as they emerged, bleary eyed, from underpasses, slouched in and out of the Mall, wandered down into the lazy ravine of Rock Creek Park. When his Franklin appeared, Artemio might not have recognized him at first. But hours later, when the sun was high and the old man took off his stocking cap to scratch his bald head, or when he took out a crooked pair of bifocals to read a day-old newspaper, Artemio would have seen what the man could become. *People are being repurposed.* That's what you said, Artemio—but what was our purpose to begin with?

The moon is high enough that I can make out a dark shape beyond my feet, partly concealed by the bush I hoped would hide me. The large round shape is perfectly still, so I sit up slowly, still wrapped in my sleeping bag, to get a better view.

His jacket and shirt are torn. His hair is matted in strange, serpentine shapes. His face remains hidden. For a confused moment I wonder if he was conjured by my own imagination, but no, I decide, it was his proximity which caused *me*, almost as mystically, to imagine *him*. His head turns, and in the moonlight I can see a few patches of pale skin on his face, but not his eyes. I wonder if they're still covered in dirt, or if, during the struggle, they were gouged out, if his face was maimed.

"Mister Franklin," I say, in case he can't see me, "it's Daniel."

Slowly, painstakingly, Franklin begins to stand, and in doing so releases a series of awful cracks, as though his body is a system of giant, hollow knuckles full of resonant fluid. His face is intact, but one ear dangles from a scrap of flesh or whatever flesh-like substance covers and protects him.

"Good morning, Daniel," he says, ejecting dirt from his mouth. He isn't quite looking at me. His hand spasms like he's trying to wave.

"What happened to you?" I ask.

"There was some confusion," he says vaguely, as though he's hesitant to speak ill of the men who did this to him, and to me, "but luckily I have our orders."

"What orders?"

"In Lubbock," he says, "the site of our next appointment."

"You're kidding."

"Never about something so serious. Whisperwood Ranch."

"What?"

"The site of our next appointment. You seem distracted, Daniel. I'll be relying on you to drive me there."

"Drive you in what? They took the truck."

"The French? Tell Anaghrisson, warrior chief of the Mingo."

"Mike and Artemio."

"Hmm. Then we must march. You'll have to don period costume."

"The costumes were in the truck." But that's the least of our worries. If we show up at this Whisperwood Ranch place, whatever it is, with Franklin looking like he does, the clients will call the police, or the local militia, or maybe shoot us themselves; that is, if they don't run screaming at the sight of him. Still, we're both headed to Lubbock, and I could use the company.

"Shall we walk?" Franklin asks.

"Tomorrow," I say. "It's too dark."

"We will navigate by the light of the moon, like explorers in days of old, exploiters of men, hearty raconteurs all."

I shake my head. "We'll leave tomorrow first thing."

Franklin starts to lower himself, but one of his knees bends the wrong way and he falls forward onto the ground with an awful, inhuman *thump*. I try to help him up but all I can do is roll him onto his back. His blousy shirt is untucked and the bottom buttons have ripped off. Bathed in moonlight, his exposed belly looks like the top of a breaching sperm whale. I watch it, trying to see if it rises and falls, if he's breathing. I wonder if he'll be able to stand up again, let alone walk all the way to Whisperwood Ranch.

I head back to my sleeping bag, but I can't imagine lying in that scratchy space between the bushes again, so I tug out the bag and lay it next to Franklin, who hasn't budged. His dirty eyeballs are pointed at the night sky. I lie down next to him, head to foot. My face is only inches from where his leather shoe with its polished buckle is bent sideways at an awkward angle. I turn so my back is towards him, and when my eyes are closed I listen closely. I can't hear him breathing, and yet I sense that I'm close to another person. It's an uncanny sense. I remember lying in bed with my girlfriend, with other women I've known, with my brother and sister. I wonder if Franklin feels anything like what I'm feeling.

The sky is gray and my head hurts. My eyes sting. I try to close them and go back to sleep but Franklin says, "There will be sleeping enough in the grave."

He's standing above me, his face improbably clean and his hair smooth against his head and neck. Even his shirt has been mended somehow.

"Daniel," he says in a somewhat scolding tone I haven't heard him use, "you're paid to perform a service."

"Nobody pays," I say. "We do it for free."

"I refer to the United States of America, which pays your salary."

He's right, of course, and I'm sure my salary will be paid, along with those of Mike and Artemio, until long after news of our dissolution makes it to DC. I picture a person behind a desk at Works Progress working up the nerve to call my mother, who's listed as next-of-kin, and tell her they don't know where I am. The truck is missing. My colleagues as well. Probably this well-meaning person will imagine that the creature, Franklin, short-circuited and killed us in our sleep: cinched our sleeping bags and crushed our skulls with his massive hands, or pried through the back of the truck cab to wrest control of the steering wheel and drive us, screaming, off the rim of a rose-colored canyon.

"When I was Postmaster General in Philadelphia," Franklin says, "I was paid only a token salary but made my rounds with pride."

"Good for you," I mutter.

Franklin nods. "It wasn't until later that the position became something of a sinecure given by Presidents to key political supporters whom, the Presidents hoped, would use the postal network to galvanize patronage."

I rise and begin stolidly to roll up my sleeping bag. While I do this,

Franklin takes my empty water bottle and stuffs it with the leafy branch of a nearby shrub. He hands the bottle to me and I put it in my pocket, thinking he's crazy. He takes my bag and hangs it around his neck by its cord. When he strides ahead of me, the puffy bag rocks back and forth across his wide back like an idiot's idea of a cape. I follow a few paces behind.

Franklin waves his handkerchief. "March of my officers!"

We don't speak. Lubbock is much closer now, but I'm too tired to be happy. We come to an empty two-lane highway (FM 179? finally?) and Franklin crosses it without stopping. I follow. Farmhouses stand in the distance.

Eventually Franklin starts to limp. His right foot has turned sideways and is dragging behind a knee that's bent at an unnatural angle. But when I catch up to him, Franklin's cheerful expression is unchanged.

"Last night you were dreaming," he says.

"Yeah?"

"You spoke in sleep of a wolf."

"Huh." I don't want to talk about the wolf.

"The religions of our Indian neighbors abound in mystical wolves. There is also the giant wolf Fenrir who, at the end of the world, rides across the sea in a boat made of shoe leather."

We come to a four-lane road and see actual cars, two of them, puttering in the distance. I watch them longingly. I want so badly to raise my thumb, though no one ever hitchhikes anymore and my mother used to tell me it was a great way to get kidnapped. I wonder why Franklin isn't stopping. Doesn't he trust strangers? He seems so optimistic. But maybe he knows something I don't. Maybe the people of Lubbock are gun-crazed, like the men at the Amarillo YMCA. I start to see the city differently. The houses are unlit. Most are empty, I imagine, and the ones that aren't are kept dark so as not to attract marauders. Family members take turns sitting by the front doors with shotguns across their laps. They lay traps for jackrabbits and feral dogs. They don't pay taxes and have no concept of the federal government. They amputate limbs. They kill trespassers without compunction.

I find myself walking close to Franklin. His leg looks bad. At the end of each slouching step, his foot scrapes against the dirt with a hiss. I wonder if I should tie some kind of splint, to keep the knee from bending further the wrong way, but my hands feel too weak to tie knots. Anyway, Franklin doesn't seem bothered by the leg. He's humming a tune.

We pass ranch-style houses on huge tracts of crisp dead grass. I wonder if I could knock on a door, ask for water. I veer away from Franklin without saying anything.

"Daniel," he says.

I stop.

"Reach into your pocket."

I reach into my pocket and pull out the water bottle. A few teaspoons of water have accumulated at the bottom. I look at Franklin, who's smiling, and remember Artemio's words: *Franklin, the real Franklin, is a genius.* I unscrew the lid and pour the water into my mouth, swish it around. The leaves have given the water an almost minty flavor that stings my gums. When I swallow the delicious water, I think I can feel it enter my bloodstream and get pumped out to my fingertips, which strike me as pinker now and somehow more alive.

Franklin takes the bottle and stuffs in another leafy branch. He screws down the top and hands it back to me. We continue.

In the distance stands a cluster of red brick buildings that look like apartments. There's a large parking lot, mostly empty, and a few spindly Live Oaks. Franklin speeds up. I can hear his leg crack with each stride.

"Maybe we should slow down," I say.

"It's already ten o'clock."

"But the gig was yesterday. Why does it matter?"

"Why does it matter," Franklin repeats, but he doesn't answer the question.

After another delicious sip of minty water, I start to wonder if Whisperwood Ranch is an airfield, and if Franklin knows by some sort of chip in his cybernetic brain that a plane will be leaving there for DC. Is it possible he made plans to meet Mike and Artemio? I hurry. I try not to think about the cracking leg.

We're heading straight for the brick buildings. There are some people out front on a bench. One of them, a man, is in a wheelchair.

Crack.

Franklin stops. His body teeters. Slowly, it tips sideways like a staved ship taking on water. I make a lame attempt to steady him but he's much too heavy, and I scoot out of the way to avoid being crushed.

His body lands with an awful *thump*, the loudness of which causes a visceral reaction inside me, a panicked thought of death; only a dead thing could fall like that. A cloud of dust has risen where Franklin lies. His leg, the one that was limping, is jackknifed sideways.

"Franklin?" I say.

He doesn't respond.

I kneel and touch his back. "Franklin? Can you hear me?"

He doesn't move. He's lying face down, but his head is turned so I can see one of his eyes. Its smooth surface bears a residue of the dirt that was smeared there in the grave. Beneath my hand I feel a rattling, and the lawnmower sound of his throat starts up.

"It matters," he says at length, "because, although the Constitution gives one the right to pursue happiness, one has to catch it himself."

I look into Franklin's dirty eye and wonder if he really means to suggest I'm going to "catch" happiness by doing this gig. How will a gig at Whisperwood Ranch, or anywhere else, make me happy again? And was I happy before, with my home and girlfriend and semi-normal job? Was the wolf not nipping at my heels even then? It's hard to remember. Feelings fade so quickly, unlike images, which linger strangely, patchily, almost forever.

"It matters," Franklin repeats, "because it is the working man who is the happy man, whereas the idle man is miserable."

"Sure," I say.

"It matters because it takes many good deeds to build a reputation, and only one bad one to lose it. Because lost time is never found again. Because hunger is the best pickle. Because—"

"Okay, okay."

The man in the wheelchair is speeding towards us. His hair is white and his face is wrinkled, but his arms, pumping at the wheels of his wheelchair, seem impossibly strong. He skids to a stop right in front of us and looks appraisingly at Franklin.

"Nurse is on her way," he says to me. "He your daddy?"

"Colleague," I say.

"It's five past ten," Franklin says. "Daniel, apologize to this man."

"What?"

"Have you learned nothing? Waste your own time all you like, but never waste another man's, for in doing that you waste a life that is not yours to waste."

The old man grunts, then squints as though he's trying to remember something. "Didn't Ben Franklin say that?"

3.

Inside Whisperwood Ranch Retirement Home and Nursing Facility, only a few of the residents are aware that a guest speaker missed his appointment yesterday. That speaker, a simulacrum of Benjamin Franklin, lies in a small, brightly lit room where he's having his leg set by a physical therapist named Trina. I, his driver, sit in one of several leather club chairs surrounding a big stone fireplace. In the other chairs sit elderly people in various stages of resting and sleep. I was dozing myself, dreaming of a wolf who portends the twilight of human history, but now a man in a wheelchair is looking for a chess set so we can play. I told him I don't know how but he said he'd teach me.

A young man in khakis and a polo shirt announces that lunch will be served in fifteen minutes. Residents begin to muster. Soon we're in a room full of long tables where we're served borsht and oily garlic bread by a woman whose polo shirt matches the man's. The borsht is extremely sweet, and I worry about my teeth. I tend to get cavities. Nearby, a man removes his teeth and places them on the table next to his plate of food.

After lunch I get taught, painstakingly, to play chess. When he isn't telling me where to move my pieces, the man in the wheelchair, my opponent and instructor, tells me about a video he saw when he was a boy in the sixties. "If it weren't for that video," he says, "I never would have saved the money to buy my first car. But in the video he goes to a dance. That's what the money's for. Remember dances?"

"Vaguely," I say, though I remember them well. I took my high-school girlfriend to a dance. We made love for the first time, one year later, after the same annual dance.

"What an organized mind," the old man says, studying the board. "Every morning he made a list of what he had to do that day. That's where I got the idea. Did it every day of my life." He takes my knight. "Nowadays I wouldn't even know what to put on the list."

"Or where to write it," an old woman adds. She and a few others have gathered around us, muttering about lists and dances and Benjamin Franklin. They get quiet when they sense that the endgame has begun. I have only two pawns and my king. The man in the wheelchair is calculatedly chasing me around the board. But my fate is suspended with a *whoosh* as, across the room, a set of double-doors swings open, rustling our hair, and my opponent and the others look up with such surprise that I wonder if the doors have been closed for years.

The wide doorway is nearly filled by a man whose once-exquisite clothes accentuate his round and regal body. The man, who doesn't look any younger than his audience, smiles and gives a gallant flip of his hand.

"All who think cannot but see," the man proclaims, "that there is a sanction among us like that of religion, which binds us as partners in the serious work of the world."

MAGELLAN

By the end we were starving. Barros and me. Magellan had long since lowered the sails, so we lay on the deck in the naked sun. Sweat trickled through fresh cracks in our skin, and the acid inside our bubbling, distended stomachs sloshed with each rock of the boat onto hidden sores, and with each slow, creaking rock came a dim chorus of moans from belowdecks, where Pigafetta and the other survivors were chained. Magellan had caught them cannibalizing the boatswain. It was an atrocity he would not tolerate, and he made Barros and me, the only crewmen who had refrained, chain up the cannibals a safe distance from each other. Now they spent their days sleeping and starving and setting homemade traps for the turkeys.

Lying on the deck I imagined the crow's nest that teetered above me to be an obscene metronome, counting off their lives. Neither Barros nor I had the energy to check on them, and what energy we did have was spent scouring inside the great wooden pepper boxes for stray peppercorns. It had been twenty days since our last proper meal. Lately, we had been chewing on a length of rope. It lay between us. I touched it with my foot to gauge its heft and said that I thought we could chew on it some more.

Barros raised his head a few centimeters to see for himself. He shook his head no, and he was right. If the rope had been a snake, what lay at our feet was its skeleton. The edges of my eye teeth were jagged from sucking on it.

"Jew."

Both of us pretended not to hear the word. Barros was Jewish. As soon as Magellan learned this, he had fixated upon it. "Every man has his weakness," he said to Barros, echoing his famous proclamation to the Lapula Indians. He whispered to me right after, "Yours is that you're a slave and a Malay cannibal. You want to take a big bite out of my ass, don't you, you hungry cannibal?" He was always whispering things like this to me. Secretly, I was thankful when he found out about Barros being Jewish.

Barros raised his shallow buttocks from the deck and rolled onto his belly. He pressed his mouth and forehead against the bleached, buckling wood.

"Don't cut your face on the deck," I said. "We haven't swabbed it for quite some time." This was a joke, based on Magellan's utter abandonment of traditional seafaring.

"Jew."

The door to Magellan's cabin was slightly ajar, framed in the forecastle by two dark, circular windows like expressionless eyes. Wheezing confirmed that Magellan was standing in the narrow shaft of darkness. Was he staring at us? Was his mouth hanging open? I could almost smell the turkey meat.

The sea was gray as dishwater, complete with scummy froth. A shiny dolphin breached the surface, and I turned to watch a thin tower of water shoot from its blowhole. When I turned back, Magellan was standing in the doorway, his pink and purple robes flapping in the breeze. He held a turkey leg. He said, "Get over here, you Jew." His voice was slurred. "Your shiny head is like," he said, then thought for a moment. His insults had become strange and abstract. "Your shiny head is like a disgusting moon."

Barros sighed. I could tell he was preparing to stand up and go to Magellan. Barros was the navigator of the *Trinidad* and at one time had wanted very much to help Magellan. I pressed my foot against Barros's leg, and he looked at me. I hoped my face said, 'Don't go talk to Magellan,' but it was so wrinkled and blistered who knows what it said. Barros mumbled something and began to sit up. Then Magellan withdrew. The cabin door closed. Barros lay down beside me again, a little closer than before. Relieved, we reminisced about how in the land of the giants Magellan had lashed his legs to the torsos of José and Pigafetta and worn his longest robe in order to look like a giant himself. The natives had discovered this stupid trick immediately, but instead of running, Magellan had pulled out his penis and swung it around. Either because of its absurd length or its many fleshy colors, the natives had been fascinated by it. They served us fruit the consistency of sand.

Laughter came from the cabin, as if Magellan were listening to our story. His laughter was like a series of short, monotone yells. It was hysterical and lasted for minutes.

Barros covered his ears. He was cracking up from it, I could tell. I took a rag out of my pocket and put it on his head, because the sun was directly above us and Barros, though young, was quite bald. He mumbled thanks. Soon, the laughter stopped.

Before the boatswain incident, we used to gather belowdecks during the hottest hours to play cards and tell lies about exotic sexual positions we had learned from native women. For a while after the incident, after chaining up the others, Barros and I still went below and attempted conversation. But the men resented us for chaining them up. The last time, Pigafetta read aloud from his journal that I was a slave and a criminal and easily the most poorly trained seaman with whom he had ever voyaged. I explained that I was not a trained seaman and had been purchased by Magellan ten years before, but Pigafetta pretended he hadn't been there when Magellan showed up pulling me, his new translator, by a rope tied around my skinny brown waist. Pigafetta waved the open journal at me. He believed that after all of us died, the journal would be discovered and the truth of my villainy would be known. I asked him, isn't the real enemy Magellan? But Pigafetta was unwilling or unable to admit this. Now, he and the others had languished so badly that their knobby elbows and knees made me gag. I worried, too, that after I climbed the ladder down to the cavernous hold, I would not have the strength to climb back up. And, of course, there were the turkeys: a gift from the Coha Baloa Indians. Once, there had been thirty of the strange creatures, mostly female. The few males made such awful noises—yelping like dogs, purring like cats, cackling like maniacs—that Magellan ate them first. He ordered us to kill them, and they faced us down like sexual rivals, puffing out their chests, worming their penis-like necks back and forth to show the reds and blues in them, spreading their dark tails in semicircles that shone green in the sun until finally, with a girlish scream, they leapt at us with their feet out like claws, and we stuck them.

"Get over here, you Jew."

I didn't dare turn my head to look at the source of the slurred, wheezing voice. Neither did Barros, who closed his eyes in horror.

"You two are like skinny wolves from Muscovy, trembling and horribly shaved. One is black and one is white. I wonder if you can have puppies together!" Magellan laughed raucously. With luck, he would stand in the doorsill flinging curses at us until he grew bored and retired again. But when the deck began to creak under his prodigious weight, I knew we were in for more substantive indignity.

Barros worried the tattered edge of his shirt. A drop of sweat rolled from his bristly chin into his ear. I patted his hand and considered how to deflect Magellan's tirade away from Barros and towards me. But secretly I did not want to do this at all. I did not want Magellan looking at me with his hungry, desperate eyes.

The smell of barely cooked turkey was overpowering, and from it I knew he was standing beside us. It was too late to hope that by ignoring him he would go away. Now it was time for appeasement. I sat up.

Magellan was holding a turkey leg, wiping it back and forth across his chapped lips. Pieces of skin clung to his strange beard, which grew exclusively from beneath his jaw like a putrid bib. He had the pelt of an exotic animal thrown over his shoulder and wore, as always, several layers of filthy and colorful robes, the bottommost cinched with a rope, barely concealing his pendulous scrotum and penis.

Magellan carefully placed his toes over Barros's, who had not raised his head to look at him. "Your penis is like," he said, then thought for a moment. "Your penis is tiny, like a seahorse smoking a cigarette." Laughter erupted like a fusillade from which, instead of smoke, rose a cloud of turkey smells and particles. "Eh?" he said. He slowly rocked towards Barros, shifting his weight onto Barros's foot. Barros sat up but kept his eyes down, away from Magellan. "Eh, Jew?" Magellan repeated.

With all my courage I said, "I believe that Barros has lost his voice from dehydration."

"If I'm talking to a Malay cannibal slave interpreter named Henrique, he will know it from the bowl of human fingers I use to make him do my bidding."

I mustered a quiet laugh, knowing that this was not an insult but a joke. Weeks before, I would have raised my hands like claws and made a snarling face, which Magellan loved. But I no longer had the energy or will to please him. Also, Henrique was not my name. *Henrique.* How had he decided on it? It sounded nothing like my real name. This is Henrique, he had said to the others after he dragged me by a rope up the plank onto the *Trinidad*. Though it was cold, he had insisted I remove my shirt to look more like a slave. Henrique is our new interpreter, he said, then laughed outrageously as the others poked my chest and pinched my trembling arms.

Now Magellan reached into his robe and withdrew the corroded metal pieces of an astrolabe. He dumped them into Barros's lap, where they lay like the bones of a rodent picked over by birds. "Where are we?" he said. "Where is land? Where is land, Barros the navigational Jew?"

Barros ran his hands over the pieces of astrolabe, inspecting each one. As he did this, Magellan turned the phrase "Barros the navigational Jew" into a tuneless, manically lighthearted song: "*Barros the navigational Jew! Barros, Barros! Barros the navigational Jew!*" The addition of song to his usual nonsense was nearly impossible to stand, so I concentrated on Barros's careful movements over the astrolabe. He fit some pieces together, tried to fit others, raked through those pieces for other pieces that surely were missing.

Please, I thought, just fix the astrolabe and tell him where we are. At least pretend to fix it and tell him we're somewhere, even if it's wrong. But Barros was like the badger who, instead of knocking, scratches at a door until a badger-sized hole appears. In his lap were half an astrolabe and a handful of pieces that may not have been in the astrolabe to begin with.

Barros mumbled.

"Yes?" said Magellan. "Yes, speak up?"

"What did you do to this astrolabe?" The question hung in the air for a moment. Barros seemed on the verge of tears. "Did you destroy it on purpose?"

"That is none of your concern!"

"Here," I said, and I took the astrolabe from Barros's lap, gathered a handful of the remaining pieces and made a show of arranging them on the half-astrolabe, like a house of playing cards. Magellan watched this, nodding with interest. Then I held the device aloft and pretended to orient it according to the position of the sun (I had never seen one used and did not know they were used at night on the stars). I put my face to the edge of the circle and squinted. The sun glinted on the brass. I chose a mark at random and slowly turned the device until the sun hit that mark.

"That is the way," I said, pointing more or less in the direction we were headed.

Magellan followed my finger and squinted into the distance. In profile, backlit by the sun, he looked every bit the hawkish captain. "What is that way?" he asked.

"The island," I said. "The island with food and water."

"Hmm," he said. He raked some turkey out of his beard and stared into the blue and gray distance where my finger had been pointing. "I believe you're right. What about you, Barros? Do you agree?"

Barros looked at me, at the pieces of astrolabe in my hand. Always I will wonder why he did not say 'yes, yes, of course' and let Magellan retire to his cabin. Instead he said, "I don't know."

Magellan blinked. His mouth hung slightly open. It was the look of a wolf caught napping after a large meal, with stupid eyes that tricked you into forgetting that it could be, at a whiff of blood or weakness, electrified into terrible violence.

Barros continued, "We should wait for a nighttime reading."

"But don't you believe Henrique?" Magellan asked. It was impossible to tell if he was joking or serious, asking for a second opinion or about to wrench out Barros's beating heart. He leaned down to put his face near Barros's face. I wondered if Barros's eyes stung from the moist cloud of Magellan's breath. Magellan whispered, as if to a lover, "I hereby appoint Henrique navigator of the *Trinidad*. Henrique, chain him up with the other turkeys."

Barros did not look up or turn his head as Magellan shuffled across the deck towards his cabin. One of Magellan's hips was bad so the foot beneath it made a hissing sound as it dragged across the planks. The door opened and shut, leaving us in silence. A seagull cawed.

"If you go belowdecks he won't know if you're chained up or not," I said. "He never goes down there." Barros knew this as well as I did.

"It's only a matter of time before he kills me or I starve to death." Barros reached his hand into my lap and petted the brass pieces of astrolabe. "Why?" he said, more wondering aloud than asking.

My answer—that Magellan was as cruel and arbitrary as nature, as life itself—was as yet half-formed, so I shrugged. Barros's stubby fingers ran the length of the great circle and up a skinny part that looked like a sundial. Other parts were so oxidized that they looked like patches of moss. I should have said, 'Why anything? Never ask why.' But I didn't understand yet that silence was my secret; that 'why' was the question that would have driven me insane when the old men sold me to him for gold and mirrors, when my sword first passed through a smooth-skinned native, when my fellows began nibbling the meat off their little fingers, when Magellan put a turkey bone in my nostril and tried to lift me by it, screaming that my penis was like a shaved baby panther and my face like a starfish's penis.

Barros took the loose pieces of astrolabe off my lap and stuffed them into the pockets of his ragged trousers until all that was left was the great circle, the heaviest piece. I thought about pitching it into the ocean before Barros could take it, but he peeled my fingers off it and slid the heavy ring under his shirt. Holding it in place against what remained of his belly, he used his free hand to squeeze mine. I did not look at him.

"Henrique," he said, "is that even your name?"

"Yes," I lied. I raised my free hand and stoically patted his. The three hands clasped together in my lap looked like a brown and pink octopus.

"I have a favor to ask you," he said, "because of my religion." He stood up, and I followed him to the railing. He sat down facing me, then pulled my hand onto the great circle of the astrolabe, which was hard and bumpy beneath his shirt. He closed his eyes. His lips were slightly parted, as if he were expecting a kiss. Was he going to say something, I wondered? How would I know when to do it? When he squeezed my hand I stepped forward just a little. His eyes opened as he tipped backwards. The back of one of his shoes caught on the railing, popped off, and twirled in the air before crashing into the sea with a small splash, like an echo of the big splash of Barros's body. The sailors had told me that, after the panic, drowning was not an unpleasant way to die. Some had come very close to drowning before being rescued, usually by Magellan, who dove like a spear and swam like a stingray. It was hard to imagine a time when Magellan saved people instead of teasing out their deaths.

I sat down on the opposite railing. The sun was behind some clouds and didn't sting my neck. The door to Magellan's cabin was open. Of course it was. It had been open the whole time, for his twisted pleasure.

I pictured him staring, smiling, pleased at the entire episode and its strong effect on me. I closed my eyes before the footsteps began, the creaking of the sun-bleached planks beneath the massive, calloused feet, the smell of turkey, the deep, phlegm-cracked breaths.

"Where's the Jew?"

His voice was close. The smell of turkey was strong. Something poked my cheek, and my mouth began to water. I opened my eyes and saw a turkey leg, now no more than a bone.

"I was going to make you two fight for it," Magellan said. He passed the bone under my nose. The smell of marrow released a hidden cache of stinging juices in my tender stomach. "You would have killed him for it, yes?"

I grabbed the bone from his hand and began to suck it. Later, I broke it into pieces with my teeth and sucked on each piece one by one for hours, like hard candy. Then I fell asleep.

When I woke the next morning at dawn he was back in his cabin. The door was closed, bathed in red by the giant sun on the rippling horizon. The black windows on either side stared at me unblinking. With the door, they formed the face of a high-mouthed insect, red and monstrous as the devil that sailors say creeps behind every corner of the city and in every island cave. Beside the cabin, off the edge of the *Trinidad*, a strip of gray crowned the horizon like an answer to the sun's red challenge.

"Land," I whispered. Could it be? I did not trust my eyes, but the strip of gray was so steady, so dull—it had to be real. "Land," I shouted. "Land!"

The cabin door creaked open. From the sliver of black he wheezed, "Land?"

"Eleven o'clock!" I yelled, having overheard this parlance, which referred to the hands of a clock. The yelling sapped me, and I pressed my palm to the railing and leaned on it.

Magellan emerged from his cabin. Seeing him, all my joy at discovering land was replaced by anger. He withdrew a periscope from beneath his robe and looked through it at the strip of land. I would never have guessed that the periscope was not broken. I relished the idea that Magellan had taken care of it, had wrapped it in clothing or laid it under his pillow; it struck me as a sign of weakness.

"Smoke!" he yelled. "There are men there!" He came towards me with his robes flapping open, his pale torso bathed in red from the rising sun. He stopped a few meters away, since he had no interest in torturing me with the meaty smell of his breath. "Wash off your tongue, you filthy Malay. Those natives will need some talking to. How many mirrors do we have left?"

"Two or three, all broken."

"Put them in a sack. The idiots won't know the difference if they haven't met any white men before. While you're down there, put on some brighter clothes. You look like a street urchin. Brush your hair too. Are you listening to me?"

I was, but I was also staring at the fragments of bone that lay on the planks between us. Magellan noticed them. I leaned my head forward and peered at him from under my dark brows, in a look I hoped was full of animal menace. He would regret having fed me, having made me that much stronger. "I'll go belowdecks," I said.

My legs and arms trembled as I descended the ladder. It was darker than I remembered and fouled by such a mixture of smells that no one smell rose distinguishably above the others. Before, the turkeys had roosted in the middle of the room, away from the men chained to the perimeter, who were constantly setting traps for them with jewelry and scraps of clothing. Now I could tell from the gray smears of guano that the turkeys strutted wherever they pleased. There were five of them, maybe six. Half of these were pecking at the slumped body of a sailor, possibly José. Another stood quite near me raising one leg then the other and flashing the elbows of her wings. Her beak swung from side to side as she examined me with each eye.

"She doesn't like you," someone said quietly. I knew from the nasal, aristocratic accent that it was Pigafetta. How many men remained, I wondered? I would not give Pigafetta the satisfaction of seeing me count, as if I cared. "What sort of land is it?" he asked.

"Gray," I said.

The turkey gurgled, as if speaking for Pigafetta. A sailor moaned in the darkness, and wings fluttered as he or some other half-dead sailor batted away a nearby turkey, who had no doubt mistaken him for carrion and begun probing him for meat.

Dried guano crunched beneath my feet as I walked to the chests. I opened the large one that had contained half-length mirrors. The few that remained rested in irregular pieces at the bottom of the chest.

Carefully, I lifted the largest pieces and put them in a canvas sack. The effort sapped me, and I knelt to rest my trembling arms on my thighs.

"What a slave you are," said Pigafetta. "Rest assured I'll record your continuing inhumanity to your fellow man in my account of our voyage. The dead turkey beside me has dried up, so I use the blood from my gums to write. Each word is precious now, but your disgusting behavior warrants a few sentences."

"Soon you'll have less to write about," I said.

"What's that supposed to mean? Aren't you coming back for us?" He looked at me desperately. "After you die, Magellan will throw your body down here for us to eat. I'll relish it, you cannibal, despite how skinny and filthy you are. How does one describe the man who cannibalizes the cannibal? José, what do you think?"

José did not respond. I gathered a few handfuls of pearls, parrot feathers tied in bunches according to color, cheesecloth bags of salt, and small wooden statues of Jesus and the Virgin Mary covered in chipped gold paint. I said nothing more to Pigafetta.

It was mid-afternoon before we were close enough to shore to drop anchor. Magellan had spent the morning manically swinging the jib of the mainsail this way and that to steer us towards the thin column of smoke. He would scream at me to help him then perform the task himself before I could figure out what to do. I spent most of the day sitting on the railing and watching this strange nautical dance, by the end of which his colorful robes lay in a pile on the deck as he scrambled here and there naked. Our brutal ordeal seemed to have made him younger, leeching away whatever fat was hiding in the corners between his powerful muscles. His body had a pleasant, almost oriental complexion. "Sizing me up!?" he screamed whenever, between elaborate maneuvers of the mainsail, he glanced in my direction. Joy at seeing land reinvigorated his insults: "I'll not be eaten by the likes of you, you shaved panther perched on the railing. Perched as you would perch in a tree in your jungle home, waiting for a nice fat white man to saunter by before leaping down and jamming your claw-like penis into his eye!" He laughed ecstatically. "Isn't that what you would do?"

I nodded.

"Good," he said. "I was right, then."

I helped Magellan turn the crank for the anchor and then the crank for the dinghy, which took some coordination because there were two ropes and I was not as strong as Magellan or as familiar with the turning of cranks. After a stream of particularly incomprehensible curses, the bottom of the dinghy splashed into the calm, shallow water. Magellan told me to climb down first while he put his robes back on. My stomach, for weeks familiar only with the sensation of hunger and pain, began to flutter as I crossed the railing into the air beside the *Trinidad*, lowered myself on the rope with shaky arms, and probed the edge of the dinghy with my toes. But before I could enjoy the strange sensation of bobbing on the waves or examine the glowing blue and shallow water, Magellan was positioning the big canvas bag full of mirrors above me, telling me to get ready, to get ready because he was going to drop it, and was I ready, and would I not flop out of the dinghy on impact and bungle the whole thing? Then the bag crashed onto my feet, and I knew from its limp shape that the largest pieces of mirror had shattered. He should have lowered it with a rope, I thought, but what was the difference?

Cursing, Magellan climbed down to the dinghy. Then, in what could only have been for show, he demanded I paddle backwards in the bow as he sat upright and facing me in the stern. Because he was so much heavier, the bow fishtailed this way and that, despite my novice efforts to correct it with the curved strokes Barros had taught me in moments of boredom. Magellan kept his hands cupped over his eyes to see what was in front of us. The effect was less than regal, and soon he had pulled me by my neck into the stern and taken my place with the oars. We made quick progress. The bottom of the dinghy hissed onto the sand and we stepped out of it.

Magellan strode ahead of me onto the beach as I struggled under the sloppy weight of the canvas bag. Before us stood a deep forest of tall trees with bare, upright trunks and broad waxy leaves that blocked the sun. Magellan walked to the edge of the trees and shouted "Hello! Hello!" The column of smoke we had seen above the treetops from the *Trinidad* had dwindled, as if the natives had left their fire to inspect us from secret places among the trees. Magellan shouted "Hello!" and "I am Magellan!" and "I am the explorer Ferdinand Magellan here with my interpreter Henrique!" several more times before sitting down in the sand, opening his robes and leaning back on his palms. I dropped the canvas bag and sat down cross-legged. "They'll come," he said. "Let them get a look at us first. You know their language, yes?"

"Yes," I lied. Why did Magellan think I knew their language? Were we in Asia, America, who knew? Magellan nodded earnestly. To this day I cannot say if it was the nod of a crazy man or of a great explorer, forever the optimist when it came to strange cultures. His commitment to his work was something the other sailors admired, but I struggled to grasp it. What did he want from these people, anyway? I was about to ask him when something moved in the periphery of my vision. Magellan retied his robes and stood. Far down the beach, a brown-skinned man stood at the edge of the trees observing us. Another stood just as far away in the opposite direction. Magellan waved his arm high above his head and shouted "Hello! Hello!" and "I am the explorer Ferdinand Magellan!" spinning from side to side to address both men. Other brown-skinned men emerged from the trees on either side, and gradually they walked towards us. I stood and brushed the sand off my ragged trousers, wishing I had changed into something brightly colored, as Magellan had suggested. I was so obviously his slave. How would these shirtless men take me seriously? After Magellan had been done away with, would they kill me too? I wished I were still so enraged by Barros's death that I did not think of myself, did not fear death. How could Magellan smile and shout and wave his arms? Didn't he understand that he could die at any moment?

Slowly, the natives encircled us. They wore rope belts with leather codpieces and had black markings on their chests like the gills of fish. Their faces were soft, nearly hairless, and the hair on their heads made fluffy caps that ended at their ears and eyebrows. There were maybe a dozen in all. One of them stepped forward. He was older than the others and alone carried no spear. He came very close to Magellan and looked him up and down. I imagined that Magellan could feel the man's hot breath on his chest. Magellan smiled and raised his hands, as if to say 'I have no weapons,' before untying his outermost robe and presenting it to the leader, held in one hand and draped over the other arm, like the pelt of a mint-green animal. The leader took the robe from Magellan, squeezed it, and held it to his nose. He frowned and muttered something, to which another man replied. Then he turned and handed the robe to this other man. Then he said something to Magellan in rapid gibberish.

"What did he say?" Magellan asked me.

"He said he would like the rest of your robes, for his other men."

"Of course." Magellan shed robe after robe and handed them to the confused leader until only one remained, made of tattered silk that had once been pearl-colored. It was very short in the thighs, possibly a lady's robe.

Overwhelmed by the pile in his arms, the leader began passing the robes to his men, who passed them from man to man in an ant line. Now, all the men had a robe, some had two. The leader gibbered something else.

"He wants the last robe," I said.

"Why? Everyone has robes already."

"I don't know. Maybe he likes how silky it looks."

Magellan untied the last robe, exposing his hairy front and penis. The leader raised his hands and shook them, frowning. Magellan stopped. "It seems he doesn't want this robe after all," he said.

"He wants the robe," I said.

Magellan cautiously pulled off the robe and handed it to the confused leader. "It was my wife's robe," Magellan said softly. "I brought it for her smell. I can't recall why I started wearing it." He turned to me. "Tell him that this is a very special robe to me, and that I want him to keep it for himself."

I hesitated, not sure if I could adequately mimic the sound of their language. Magellan stared at me urgently, for the leader was touching and sniffing the silk robe with a look of utter revulsion. Finally, I said something in my own language, hoping it would sound like just as much gibberish to Magellan. I said, "Three birds were sitting in the bottom of a boat when a fish jumped in and joined them." It was the beginning joke that had been popular on my island ten years before.

"That sounds like Malay," said Magellan.

"The two languages are similar," I lied. "Their dialect is delivered more rapidly, but I think they can understand me. See? Look at his face."

The chief's face had gone from revulsion to confusion and, finally, to what might have been resignation—resignation that Magellan and I were idiots, I imagined. During our conversation, one of his men had dragged the bag away from my feet and opened it. He and a few others were passing around pieces of mirror and statues of Jesus and the Virgin. The statues seemed to please them. Seeing this, the leader raised his palms at Magellan and slowly (reluctantly?) spread his lips in what might have been a smile, or at least a gesture of appeasement. He said something.

"He says thank you," I said.

The leader said something else, something longer that involved gestures and waves towards the forest.

"What is he saying now?" Magellan asked. "Is he inviting us to their village?"

I knew that the longer these people spent with Magellan, the more they'd be endeared to his jovial façade, and the easier it would be for him to exploit them somehow, to trick them out of gold or daughters or thirty wild turkeys. I wished I did speak their language so I could tell them Magellan was evil and that the nature of evil was unknowable. If they could have seen what I saw, they would have killed him without any trick by me.

The leader stopped talking, having gotten nothing for his efforts. He stared at the sand for a moment before beginning to repeat the same sounds and gestures. It was hard to determine his tone because he seemed to have difficulty looking at Magellan, who was now completely naked. I suspected from my own experience that the big, hairy body of the white man was disgusting to him. I decided to use this to my advantage.

"Well, you cannibal," said Magellan, "what is he saying?"

"He wants to see your penis."

"What?"

"It is curious to him. He wants you to hold it out so he can see it better."

Magellan frowned a little and glanced over his shoulder, as if to make sure that no one besides these natives was watching. The gesture humanized him, and I tried not to think about it. The flabby penis lay in his hand like a pink and purple sea slug. Magellan sort of pushed it towards the leader like a tray of food. The leader raised his hands over his face and made a wilting noise. Then he barked something at the man to his left, who rose from inspecting mirror fragments in the sand.

"I don't think he likes this," said Magellan.

"But he does," I said. "He's telling that other man to take a look."

As if on cue, the other man *did* take a look before likewise covering his face and uttering a few sour words. The leader pointed at the penis and yelled, but he was careful not to look at Magellan's face.

"What is he saying now?" Magellan asked.

"He wants you to make it hard."

"What?"

"That's what he said. I won't look, if you want."

Magellan thought this over. "It must look big and strange to them, eh?"

"It must."

This seemed to please Magellan, and he began to rub the back of his hand over the top of the penis. As promised, I averted my eyes. The leader and his man continued to mutter to each other. I imagined they were unable to comprehend Magellan's behavior and wondered if he was crazy or somehow insulting them. I hoped for the latter. Soon the other natives had risen from the sand and were watching too. Their faces were either blank or sour looking, as if they had just chewed a mouthful of spoiled food. I stole a glance at the penis, which was getting longer and stiffer. It was magnificent, really, easily the longest penis I had ever seen. The pinks and purples stretched until the sheer surface looked like that of a marble column. The natives were silent. All but the leader were staring at the penis, which was now fully erect. The leader looked at Magellan, a blank expression on his face. Then he looked at me. I was startled but tried to keep my face as blank as his. I wanted to say, 'Hey, I'm like you. Leave me alone, okay?' But if I had ever been like him, I wasn't any longer. He glanced back and forth between Magellan and me, as if confused. But what was he confused about? How one man could be so large and menacing; the other, so small and weak? Couldn't he see that Magellan was evil, vicious, arbitrary and violent as a thunder cloud, and that I, though possibly corrupted by him, was no more than a slave? Then, silently and without warning, the man to the leader's left produced a spear and, as quickly as he had produced it, drove it through Magellan's stomach. Magellan gasped and writhed only for a moment, then hung from the spear like one of his own stuck turkeys. I had taken two steps back without thinking, expecting that Magellan would turn to me with one final confusing insult. But he didn't. The natives chatted briefly. Then two of them carried Magellan away, followed by the others, who took the mirrors and statues. I stayed behind and was ignored.

Later, I gathered as much fruit as I could fit into the dinghy then paddled back to the *Trinidad*. I dumped some fruit belowdecks so the men could see it before I unchained them. Pigafetta and a small man named Colombo were the only survivors. Pigafetta promised to take out the parts of his journal about me. After they had eaten their fill, they set about tacking along the coast of the island. I was too shaken to help. What shook me wasn't the evil of Magellan but the mystery of him, which was also the mystery of all of us and of life. As Pigafetta and little Colombo swung the jib and furled the mainsail, I looked not at the island where Magellan had just been murdered but out at the open sea. Scummy waves crashed against the prow, and a turkey yelped beneath me, as if in warning.

IN THE PRESENCE OF THE ACTOR

John Phillip Braxton has appeared in thirty-seven films and over a hundred theatrical productions. He has played every major role in Shakespeare, from Petruchio to Prospero, and is Jean-Paul Sartre's favorite English-speaking actor. After seeing his 1956 portrayal of James Tyrone in the Broadway debut of Eugene O'Neill's *Long Day's Journey into Night*, Brooks Atkinson of *The New York Times* called Braxton "the finest actor the United States has ever produced, whose unparalleled range is now cemented."

Today, at eleven o'clock in the morning on October 20th, 1961, John Phillip Braxton is asleep in a motel room on the outskirts of Los Angeles. A thin mattress sags beneath him. Sunlight through flimsy yellow curtains gives the room a warm, candlelit quality.

The bedside phone begins to ring. The person calling is Braxton's agent, David Rosen, whom Braxton describes as a conniving flatterer. Through Rosen, Braxton has been hired for fifty-six dollars, plus expenses, to coach actors in a film called *Terror of the Haunted West*, being shot in the nearby desert.

Braxton sweeps the clamorous phone off the table and attempts, by raising the sheets over his face, to return to sleep.

The second time the phone rings, I take it upon myself to answer.

"Is this that writer?" Rosen asks.

"I'm afraid it is," I say.

"You tell Braxton we aren't paying him to sleep 'til noon. What the hell does he do all night anyway?"

I begin to describe our adventures of the previous night—a steakhouse, a cocktail bar, a karaoke lounge where Korean businessmen lavished Braxton with attention—but Rosen isn't interested. He says, "Tell Braxton that Ted locked himself in his trailer. He's gotta talk to the kid. He's the acting coach for God sakes."

Braxton whips down the sheets and sits up in bed. His eyes are puffy from sleep, and his silver hair is stacked on his head. He pulls the phone from my hands and holds it awkwardly to his mouth. "Of course Ted locked himself in his trailer," Braxton says, "he read the script! One day I'll gather all the so-called writers and load them onto a Burmese slave ship."

"Then what?" Rosen asks. "You'll write all the movies yourself?"

Braxton drops the phone on the floor. He may find Rosen's comment hurtful, since he's been trying to supplement his income as an actor with that of a screenwriter. Braxton claims to have written several stirring screenplays, each with a hardboiled plot, titillating romance, and "plenty of lengthy monologues into which any actor would gladly sink his teeth." He sends these scripts to the attention of Rosen's assistant.

Braxton showers then sets about his daily ablutions: tooth brushing, hair combing, shaving followed by vegetable glycerin balm, facial exercises, vitamins, a light rinsing of the wrists and neck, five "Peter Piper's," two "Unique New York's," and all manner of creams and gelatins that I won't bother to enumerate but culminate, as always, with a ceremonious clasping of his eagle necklace behind his smooth, upright neck. The golden eagle is the only item to which Braxton seems to bear any sentimental attachment. He explains that the actor's life is a transient one, and that wearing many disguises causes "the disguises of life" to lose importance.

The phone rings again but we ignore it. Now donning a black turtle-neck and crisp gray slacks, Braxton loads his tattered copy of the script into his calfskin briefcase (joking, as always, that he'll have to disinfect the briefcase when shooting is over) and we set out the door.

I accompany Braxton, who refuses to be driven, to a dilapidated diner where we enjoy a leisurely breakfast of eggs, coffee, toast, grapefruit halves, florets of broccoli, and assorted breakfast meats. There, he explains to me that the director, Roger Kitchen, is the real source of the trouble with Ted. "No doubt Kitchen has bullied poor Ted into an artless state," Braxton laments, "as the cruel sun of the American West drains life from the sand." For dessert, Braxton orders a slice of buttermilk pie.

While I pay the bill, Braxton examines a section of script. Though he tells Rosen it's such dreck he can't read it, the truth is he reads it almost constantly. He pays particular attention to the lines of Ted's character, whose words he rolls around his mouth like succulent candy.

After lunch we walk along the shoulder of a six-lane road. The sun is high and burns through the thin haze, causing the pale concrete to shimmer. Braxton, who never sweats, walks jauntily ahead while I trail behind. Sometimes he comments on buildings we pass, like a tire shop where the greasy-smocked proprietor once gave him a cup of water, or a cocktail lounge where "a real-life gaucho" asked him to dance. This starts him on a lengthy monologue about homosexuals and Montgomery Clift, whom he admires. He mimics a little back and forth between Clift and Burt Lancaster in *From Here to Eternity*. "A man don't go his own way, he's nothin'!" Braxton concludes in Clift's reedy voice, then says it's a shame a young man like Clift doesn't get good work anymore.

When we crest the hill that marks the end of the ragged town, Braxton stops. He grabs my sleeve and points at the sky. "Do you see that?" he asks.

I see only haze and a few streaky clouds. "What is it?" I reply.

"Open your eyes, man. Up there! The dark spot!"

I see no dark spot, but this is not unusual; Braxton often asks if I see this or that horror, or hear a bloody scream. I never do.

"Like a filthy hair-clogged drain," Braxton whispers, "in a bathtub full of swirling clouds." He pauses for a moment while I write that down, then journeys onward.

Coming down the hill we can see the white trailers and tents to the side of the highway, where the scrubby desert stretches to the horizon in a great swath of tan. Men and women in gauzy clothes hurry between buildings, and a few skinny lights are arranged in a ring. Closer, Braxton calls my attention to two horses moored to posts behind a metal shed. "Today is horse day," he says excitedly.

As we stroll into the compound, Braxton is accosted by a small woman named Doris Jones, the line producer, whom he describes to me as a spinster Negress.

"It's almost four," she says. "Why didn't you take a cab? We're giving you a per diem."

Braxton says he spent it on breakfast.

"We have caterers," she says, then waves to the craft-service table where burritos wrapped in tinfoil droop in the sun.

Braxton shudders haughtily. Jones grumbles about his ungratefulness then leaves. Later, Braxton will stand guard while I slide a few burritos into his briefcase.

Next comes David Rosen, who wears cowboy boots over tight slacks

("Wild Bill Shylock," Braxton calls him) and is combing his thin hair against the sandy desert wind. "Good to see you, Phil," he says. "The kid's still in his trailer. You gotta talk some sense into him."

"I *got* to do nothing," Braxton says. "I take it the young man is struggling with his poorly written character?"

"Sure."

"Good, because if he's struggling with the charlatan directing this film, then I won't be any help. In fact, I might drive Ted to suicide with my myriad tales of how much *worse* it can get in the hands of that criminal." Braxton describes a shoot in Mexico where Roger Kitchen fed the cast and crew "garbage fried in lard" for two weeks and made Braxton give line-readings to natives who later brained Kitchen with a coconut for scaring one of their donkeys into the forest with a giant rubber crab monster. Braxton retrieves the script from his briefcase and flips through it. "I have a few questions," he says. "The aliens, of what sort are they?"

Rosen sighs. "Alien aliens. Just make Ted act afraid, then heroic in the part at the end."

"You can't *act* heroic. One performs heroic acts, and that *makes* one heroic." Braxton steps away from us disdainfully and makes a loop around the craft-service table, gesticulating to himself. Rosen watches with patience. He tells me that, long ago, Braxton decided to embrace the medium of film, in all its goofiness, and started reading science-fiction magazines with the fervor he used to reserve for Shakespeare and Ibsen.

Braxton returns to us with a calculatedly serene look and says, "Are they tall aliens with lengthy proboscises? Giant cockroach aliens with bulletproof chitinous casings? Titanian slime molds that read minds?"

"I don't know, Phil."

"Haven't they shot any of the scenes yet?"

"The aliens don't show up until the end, obviously." Rosen is referring to the common practice of saving the creature until the third and final "act" of a film, to save money on special effects and costumes. He calls out to a young woman in blue jeans, the costume girl.

"Yes, Mister Rosen?" she says, coming toward us. She has fashionably short hair bound with a red bandanna.

"What do the aliens look like?" Rosen asks.

"I'm sorry but I'm not supposed to say. Mister Blaisdell told me to keep the aliens a secret so everybody would be scared when—"

"He wants to keep them *secret*," Braxton says, "so it will be too late to send his lazy bones back to the drawing board."

They're referring to Paul Blaisdell, who creates all of Roger Kitchen's monsters and is famous for his budgetary mindfulness. During filming of *It Conquered the World*, when Beverly Garland threw a tantrum and destroyed the stumpy Venusian creature with a single kick to its head, Blaisdell replaced the head with a painted traffic cone.

"I'm sure Mister Blaisdell knows what he's doing," the costume girl says, but Braxton has already started for the trailers. Rosen, satisfied, goes for the burritos.

I catch up to Braxton by a cluster of small trees.

"Shh!" he says. "Do you hear that?"

I listen but hear nothing.

"Hissing," he says. "It's coming from the trees, I think. Don't go in there."

I say I won't, and we continue to the trailers. There are three. Each is white and set apart from the others by a few paces. Ted's is the most dilapidated. Braxton knocks on its door.

"Go away," comes a muffled, youthful voice.

"Open up this instant," Braxton commands, and Ted does so with the alacrity of a student welcoming his master.

Ted—Theodore Gorecki—is a promising new talent Kitchen found sacking groceries in San Bernardino. He's big and handsome and has a childishly expressive round face, but today he looks wretched. He wears nothing but a robe and a baseball mitt, in which he holds a dirty tennis ball. Averting his eyes he says, "Gosh, Mister Braxton, I just don't know about this script and—"

"We're in trouble," Braxton says. "There's a creature in the woods."

"What?"

"Let them shoot your godforsaken scene so we can get out of this place."

"It's a big scene. There'll be lots of takes."

"Tell me, Ted, how many takes were there when Gielgud played Cassius at the Royal National Theater?"

"Gosh, Mister Braxton, I don't know."

"One, Ted. It was a play."

Ted squints.

"My point is that the excellence of your acting dictates your terms. Act well enough and you'll be on a plane tonight."

"But we still have all the scenes on the beach, the ones where the aliens capture the bikini lady to plant baby aliens inside her and I try and run 'em over in a dune buggy."

"You haven't shot those yet?"

Ted shakes his head. "And I don't know how to act it."

"Remember your training!"

"Yes, sir."

Later, Braxton will explain to me that he hated to snap at Ted but needed to get through to what he calls "the second, deeper Ted," the Ted who, "despite his torpid, childlike brain, wields a certain animal bravado for which many finer actors would sell their mothers to Arabian caliphs."

"Tell me," Braxton says, "what is my seventh rule of acting?"

Ted straightens his sloping shoulders and addresses Braxton from his diaphragm: "The power to act is the power to be any man at any time with any skill, no matter how archaic."

"Very good," Braxton says, then leads Ted in some breathing exercises. Watching them, I wonder if it was the seventh rule that allowed Braxton, in Stratford playing the blacksmith in *Tis Pity She's a Whore*, to hammer an actual sword sharp enough to slice the little finger off a property mistress. At our first meeting, in his bachelor's apartment in the Echo Park neighborhood of Los Angeles, Braxton told me that an actor has a better understanding of how it feels to do things, to *be* things, than the man who actually does them. "A man who lived through the horrors of bubonic plague didn't spend his life preparing for those horrors," Braxton said. "He was probably illiterate. He couldn't make sense of that experience the way I can, as a trained actor."

Braxton and Ted have assumed neutral position—legs shoulder-width apart, arms at the sides, head down, eyes closed—and are taking deep breaths. This is not unusual, but there's something strange about Braxton's face, something especially intense, as if these exercises aren't for Ted's benefit but his own. They begin whispering words into each other's faces, a technique popularized by Stanford Meisner of the Group Theatre.

Abruptly Braxton cries, "What was that!?"

"What was what?" Ted asks.

Braxton goes to the end of the trailer and presses his face to a small, dirty window. "The sky!" he says. "Why, it's the sickly sepia color of a forgotten photograph. And in the center—oh my—" He recoils from the window and presses his back against the wall of the trailer. "In the center of those swirling brown clouds a bright object was hovering. I don't know what it is, but I know it's up to no good. No good, I tell you!" With characteristic burning introspection he concludes, "What sort of hell has been unleashed on this Earth?"

"Hey," Ted says, "that's from the movie."

"Put your clothes on. We're shooting this goddamned scene. Where's Kitchen?"

Ted goes to the closet. "I can't find my costume."

"You're an actor, goddamn you. Wear a gunny sack!"

There's a knock at the door. Braxton looks through the peephole, then opens the door and pulls Rosen through it by his shirtfront.

"Take is easy," Rosen says.

"Did you see it?"

"See what?"

"The alien craft!"

"What?"

"The sky? The darkness? The swirling clouds?"

Rosen nods. "Riiiight," he says loudly, as though for Ted's benefit. "Flying saucers." He winks at Braxton and whispers, "Thanks for this, Phil."

Shockingly, at this point Braxton attempts to punch Rosen in the stomach, but Rosen spins away from him and gets behind a chair. "Okay, Phil, geez," he says.

Ted emerges wearing the gray suit and red necktie of the character he's playing, a state senator. A pair of wire glasses is perched on his broad athlete's nose. He pulls down on the suit, which is bunching in his armpits. He looks awkward and desperate.

"Here," Braxton says, then unclasps his eagle necklace and, with great solemnity, clasps it again behind Ted's thick neck. The eagle rests proudly atop the scarlet bed of Ted's necktie, and Ted squishes down his chin to regard it. I would be lying if I didn't admit that this causes in me a twinge of jealousy. I've been Braxton's companion for several days and fancy we have a strong bond. I know, at least, that I'm his intellectual match in a way that Ted simply cannot be. But the bond between an actor and his master is peculiar in its strength.

"There," Braxton says, patting his trustworthy eagle, then he tells Ted a story he's never told me before: "The necklace was given to me after a particularly stirring performance of Kyd's *Spanish Tragedy*, in which I, as the Marshall Hieronimo, having gone quite mad at the conclusion of the murderous play-within-a-play, actually bit out a small piece of my own tongue and spat it onto the stage. Real blood is darker and more watery than stage blood, and it kept dribbling down my chin. This went unnoticed by all but a lovely young typist seated in the front row with her parents, who afterwards commented—very astutely, I think—that mine was an art not of man but of nature, and that watching me act was like watching an eagle rip the innards from a prone carcass. Before she left for art school in Paris, she presented me with a token of the very remark that had begun our lengthy romantic entanglement: the eagle, which daily challenges me to climb to heights of performance where only the most powerful artists dare to soar; which daily reminds me that in my core, revealed only on stage—and even then, quite tremblingly—is a majestic and bloodthirsty animal; which daily chides me to—"

Rosen interrupts the actorly reverie by opening the door and pushing Braxton through it.

A few yards from the trailer, Roger Kitchen is listening to a supporting actor named Jim Weatherby who, according to Braxton, made his name by being fat. Kitchen is tall and has the tidy look of a graduate student, which is what he was until he began making budget-minded pictures for Jim Nicholson and Sam Arkoff in 1954. Now, he's in the middle of a lucrative series based on the work of H. P. Lovecraft and starring Boris Karloff. *Terror of the Haunted West* is being shot in five days using leftover rentals from one of those films.

"I was thinking about maybe a mustache or an eye-patch," Weatherby says.

"Hmm, yes," Kitchen says, but it's plain he's only waiting for Ted and has been accosted by Weatherby, whom he indulges through tinted glasses.

Unexpectedly Braxton chimes in: "I think you're right, Jim."

"Really?" Weatherby says.

Braxton inserts himself into the narrow space between the two men, drawing the attention of several hangers on. He strokes Weatherby's cheek with the backs of two fingers and says, "A broad and noble mustache that extends past the line of your jaw and onto your neck like the wings of a swan."

Weatherby frowns.

"You heard the man," Kitchen says, and the pretty costume girl emerges from behind Kitchen and begins patting Weatherby's face with a circular sponge.

"Glad you could join us, Phil," Kitchen says. "How's the hotel? You look thin."

Braxton visibly chafes at this remark but holds his tongue. Weight is a serious subject among actors, and there is a certain type of older man who one day becomes a skeleton of himself. Braxton's luxurious meals are, in part, a bulwark against this. But Braxton only laughs and says, "I've been the same weight since first I stepped onto the stage as the star-struck Dane."

Kitchen matches Braxton's soft laugher. "And when was that?"

"Nineteen-forty or thereabouts," Braxton lies.

"Sure," Kitchen says, then tells the same story he told us yesterday, and the day before, about going with his parents to the movies and seeing an English adaptation of *A Midsummer Night's Dream* in which a young actor named John Phillip Braxton, the only American in the cast, played Lysander. "He spoke Bill Shakespeare so naturally," Kitchen says, "it was like he was sitting next to me on a train and decided to talk to me about love."

The actors and crew twitter appreciatively and cast friendly glances at Braxton, who seems genuinely embarrassed, as if the early British talkie were a youthful indiscretion. Kitchen's mouth is neutral, but from where I stand I can see behind his dark glasses, where his small eyes are wrinkled with mirth. I'm reminded of a pig's eyes.

Braxton fidgets then turns abruptly to some trees. "Ted," he says, "do you see them?"

"See who?" Ted says, then shoulders through the crowd to where Braxton is standing. Braxton pulls down on Ted's necktie until they're cheek to cheek, both men staring at the meager clump of trees.

"A forest of horrors," Braxton whispers. "You can hear them hissing. Watching us and waiting."

"Waiting for what?"

"Waiting for us to sleep so they can plant their little shrimps inside us. You know the rest. We all do, don't we? The Professor certainly does."

Ted looks confused. I should admit that I, too, am confused.

Kitchen touches my shoulder. "You getting this?" he whispers.

I nod curtly, disguising my confusion with diligent note-taking and the impassive expression of a journalist. The truth is, I wonder if Braxton is coming unhinged, if the stress of his fringe existence in Hollywood has somehow combined with the heat and Kitchen's despotic presence to push him finally—and irrecoverably—into dementia.

Suddenly Braxton turns on us with a look of such naked terror that a few in the crowd step backward. "They're camouflaged," he says. "Don't you see?" He walks up to Weatherby, who grabs the sleeve of the man next to him. "Can't you see them?" Braxton asks. "Can't you see their shiny black eyes between those trunks?" No one responds. Braxton looks confused. Then he backs away from us, as if *we* were the monsters. Then he runs.

Kitchen is gone from my side in an instant, hollering for the crew to follow. The entire entourage of twenty or so people shuffles toward a clearing where Braxton staggers aimlessly. I wonder why he's chosen this place until I see the skinny poles with big black boxes on top: lights. A bearded man runs up to them and fiddles with the cords. The sun has set behind a long, dusty hill, and the sky is a vivid purple peculiar to the California desert. There's a terrible crack, and Braxton is coated in white light. He runs a balletic circle around the illuminated area then stops at Paul Blaisdell, who's wiping a shiny lasergun with a rag. "Give me that," Braxton says, and Blaisdell hands it to him without ceremony. Braxton waves the lasergun over his head and marches strangely, as though entranced, toward the center of the lighted circle. Around him the shrubbery looks shiny and moonlit, like something from a richly staged opera. He gazes up at a space between two bright lights, but what does he see? I glance at the script held by Kitchen's assistant and read, "*DEAFENING WHIZ as giant silverfish-shaped SPACECRAFT weaves among treetops. CREATURES scamper beneath. SENATOR JOHNSTON braces with dignity for potential atrocities.*"

Braxton twirls to face us, furious anger contorting his face. "Get back!" he shouts. "Get back, you people! This is *my* fight!"

People glance at each other. Some leaf through their scripts.

Braxton smoothes his silver hair from his forehead, which is high and noble like that of a Civil War general, once rakish in his youth. His hands are shaking.

"Show yourselves," he says, nearly whispering. He waves the shiny gun with broad, manic movements. "You afraid of me? Fine." He throws the gun on the ground and it skitters over the flat dirt. Suddenly he gasps and takes one step backward, and who wouldn't? For in the script I read, "*REVEAL CREATURE: tall and silver, hairless, pinheaded, with expressionless black shark-type eyes, possible wavy tendril mouth [Blaisdell? $$$?].*"

"I'm not going to hurt you," Braxton says. Then his demeanor changes. He walks forward. "No," he says. "Don't leave. We can learn so much from each other!" He runs toward the lights and falls to his knees, looking upward so desperately that I don't even have to read along to know that the creature's "*silvery head cranes sideways, struggling to understand impassioned SENATOR JOHNSTON, and hisses before being sucked into SPACECRAFT like noodle into mouth of child. Spacecraft WHIZZES INTO SKY!!!*"

Braxton leans forward, his face in his palms, and quietly begins to weep. Someone claps, but Kitchen shushes this person. Slowly Braxton stands up, dusts his knees, and surveys the crowd. "We've got nothing to be proud of," he tells us. "Man is weak, probably the weakest creature in the universe." His gaze is stern, full of loathing for us and for himself. "Our guns haven't done anything today but scare away a superior race, one that, perhaps, would have given us a gift tantamount to fire or the wheel. I suppose we should have listened to the Professor, or at least taken the serum he developed, but now it's too late. They're gone. We're alone, and together we march toward our inevitable, private little destructions. Wasn't it Emerson who said, 'A man of genius is privileged only as far as he——'"

At this point Braxton begins a series of wild contortions and throws himself to the ground, where he rolls around in the dirt. I grab the script from the assistant, flip to the last page and read, to my horror, that "*Departure only a ruse! Creature has used telepathy to IMPREGNATE SENATOR JOHNSTON with tiny shrimp-like alien fetuses!!!!!!*"

"Help me!" Braxton screams. "Help me!" Then, with disquieting understatement, he expires. For a moment I think he's really dead. I wonder if Braxton too thinks he's dead, for an instant at least. If so, he has died a thousand times. What effect must this have on a person?

A single clap issues from behind me, followed by several and then a crescendo of applause and whistles and hooting.

"Well, Ted," Kitchen says above the din, "think you can do that?"

"I sure will try, Mister Kitchen."

While Kitchen shoots take after take of Ted hollering at a man in a silver gorilla costume, Braxton gorges himself on burritos at the craft-service table. I go there to congratulate him on his performance. He seems dazed. "It isn't over," he murmurs.

David Rosen comes up and the two of them make plans to get very drunk. After that, no one approaches Braxton for a time. I wonder what people think of him: if, like me, they find his fierce commitment to fantasy somewhat troubling. Then I notice the costume girl lingering at a distance. Cautiously she slides up to Braxton and says, "I remember seeing you as a girl, with my parents."

Braxton is startled. He dabs the corners of his mouth with the back of his wrist, then winks at her.

She blushes, perhaps unaccustomed to such gentlemanly trespasses. "You really are the greatest," she says.

He looks up at the sky, which is dark except for a purple streak left by the retreating sun. "Someone had to teach humanity a lesson," he says somberly, "lest the terrible events of this week lead to nothing. If only the Professor could have been here."

She nods seriously, but I can tell from her expression that she's trying to piece together his cryptic meaning. So am I. Only later will I realize that he hadn't stopped acting, or rather that he couldn't stop.

Once, early in our time together, I asked Braxton how he cried on command. It was a naïve question and one I wouldn't ask today, because it trivialized his art, but he answered that crying was simply "a matter of *experiencing* something in your head that isn't actually happening to you. It's a triumph of the mind. The only trick is if you're a person like me who doesn't cry very often. In order to cry, I must first become someone who cries and then imagine what would make *that* person cry. It's quite difficult. Sometimes—" He hesitated, as though surprised by what he was about to say. Then he stood up and went to the window of his apartment, which overlooked a reservoir of mysterious calm. "Sometimes I picture myself on a sort of ladder, and I can see myself, my *real* self, far below. He waves at me and I know he isn't experiencing these things. He's a happy person, I think."

When the costume girl is gone, Braxton tells me she reminds him of the girl who gave him his necklace. "A supple young creature," he says. Then he touches his chest where the eagle used to be. "Where did it go?" he asks.

I tell him he gave it to Ted. He asks me who is Ted.

"Ted Gorecki," I say and point to the circle of light where Ted is on his knees imitating Braxton's performance.

Braxton watches for a moment. "Of course," he says, "one of my finest students, with a certain animal bravado for which many finer actors would sell their mothers to Arabian caliphs. Well, what are you staring at? Write that down."

FATHERS OF CAMBODIAN TIME-TRAVEL SCIENCE

1.

What makes the whole weird episode so improbable is that I never had any interest in Time Windows. Sure, I saw the ads with the blonde woman staring dreamily at the child version of herself, and yes, my own agency designed those ads, but it was different designers at the agency. Designers who wore vanity glasses and sometimes called me cat, like *This cat's alright*, or *You're one old-school cat, you know that?* I did know that. At forty I was the third oldest person in the office, after Mr. Courtney and Mr. Courtney's assistant, Martha, who was actually Mr. Courtney's wife's cousin and spent all day selling crafts online. It was that kind of agency. Our specialty was public transportation. When you see a smiling doctor or dentist staring from the interior wall of a bus, chances are we put her there. Chances are we chose her lab-coat and styled her hair and came up with how best to describe her brand of rhinoplasty, liposuction, cosmetic dentistry, erectile enhancement, laser hair-removal. All our young talent were hoping to get poached by bigger, full-service agencies. All of them except me. I was still dazzled to be living in Atlanta and designing ads for a living. Though it wasn't the life I had imagined growing up.

I grew up in a tiny city in Indiana where people were divided by class according to whether they wore pleated Walmart khakis or Dickie work pants. I wanted to be a basketball coach like John Wooden, who went to my high school, but I was an oaf and had to play football. I was recruited by Georgia Southern of all places but my senior year in high school I got five concussions and had to retire. The coach at Southern felt sorry for me, bless him, so he didn't drop my scholarship and I worked in the weight room, spotting athletes and wiping down benches and basically trying to be invisible, despite my height and increasing bulk. I lifted obsessively. I still have stretch marks on my chest and thighs. Late at night, alone in the weight room, I would zone out in this way I came to associate with my concussions, like my brain had come loose inside my head. That was when I got my best ideas.

I majored in design because I liked to do art but wasn't good enough at math to be an architect. I got an internship, which led to a job doing Adobe for a company that made billboards, and then to Courtney Associates LLC, where I'm the longest tenured designer. Longest tenured but not the best, I admit, which was why I was surprised when Mr. Courtney summoned me to his office and declared without ceremony that I would be the lead on Time Windows, moving forward.

I was flattered, but also confused. The ads with the blonde woman and her child self were less than a year old. Did the Time Windows people already want more ads? Different media?

Mr. Courtney got an Evian out of his mini-fridge and unscrewed it by the window, which faced a skinny brick building like ours. Architects could be seen inside it, hunched over high desks with bright adjustable lamps.

"Fucking Time Windows," Mr. Courtney muttered. He combed his fingers through the gray hair over his ears, which was the only hair he didn't dye strawberry blond. The dye-job made him look a little like Robert Redford might have looked if he lost fifty pounds for a role as a dying man. Mr. Courtney did triathlons. On the walls were half a dozen framed photos of him in exotic locations with his thumbs up, post-race, looking sunbaked and crazed.

"They were great ads," Mr. Courtney said.

"Yes, they were," I said softly.

"But they didn't work."

"Sir?"

"They don't work."

"But everywhere I go people say—"

"It's all talk. Nobody's going to pay five grand for something that advertises on a bus."

"Five grand?" I whistled, which must have been a corny thing to do because Mr. Courtney winced. "I'll reach out to Dietrich for a debriefing," I said. "I assume Martha has his new contact info?"

"No contact with the old team," Mr. Courtney said. "I want you starting from scratch."

"Should we open new files?"

"I'd prefer it. And I'd prefer you not look at the old files, though I'm sure you will."

I took this as a challenge. I *wouldn't* consult Dietrich's files.

Mr. Courtney stepped away from the window and fetched some papers off his desk. Our meeting was ending, which made me a little sad. I felt like we were hitting it off by our standards. Mr. Courtney headed toward the door with his papers, and I wondered if I should speed past him before there wasn't room for me to get through the door without hip-checking him or awkwardly asking him to pardon me, but before I could make my move he said, "The new team is you, Lizzie and Demarcus."

"Demarcus? The intern?"

"They want Demarcus."

That Mr. Courtney said "they want" meant the Time Windows people had requested me by name, Lizzie too, and even Demarcus, though how they knew what Demarcus did around the office I had no idea. Mostly he made coffee and picked up Mr. Courtney's daughter from school. Also, he had these hearing aids that looked like normal hearing aids but I saw them advertised online and knew they were earbuds in disguise.

"So they're familiar with my work?" I asked.

"Oh, of course, Mike, who *isn't?*" Mr. Courtney turned and began speaking with Martha, who was reading a fat *Vogue*.

It may sound like Mr. Courtney disliked me, and he did dislike me—hard as that is to admit, considering my years of service and repeated sincere attempts to ingratiate myself with him—but he respected me. I was sure of that. He made me project manager on all the conservative accounts like credit unions and discount clothiers, which were the accounts (and clients) he wanted as little to do with as possible. Recently I'd done a series for the personal injury lawyer J.J. Deckle, featuring the corpulent Deckle in a gray suit leaning on the edge of his desk and looking up from a giant law book, as though the photographer had appeared in his office unannounced. The bemused expression on Deckle's faces said, *I don't have time for this, so busy am I with the law, which I love, but my other great love is people, and you, my friend, my potential client, are a person first and foremost, meaning you're alright by me.* Deckle loved it. He called me Big Mike and insisted we hold our meetings at five o'clock in order to drink cocktails (he had a notion from TV about how admen operated). Anyway, what

Mr. Courtney understood, and what Dietrich and his ilk *didn't* understand, was that clients like Deckle were our bread and butter. They could be relied upon. They weren't looking for art, just competence, and we delivered.

I went straight from Mr. Courtney's office to Lizzie's desk. Lizzie wrote copy for most of the art I did and was my closest friend at the office, though we never saw each other outside it. She was a nice Jewish girl from Roswell, one of the ritzy suburbs where people don't have accents. Her parents had moved there from Philadelphia in the eighties so her father could practice law in the decreasingly anti-Semitic Atlanta area. During our creative process she was always asking if I needed water or to take a quick break, as though I were a lumbering dog and might collapse at any moment. I would act annoyed at her fussing but secretly I cherished it.

Lizzie was leaning back in her chair with her keyboard in her lap and her eyes closed, which meant she was thinking. Her desk was clean except for a framed photo of her and her sister on a motorboat. I cleared my throat to get her attention. She swiveled to face me, opened her eyes, and said in a breathy voiceover voice, "Reach out and touch yourself."

"Like it, don't love it," I said.

"But it's perfect for these chicks." Lizzie brought up the bus ad on her computer screen, and each of us took a moment to consider the blonde woman and little blonde girl staring at each other in profile through an empty picture frame. They were actors, a mother and daughter team who looked remarkably similar, but the daughter's brown eyes had been less striking than the mother's green eyes, and so the designers had copied the mother's iris, reversed it, shrunk it, then cut and pasted it onto the daughter's eyeball. The effect was flawless by any objective measure, but I had convinced myself when the ad came out that even if I hadn't known the truth I would have recognized that the daughter's eye wasn't her own.

"Seriously," Lizzie said, "it looks like a service where you go back in time to ogle women or young girls—your choice!"

I laughed, but I was still thinking about the green eye. It was a knowing eye. A hardened eye. It made me wonder if a person's age and experience were reflected in his or her irises.

"Totally creepy," Lizzie said, "and the hair?"

"What about it?"

"It's exactly the same color."

She was right, and the effect was unnatural. The blonde should have faded with age, to dishwater blonde or even gray.

"Lots of women color their hair," Lizzie said, "but who brings a childhood photo to their stylist and says make it just like *this*?"

I nodded, wondering if this detail was another source of the ad's subtle creepiness. The woman's colored hair meant she wanted to look not just younger but *exactly as she had looked as a child*. Combined with her use of Time Windows, the hair suggested a systematic (and expensive, therefore desperate) attempt to recapture lost youth. It made the communion depicted in the ad, enabled by Time Windows, not an instance of benevolent technology but a symptom of human frailty. It took the focus off Time Windows and placed it squarely on this desperate person who, for whatever reason, had decided that the woman she'd become was inferior to the girl she'd been.

"Think we could change the name?" Lizzie asked.

"What's wrong with Time Windows?"

"It makes me think of peeping toms."

"People besides peeping toms use windows."

Lizzie shrugged. "Time windows. A window through time. A window into the past. Into your childhood. Into yourself." Lizzie spit-balled while I doodled. Then we did what people in the business call word association: *time*, for example, might lead to *clock, alarm, deadline, failure, termination*. When we got hungry, we broke for lunch.

It was then, eating Korean tacos on a bench overlooking a parking lot being jackhammered to make way for a condo tower, that Lizzie admitted how excited she was about the project. She said she mentioned Time Windows whenever somebody asked what sort of work we did, even though she hadn't worked on Time Windows herself and wasn't too fond of the work the others had done.

"Well," I said, "the Time Windows people must have liked it okay."

"What makes you think that?" Lizzie asked.

"They're using us again, even though the ad didn't get results."

Lizzie shook her head. "They're using us because we already know their secrets."

"You mean that it's a scam?"

"I'm serious. Dietrich and them went out there. They saw the whole operation. They weren't supposed to talk about it but Miko told me the shit was for real."

I nodded, holding my tongue.

"This time-rip thing," Lizzie said, "I mean, it's pretty fucking crazy, right?"

"Yep," I said.

"So, what would you say?"

"To my child self, you mean?"

She nodded.

"I'd tell him not to be a pissant."

"Come on."

"I'm serious. Honestly, I'm not too keen on the whole thing. I guess I'd like to leave the past in the past, you know?"

2.

I might have succeeded in leaving the past in the past if it weren't for what happened two days later. What happened was I got a padded manila envelope in the mail from Marianne McCutcheon, my second grade teacher. I hadn't seen Mrs. McCutcheon for thirty years and would have guessed she was dead. Back then she was already stooped and had long silver hair, which she combed while she watched us during recess. We thought the hair had magical properties and that Mrs. McCutcheon was a recovering witch.

I took the padded envelope into my condo and set it on the kitchen counter, where I sliced it open with a boning knife and slid out a shallow gray box. To touch something from a person I hadn't seen in so long gave me an uneasy feeling. I opened the box carefully, as though whatever was in there might spring out and knock loose some stuff I didn't care to think about.

Inside the box was a letter, and beneath the letter was a wheat penny, a Fleer 1987 Steve Stipanovich basketball card, and the grimy skeleton of a frog. I felt a rush of nostalgia. These had been my treasures, the skeleton especially. I had grown frogs from tadpoles in a little fish tank, and whenever a big one died I told my grandpa and together we cleaned it with boiling water and special taxidermy chemicals.

Under the treasures was a sheet of red construction paper folded in half like a greeting card. On its front was written in big block letters "*TO ME FROM ME.*" I unfolded the card, and on the left side was a drawing in marker of Hulk Hogan riding a shark like a surfboard. On the right side was a note:

> *Dear Me,*
> *This penny is the first penny I ever earned. Dad told me to keep it*
> *but I dont need it. Mrs Macuchin says dont waste it on nerds.*

Nerds meant Nerd candy. I thought about the delicious candy and about my father, who told me if the first penny you ever earned was a wheat penny you'd be a rich man. But the father in my mind wasn't the father from back then; it was the little old man at home with my mother, flipping channels on the TV. I wondered why I had been so willing to bury my wheat penny. I kept reading:

> *I hope stuff is boss in the future. I hope you aren't a big fat loser!*

That was it?

I turned over the card—nothing on the back.

The lack of content was disappointing. Where were my hopes and dreams? Also, although I didn't consider myself a big fat loser, I recognized that to a second-grader I might have *seemed* like a big fat loser. The "loser" part was subjective, depending on how the second-grader felt about being forty and single and in advertising, which was an exciting and changing industry in my opinion but might have been boring to a second-grader. The "big" part was objectively true, and some would call me fat, I'm sure. If you saw me you might not think "boy what a fatso," but that's only because so many people are fat nowadays. And the changing standard by which a person is judged to be fat doesn't change the reality of the object itself, fat, which is an inarguable thing you can grab and squeeze and watch jiggle around beneath the pale skin on your hairy stomach, provided you can work up the courage to pull up your shirt and take a goddamned look at yourself.

I opened Mrs. McCutcheon's letter. Because the paper had no lines, her cursive script sank down on the right side such that the whole thing looked like a weird claw with *Dear Michael* for a thumb:

> *Dear Michael,*
> *They're razing the schoolhouse, so I dug up the time capsules.*
> *I got your address from your parents. Are you still in touch with*
> *Tim Benahan? I can't find him. You were such chums. I can't find*

*Lauren Bogucki or Chappy Mendoza either, but I don't remember
you being chums with them. Poor Wilfred Johnson died in a house
fire, so I gave his capsule to his parents.
All the best,
Marianne McCutcheon*

I was startled. I didn't even know the school had been closed, let
alone slated for demolition. I called my mother, who confirmed the news.

"There's gonna be an LA Fitness," she said.

"What about the children?"

"The ones that's left go to Schmidt."

"*Schmidt?*" Adolph Schmidt was the school on the good side of the
tracks. I remembered a shaded playground with multiple tire swings.

"There aren't many kids around here anymore," my mother said,
"just old farts like us." She said this loudly, as though it were a joke for
my father's benefit. If he laughed, I didn't hear him. She said, "Well, if
that's all—"

"Did the Benahans move?"

"I have no idea."

"I thought you and Dad were friends with them."

"That was a long time ago. We lost touch. Why don't you ask Tim?"

"Mrs. McCutcheon can't find him. She's got these time capsules…"
I tried to explain but my mother didn't seem to be listening. She said,
"Time machines is all the rage nowadays. Is Tim on Friendster?"

"I don't know. We lost touch."

Tim Benahan wasn't on Friendster. He wasn't on HRnet either, not
that I expected him or anybody else from my hometown to be on a
networking website for professionals. Probably Tim had become a
truck-driver like his father, a squirrely man who played catch with us and
would say "go long" until we were exhausted. Tim had been small like his
father, which was why in middle school, when I started playing football
and basketball for the school teams, we stopped being friends. I know
that sounds stupid but that's how it was where we grew up.

"How's work?" Mom asked.

"Fine," I said, wondering how best to get off the phone without
being rude.

"How's that Lizzie girl?"

"Well. We're working on a new account."

"You two work so good together."

I wasn't in the mood for this line of questioning. I didn't have the energy to fend off Mom with my usual rigmarole about workplace harassment and how a woman didn't deserve to be cornered and asked on a date for the sin of having a rapport with a male coworker. Besides, what would a successful young woman like Lizzie want with a middle-aged dinosaur like me?

"I wonder if Ellen Kearney got a capsule," my mother offered.

"I have to go."

"Mikey—"

"That's Mr. Courtney on the other line. I have to take it."

After I hung up, I took out my stationary to write a thank-you note to Mrs. McCutcheon, but I couldn't stop thinking about Tim. It surprised me how little I knew about him. We had gone to school together until we were eighteen—adults, basically—but when I tried to imagine adult Tim all I could picture was a little kid lost someplace where even Mrs. McCutcheon, for all her witchcraft, couldn't find him.

3.

When the time-rips were discovered, everybody was pumped. We didn't yet know how crappy they would be. 9,999 times out of 10,000 they showed the dark and lonely vacuum of outer space, the novelty of which wore off quickly. Rare was the glimpse of land or sea, let alone house or city. Animal or person. The hairy back of a hand. A man's leg mid-stride, which might lead to such questions as what do they wear in the future? Long johns? But, of course, it might have been the past, and the man might have been a long-johns-wearing cowboy or stevedore. What with the earth's rotation, you might have seen a trousers-wearing Visigoth on his way to sack Rome!

The first recognizable human was Rick Zorn, though many still insist it wasn't Zorn, just an old guy in Romania. But Zorn visited Romania on three occasions: once on vacation in 2004 and twice for film shoots, in 1992 and 1996. His third wife confirmed that the 2004 vacation had included a stint at a chalet on Bâlea Lake, the view from which—of the Făgăras Mountains, gunmetal and crumbling, shrouded in rising mist from the bright alpine lake—matched the time-rip backdrop almost exactly. Elderly Romanian Zorn was looking sort of downward at something, like a flower maybe, or a bug on his shoe. Zorn or not, the sighting was huge. Finally the time-rips were *showing* us something.

When you paid a company like Time Windows for a glimpse, it was understood that you were paying for the first "real" glimpse, not a peek at outer space. So you might be paying for ten glimpses or a thousand. Hence the cost. The companies claimed to have harnessed and filtered time-rips by way of their special patented algorithms, the result of which was you could see whatever the company advertised. The most famous of them, Glimpses of History, offered to show you, on demand, London in 1940, just before the bombing, or the Acropolis in 432 BC, or a field outside the city walls of Jerusalem in 33 AD where, if you were lucky, you might see some folks getting crucified.

Time Windows's thing was making it so you could see a child version of yourself and talk to it. Beyond that, I didn't know much about the company. So the first thing Lizzie and Demarcus and I did was try to find out as much about Time Windows as possible, not just the service but the company and the people behind it.

The website wasn't informative. The front page showed a dewy camellia bush with a pixilated cursive logo: *"Time Windows..."* It looked like the website for a funeral home. The only links that weren't broken were "Contact" and "About." The "About" link took us to another camellia bush with the text, *"The minds behind Mr. Vinegar the fruit fly bring you a breakthrough time-travel algorithm that puts you in touch with your child self to convey a message, perhaps, or simply to gaze with wonder."* The "Contact" link gave a phone number and P.O. Box in Monroe, Georgia.

The location was surprising. But Monroe was only an hour from Atlanta, Lizzie pointed out, and there were lots of rich people in the Atlanta suburbs who wouldn't have minded dropping five grand to say a few words to themselves as kids, like don't do too much Botox or put all your money in Compaq. Plus, Georgia probably offered time-rip companies a gratuitous tax break.

The search term "Time Windows" led to a young adult sci-fi series in which teens escape troubled home-lives into dramatic historical events such as Paul Revere's ride, where they lend a hand by, for instance, re-shoeing Paul Revere's horse. After lots of scrolling we found a message board on which a potential customer asked, *"Hey, has anybody tried Time Windows? The deal in the bus ads? It sounds too good to be true, but with the Mr. Vinegar deal, who knows?"* The responses weren't helpful. Like this, from Forever61: *"never use—body snatchers from china!"* Or this, from

YachtDaddy: "*Time is just a dimension (the 4th) no different than space.*" Or this, from OriginalAxeMan2000: "*Mr Vinegar is a lie!!!! :(.*"

"Who the heck is Mr. Vinegar?" I asked.

"A fruit fly," Demarcus said.

Lizzie said, "I can't believe you haven't heard of Mr. Vinegar."

"Sorry."

Demarcus cued up a video called "Mr. Vinegar's journey."

The video, which had thirty million views, showed a fruit fly in a shiny terrarium. The fly got blurry looking, went back to normal, disappeared, then reappeared. Then, for the rest of the video, a handsome young Chinese scientist explained that Mr. Vinegar had been zapped back in time 12.6 seconds, which was why he disappeared, and that Mr. Vinegar had gotten blurry before that because there were two overlapping Mr. Vinegars 12.6 seconds in the past. As proof, the scientist pulled out a photo that showed how the blurry Mr. Vinegar was really two overlapping Mr. Vinegars.

"Geez," I said, "is this for real?"

"Who knows with this stuff from China," Lizzie said.

"Cambodia," Demarcus said. He opened the Mr. Vinegar Wikipedia page, and the three of us began to read it. The scientist was a man named Nol Rithipol who worked at a Cambodian university but had collaborators in China and Canada. Dr. Nol had large eyes and wavy black hair, and his furrowed brow gave the impression of a deep thinker. There was a link to the journal article in which Dr. Nol described his results. We tried to read the article but found it impenetrable, and after a few minutes crowded around Demarcus's computer, breathing all over each other, I said, "We should get back to work."

"We *are* working," Lizzie said.

"This Vinegar business has nothing to do with Time Windows."

"They both involve time-travel."

"Yeah, right."

"Demarcus," Lizzie said, ignoring me, "just as the lawyer must believe her client's story, the advertiser must believe in the product or service she advertises. A great adman once told me that."

I was the one who told her that, and I needed the reminder, clearly, but I couldn't believe that Lizzie—smart, sophisticated Lizzie—was even entertaining the possibility that Time Windows worked. To me, the question wasn't whether it worked, or how it worked, but if the *scam* worked well enough that our ads wouldn't be undermined by word of mouth.

But whether or not Time Windows was a scam, we needed art, so when Lizzie and Demarcus broke for lunch I went to the flex room. I kicked the beanbag chairs out of the way and set up my easel and drawing pad. I wrote TIME WINDOWS and a bullet underneath to start a list, but I couldn't think of anything to put on the list so I drew a big oval (the adult) and a small oval (the child). Then I crossed out the ovals. They were too much like Dietrich's ad. Then I turned down the lights and paced back and forth, hoping to make my mind go blank and get an idea, but I couldn't shake the image of Tim Benehan's face floating open-mouthed as though witnessing a horror. Frustrated, I flipped the page and started drawing disembodied heads of different shapes and sizes. One had a mustache. Another wore glasses. Yet another had wavy black hair and a furrowed brow. I stood back from that one, surprised to see the face of Nol Rithipol, the Cambodian scientist of Mr. Vinegar fame. I chuckled at the idea of showing Dr. Nol, the client, a Time Windows ad featuring his own face. It was a solemn face. I took out my phone to learn more about Dr. Nol and was surprised to discover he had his own Wikipedia page. It showed photos of a wizened Dr. Nol speaking here and there around the world, but not about Mr. Vinegar—about what happened to his family in Cambodia.

Dr. Nol was from a prominent military family in Phnom Penh, I learned, and when he excelled in school he was able to study medicine in France. His father, a general, sided with the anti-communists in the coup and ensuing civil war, and at first this seemed to Nol a stroke of good fortune. After the anti-communists took power and the U.S.-backed Khmer Republic was established, Nol was able to travel to and from Phnom Penh to see his wife and their baby. Years later, on stage, he told the story of the last time he visited them, in early 1975, and of a trip he took with them to the small city where his wife grew up. Early one morning they walked to the top of a hill, for a view of the sunrise over the mountains, but what they saw was smoke. Dozens of columns of smoke drifting skyward. For a moment he thought trees were being cleared to make rice paddies, but then he realized the smoke was coming from the surrounding villages. The villages were on fire. And the thin, wraith-like columns of smoke receded in the distance as far as he could see, which gave him the uncanny impression that every single village in

Cambodia was burning. When they got back to the capital, he set about trying to arrange for his wife and son to join him in France, but for now he had to return alone and resume his studies.

I was reading about Dr. Nol's thwarted attempts to return to his homeland, and about the rumors he heard of the savage cruelty of the Khmer Rouge, when Lizzie came into the flex room and said, "Nice drawings, but where are the kids?"

I looked at the drawing. "That's one," I said, pointing at a small face.

"That one's just small," Lizzie said. "It has a big nose like a man. What's the problem, Mike, they didn't teach kid-drawing at art school?"

"I didn't go to art school."

"Touchy, touchy."

What could I say? I wanted to know what Dr. Nol found when he finally returned to Cambodia. But then Demarcus got back from lunch and Lizzie started a brainstorm session.

While we sat in the beanbag chairs, she dimmed the lights and told us to close our eyes. "We've got to get into the head of the customer," she said. "So, if you could go back in time and talk to a yourself, what would you say?"

Nothing, I wanted to tell her, *the kid called me a big fat loser.* But instead I said, "What age?"

"Any age."

"How long do we get to talk for?"

"Let's say five minutes."

"It would help to know for sure, because if it's longer I'd tell me a little about myself."

"Five minutes."

"Fine." But I needed more than five minutes. I would have to convince myself, early on, that just because I was fat didn't mean I was a loser. Unless—"Wait a minute," I said, "are you sure we can see each other? Like, can the kid me *see* me?"

Lizzie sighed.

Demarcus piped up: "I think we can. In the bus ad they're looking—"

"Forget the bus ad," Lizzie said. "Okay, Mike, you first."

"Me first what?"

"What would you *tell* yourself?"

"I guess I'd tell myself to work hard, but to have some fun too."

"Wow, exciting."

"It's good advice!"

"Everybody gets advice like that a thousand times. It's no reason to pay a bunch of money to see through a time rip. Think harder. Demarcus, how about you?"

While I thought harder, Demarcus told us how he wished he hadn't gone to an expensive private college. He said his friends who went to State (Ohio State? Florida State?) had lots of fun and barely any student loans to pay off. They got good jobs, too. Demarcus paused reflectively. "But maybe I shouldn't tell myself that," he said, "because what if it got me thinking I didn't have to work hard in school because I was gonna go to State anyway? Then what if I didn't even get in to State and ended up someplace bad, or no place at all?"

There was something heartbreaking about that to me. "Someplace bad" combined in my mind with "no place at all" to become a sort of wasteland wherein Demarcus, who had a childlike face, wandered with a few other young people turning over dumpsters in search of empty cans with food residue inside them. The sky was overcast. Dirty snow covered the barren ground. When starvation set in, the weakest among them would have no choice but to join the black-clad guerrillas who had torched their homes and families.

"Interesting," Lizzie said. "What I like is the positive aspect. You're telling yourself to *have more fun.*"

Wasn't that what I just said?

"That's something a lot of people can relate to," Lizzie said.

"Like me," I muttered.

"Pardon?"

"I said that already, about fun."

"Do you want some water or something?"

"No."

"You're grumpy. How about candy?"

"I don't want candy." But I did want candy, and Lizzie, sensing this, went to the kitchen for a bowl of peanut M&Ms, which the three of us shared.

When we got back to brainstorming, I didn't close my eyes. Since there wasn't a table in the room I had a good view of Lizzie sitting across from me with her hands clasped in her lap and her legs flopped out in front of her. Probably she was thinking about important career advice, like not to waste two years as an editorial assistant before going back to school for copywriting. I kept getting flashes of what she might look like beneath her tasteful skirt-and-blouse combo, so I looked away, embarrassed, and stared for a while at the acoustic ceiling tiles. The whole thing was ridiculous, I decided. Who cared about seeing his or her child-self when on the other side of the world men and women might be toiling in rice paddies while their villages burned? While their *actual* children were trained to be unfeeling zombies? I thought of Lauren, Chappy, and Wilfred. I thought of Tim Benahan, my chum. One time we carved our names with scissors into the wooden hutch where we hung our winter coats. We got in such bad trouble that I didn't like to think about it, but I was thinking about it, and I remembered that our teacher at the time, Mrs. Rohr, said I was in extra trouble because Tim looked up to me.

4.

I wanted to start running again, but my doctor told me I had to lose fifty pounds first or whatever cartilage I had left in my knees would be obliterated. But how was I supposed to lose fifty pounds if I couldn't run? Who had time to drive back and forth to a gym? I worked sixty hours a week, and not at some tech startup where you could do pilates during lunch and wear stinky gym clothes the rest of the day. At Courtney Associates LLC, I told my doctor, you had to look sharp. And that's how I ended up with the machine.

Though advertised as a private indoor cycling studio in my home, the object sitting in the middle of my living room looked a lot like a stationary bicycle. Approaching the sleek little bike from my bedroom, where I'd changed into a cutoff sweatshirt and some drooping Georgia Southern basketball shorts I hadn't worn in years, I felt intimidated. Could it really support me? Was I sure I hadn't accidentally bought the women's size?

I placed my feet on the pedals and raised my butt onto the narrow seat. I'd already adjusted the seat so I wouldn't have to monkey around with it and lose my gumption at this very crucial moment, which I hoped would be the beginning of a major lifestyle change. I was pleased by how solid the contraption felt beneath me. I turned on the monitor and was instructed to select a coach from among the dozen or so on offer who could teach my online class. This, too, I had decided beforehand. Ramón had looked like the oldest coach and might, I thought, be slightly less dispiriting to stare at while sweating and grunting and feeling every bit Ramón's age, but now that Ramón's stern face with its salt-and-pep-per stubble was eyeing me from the little monitor, I opted quickly for someone younger and friendlier. Someone female. Christie. Christie's ribs weren't visible beneath her shiny outfit, and her profile promised she would empower me to break through self-imposed limitations and embrace my authentic self.

Christie told me all the buttons I needed to push, and I pushed them, and when I started pedaling it actually felt pretty good, like doing a bunch of tiny squat presses one after the other. My legs weren't going nearly as fast as Christie's, though. Or as fast as the legs of the other people in my online group, according to the numbers that were scrolling across my screen. Dan in Cleveland had already burned a hundred calories. I'd burned six. Then my phone buzzed, and even though I don't normally answer calls from numbers I don't recognize, I answered this one right away.

"Mike Muhler," I said, dismounting.

"Michael?" came a frail and spacey female voice.

"Speaking. May I help you?"

"This is Marianne. Marianne McCutcheon?"

"Mrs. McCutcheon?"

"Marianne, please."

I felt embarrassed to be caught wearing a cutoff sweatshirt and basketball shorts. I fought the urge to ask if I could call her back after showering.

"How are you?" she asked.

"Good," I said. "Well, I mean."

"And your parents?"

"Well. Thanks for asking. And your… husband?"

"Wife. She passed last winter."

"I'm so sorry."

"Don't be. She awaits me in Thulerat."

"Pardon?"

"The sphere where souls rest before deciding on their new bodies."

"Ah yes, Thulerat." I wracked my brain for topics other than Thulerat. I was in a people business, wasn't I? I chatted up clients all the time, clients I had nothing in common with other than my race and gender, and here was a person I had spent literally hundreds of days with. Thousands of hours. A person from my past. What was wrong with me?

"I was wondering," Mrs. McCutcheon said, "if you've had any luck finding Tim."

"What? No. I guess I haven't really been looking, though."

"Oh." She sounded so disappointed! "It's just, well, I haven't had any luck with his parents either."

"Did they move away?"

"It's possible, but my wife hired Stuart for a job as recently as five years ago."

"Stuart?"

"Mr. Benahan. He was a handyman."

"I thought he drove a truck."

"That was before, well, you know."

I didn't know.

"Before he lost his license," she said. Then, when I didn't respond, she added in a whisper: "the DWI's."

Memories of Mr. Benahan flashed through my mind: the games of catch, the grill in their back yard, the way he playfully swatted his Reds cap at Tim and the other kids (Doug? Lisa? Liza?). Had there been a beer in his hand? Even so, did that mean he was drunk? Lots of people drank beer. I drank beer, lord knew, especially back then. But Tim hadn't, I remembered suddenly, and my heart sank. Drinking had been another of the reasons we drifted apart, when in high school I started going to beer parties and Tim acted real prissy about it.

"My God," I said, thinking of the ephemeral beer parties and of Tim sitting home alone, wondering if his best friend would go the drunken way of his father. Maybe Doug, the older brother, had already gone down that ignominious road. He had sideburns, I remembered.

"I know you don't have any special information," Mrs. McCutcheon said, "but I felt like I could call you. You're the only one who wrote me back."

"The thank-you note?"

"It had your phone number."

I couldn't believe no one else had written Mrs. McCutcheon a thank-you note, after all the work she did rescuing our time-capsules and tracking us down. I pictured her standing in the rubble-filled schoolyard, stomping a shovel into the dirt. She was an old woman!

"I'll try harder," I said. "I'll make some calls. Any luck with Lauren and Chappy?"

"Lauren is an accountant in Chicago."

"Wow. Good for her."

"Chappy ran a mink and ermine farm with his brother, Rigoberto, but it got shut down."

"Fur must be a tough business."

"Those boys always had a can-do attitude. Their mother says they're down in Mexico trying to get the operation going again." She sighed. "What a lovely woman. It was great to catch up with her."

After we hung up, I felt guilty. I opened my laptop and did a search for Doug Benahan, Lisa Benahan, Liza Benahan, Eliza Benahan. There was a Douglas Benahan, age forty-five, listed on the sex and violent offender registry in Marion County, Indiana. The age was about right, but the man in the photo was so decrepit beyond his years, with thinning hair and tiny eyes shrunken by thick glasses, that he did nothing to knock loose a memory of Tim's big brother.

I did a search for private investigators near me, doubtful that the cigarette-smoking, cheap-suit-wearing men of my imagination would deign to build websites, but sure enough I found many investigative agencies online, as well as services dedicated to locating and selecting investigative agencies based on my criteria. I chose one of these services at random and put in the zip code of my hometown, but the investigators it recommended were all over America and seemed to prioritize infidelity and child-custody investigations over the finding of missing persons. Maybe because it was so hard to find missing persons? Still, I wanted to make at least a token effort, for Mrs. McCutcheon's sake, so I signed up with the second cheapest, Double A Detection, which charged a flat fifty-dollar fee and would contact me if more money was required. Without having to get on the phone, I entered Tim's name, age, last known address, and my best attempt at a description.

Within seconds an e-mail from Double A Detection appeared in my inbox: *Hello*, it began,

> *Thank you for requesting our help to find TIM BENAHAN. People go missing for various reasons, such as personal choice, illness, stress, abduction, foul play, and drug- or alcohol-related reasons. We understand the frustration and anguish in locating your relative, past love, runaway child, witness, or debtor. There are many 'unknowns' in the field of missing persons, but we have a worldwide database that provides us with billions of records. Please rest assured our team of*

investigators previously active in the fields of law enforcement, military,
corrections and/or security personnel are pleased to help. We at Double
A Detection are honored to have you as our client. Now, let us find
TIM BENAHAN!

Right away I felt sorry for not trying harder. I thought about Dr.
Nol, who'd spent years wandering Cambodia in search of his missing
wife and son before conceding the probability, based on overwhelming
circumstantial evidence, that they were dead. Would Dr. Nol have let
himself off the hook for fifty bucks' worth of online sleuthing? Of
course not. But Dr. Nol had been searching for his family, I reasoned,
whereas I was searching for a childhood friend I hadn't seen in twenty
years. Did that make me a bad person? Maybe, but wasn't a person who
writes thank-you notes actually a *good* person?

Rather than get back on the exercise bike, I took out my easel, set
it in the middle of the living room, and started sketching with charcoal.
I drew the nondescript faces of children, floating in space at first, eyes
wide, mouths open, and then inside of geometrical designs that looked
like tiny cages. I kept drawing until the geometric cages took over the
faces, covering them almost completely, like masks. I kept drawing until
charcoal had piled at the base of the easel and the page was so crowded
with obscure masked faces that they looked like an alien hive. A hive
of the dead. Dr. Nol's son was among them. And Wilfred Johnson, still
untouched by the house-fire that would kill him. And the little blonde
girl from the Time Windows ad, the one whose brown eyes weren't quite
pretty enough. And I saw in every fragment of every eye and mouth the
face of Tim Benahan. But he wasn't really there, I decided. He wasn't
dead. Then, as though to assure myself of this fact, I used the side of
my palm to fuzz out a space in the center of the seething hive, and within
that gray smear I meticulously drew the face of a living, breathing boy.

5.

When I showed the drawing to Lizzie the next day, she looked at the face
and said, "What's with the mist?"

"What mist?" I asked.

She pointed to streaks of gray where the hive of other faces had
been.

"Oh, that's meant to be, like, memory," I said, regretting it immediately. It sounded so corny! I tried to think of something more intellectual.

"Time too," I said. "Like, the clouds of time."

Lizzie stared at it, and I feared the worst. *The clouds of time?*

"I like it," Lizzie said. "No, I love it."

"You do?"

"The kid looks weak and lonely. That's the appeal, I think. You've got to reach back in time and reassure the little guy. I mean look at him. Those eyes! You gotta tell him everything's going to be okay, and if you can afford Time Windows, chances are it is."

Suddenly the boy's dark eyes looked exaggerated, like those of the needy kids calculatedly chosen for Save the Children ads. It made me feel crass. "I guess I hadn't thought of it like that," I said.

"Who is he, anyway?" Lizzie asked.

"I don't know," I lied.

We showed the drawing to Demarcus, who liked it too, then we gathered around Demarcus's computer. Demarcus, who proved impressively agile with Adobe, chose some muted colors for the kid's clothes, pale white for his face, and a sky blue for his irises that Demarcus duplicated for the text and Time Windows logo. The blue was Lizzie's idea. She explained that sky blue was almost connoted by the word *window*. I considered this a conciliatory gesture, design-wise, since the background of my drawing looked more like outer space than blue sky, and the Time Window in my mind looked out on the endless abyss of the past.

Later, we presented the design to Mr. Courtney inside his darkened office, with the mock-up projected on a retractable screen. While Mr. Courtney stared at the mock-up, legs crossed, chin in hand, Lizzie cycled through copy: "Remind yourself to honor your parents, to cherish your friends. Remind yourself to do well in school, but to have fun too. Remind yourself to savor every moment in life."

When Mr. Courtney said nothing, Lizzie explained that the word *remind* was key because *to remind* represented a tangible act that would be worth the money. Dietrich's team had placed too much emphasis on the novelty of *seeing* the child self, she went on, when the heart of Time Windows's appeal was in *communicating* with the child self in a positive way.

"Positive?" Mr. Courtney scoffed. "Who is this poor kid?"

I said nothing.

"And *where* is he? Bergen-Belsen?"

I laughed uncomfortably.

"*Remind* is a nag word. It's what your mother does." Mr. Courtney stood up and sauntered over to his window, where he clasped his hands behind his back and stared at the brick building across the street, as though a great secret were somewhere inside it among the architects. He rubbed his stubbly jaw, thinking deeply, or trying to appear to think deeply. It was possible he had thought of what he was going to say long before we came into his office. It was also possible what he said would be brilliant. I braced myself. At last he cleared his throat and said, "This is *you* you're talking to. You and your child self are buddies. Pals. You don't *nag* each other. In fact, you're so close to your child self that you don't have to *remind* him of anything. *He knows.*"

Mr. Courtney turned to us slowly, as though to emphasize this last part, or maybe to gauge its brilliance by our reactions. Lizzie and Demarcus were nodding, so I nodded too, even though my child self and I *weren't* pals. My child self called me a big fat loser. And sure, the criticism had spurred me buy an exercise bike and set up an online dating profile, but what now? I was still fat and single and stuck in an office listening to my boss's high-handed prattle.

Mr. Courtney sighed. "Okay, Mike, what's the problem?"

"There's no problem," I said. "I like it, the thing about closeness. That's key, I think."

Mr. Courtney stared at me.

"Okay, well, I don't feel close to my child self. I barely even think of him."

"Then you're a weirdo. Normal people look back fondly on childhood. Isn't that so?"

"Sure," Lizzie said.

Mr. Courtney looked at Demarcus, who had a laptop open in front of him and was taking notes. It took Demarcus a while to notice Mr. Courtney, and when he did, he glanced at Lizzie before responding.

"Um, I guess I look back like that," Demarcus said. "Fondly or whatever. I got to play sports back then, which was fun."

Each of us took a moment to remember sports.

Mr. Courtney said, "Hear that, Mike? Everybody except you wants to be a kid again."

I smiled, accepting the joke at my expense. "It isn't that I look back *un*-fondly," I said, "it's just that, well, I don't have too many memories of childhood. The concussions..."

Lizzie and Demarcus were watching me, waiting for me to elaborate about the concussions, but I didn't want to tell my frigging life story.

"Maybe I'm atypical," I said, shrugging bashfully. "Their target users probably do want to be kids again."

"And who are their target users?" Mr. Courtney asked.

"Not me!"

Lizzie and Demarcus chuckled. Mr. Courtney did not.

"Seriously, Mike," he said, "if you have this insight about the target user, please fill us in."

Why was he coming on so strong? Was he trying to embarrass me in front of my team? I hadn't meant to criticize his idea. I just didn't feel close to my child self!

"Who are the target users?" Mr. Courtney persisted. "Who are these crazy people who feel such sympathy for themselves as children?"

"Oh, I don't know," I said with mock bluster, "rich people?"

"And rich people are all the same?"

"Of course not. Some spend their summers frolicking in the Hamptons, others on St. Simons. Some go to Harvard, others Emory. Some ski, others ride horses."

Mr. Courtney glowered. Harvard and the family compound on St. Simons were common knowledge, but Mr. Courtney had told me about the equestrian lessons in a private moment, after a meeting with a real estate brokerage owned and operated by a prominent Atlanta family. The meeting had been with a father, son and grandson team, all of whom had thick white necks pinched by starched collars. I'd watched with wonder as Mr. Courtney bullshitted with them about the Atlanta polo scene, or lack thereof. The joking consensus seemed to be that Atlanta would always be a backwater when it came to competitive polo.

"I'll have you know that my childhood was as difficult as anyone's in this room," Mr. Courtney said.

Lizzie shot me a look: *What did you do?*

"I started seeing a therapist in middle school," Mr. Courtney was saying. "My father..." He trailed off, turning back to the window.

I was ready to stand up and lead my team out of the office, when Mr. Courtney turned to us and said, "No tag lines. Just 'Time Windows' in tasteful bold sans serif. Everybody knows what it is by now. They'll know that the kid in the ad is them. They'll start thinking about what they want to say. It's impossible not to. Hell, I'm thinking about it right now."

He stood for a moment in silence.

"What would you say?" Lizzie asked, earnestly.

"That's a personal question, but it doesn't matter anyway. It's the act itself that matters. It isn't about the effect you have on child you, it's about the effect child you has on you. Child you was the only person who ever really understood you..."

This was a subtle insight, I thought, but Mr. Courtney kept talking about the closeness of the child self until I zoned out. I was staring at the ad mock-up and thinking about the kid. About Tim. *There are many "unknowns" in the field of missing persons,* Double A Detection had informed me. *Personal choice, illness, stress, abduction, foul play, and drug- or alcohol-related reasons.* In my mind the gumshoes of Double A Detection were searching for Tim inside crack houses, dumpsters, barren fields. They were poking with sticks through a pile of bones and skulls.

"I'll call the Time Windows people to set up a meeting," Mr. Courtney was saying. "Talk to Carol Chen about a casting call for some kids. I want real photos for this. No internet stuff."

And so it was: on the heels of good news, bad. We were happy Mr. Courtney liked the idea, and excited at the prospect of meeting with the mysterious client, but first we would have to deal with child actors.

6.

The first and only date I arranged online was with a woman named Amy who messaged that she liked my eyes. The message had no caps or punctuation and was sent at two a.m., which made me wonder if Amy was a lush or crazed midnight internet person, but her profile offered actual information, unlike most women's profiles, and in photos she was pretty but slightly overweight, which made me feel less self-conscious about my own weight. She was a paralegal, divorced, and had grown up in Rochester, New York. I responded to her message with a longer, more formal message of my own. It was a version of the same message I'd sent to half a dozen women whose profiles intrigued me, but whereas those women ignored my message, Amy responded: *"You seem very passionate about your work! I admire that. I love my work, but I try to remember to have fun too. Lucky for me my coworkers are a great bunch. Do you like bowling?"* I replied that I couldn't bowl because of a football injury (true—I couldn't bend low enough to put the ball on the wood) but that in general I liked to try new things (less true), and Amy replied that we should meet at a new Sichuan restaurant on Buford Highway.

I spent a long time picking out what to wear. To work I wore pleated khakis, button-down shirts and penny loafers, what Mr. Courtney called my uniform. In theory, this uniform should have made life easier, since I never had to worry about what to wear, but pleated khakis had gotten harder to find, and the penny loafers didn't offer much support to my large and flattening feet, so recently I had introduced to my curated wardrobe the kind of bulky white New Balance sneakers worn by my father and half the other old men in Indiana. But for the date with Amy I would wear the loafers, and with some reluctance I withdrew from my closet the single pair of flat-front khakis.

The restaurant, which was in a strip mall, struck me as dangerously authentic. Through a cutout in the back wall I could see two surly-looking Chinese men toiling in the kitchen, and the steam that wafted across the dining room from the cutout stung my eyes. All around me Asian families were chatting loudly. I was early, so I sat down at a corner table and perused the menu, which didn't feature any of the sweet and gooey things I was used to eating.

Amy was fifteen minutes late and made a loud noise as she came through the swinging glass door. She sped toward me, apologizing. We shook hands and she sat down. She grabbed a menu and starting reading, as though she had to catch up, and her absorption in the menu gave me a chance to look at her. She was prettier in person than in her photos. There was about an inch of gray at the top of her head, where her brunette hair was parted, and I wondered if she had decided to stop dying it (a choice I admired, frankly) or if something traumatic had happened. I thought of photos I'd seen of young POWs returning from Vietnam, their long hair white at the roots. The word *torture* flashed in my mind. Then *Tuol Sleng*, the torture and execution center in Phnom Penh where prisoners had slept chained to iron bars. The inquisitors there had used farm implements instead of guns, to save bullets.

When the waiter approached, Amy ordered baijiu without looking at him, and I told him I'd have the same. For the rest of the meal, Amy drank quickly and constantly: first the baijiu, which tasted to me like toothpaste water, and then a sweet, slightly viscous Chinese wine. I struggled to keep up and was thankful when the food came, hoping it would settle my stomach.

It didn't.

The sauce on a noodle dish was so spicy that when a fleck hit my cheek it actually burned the skin. The small red mark on my face would last for three days, and whenever I saw it I would think of Amy: the way she gobbled her food, glugged her wine, and paused only to ask perfunctory questions about "the ad biz," as she called it. I had no idea where the evening was going, or if I wanted to see her again, though I was beginning to find her very sexy. A dark tattoo peeked out from beneath the unbuttoned top button of her work blouse. But I tried to tamp down those feelings because she didn't seem interested in me. I wondered if she had taken one look at me when she came through the door, late, and decided to get through the meal as quickly as possible. But then, after the meal was over, after we split the check, after I went into the bathroom to try and fail to use the toilet and then to wash the sweat from my face, we were standing in the dark strip mall parking lot and she offered me a cigarette. I hadn't smoked in years but I took one, she lit it, and we smoked.

Amy asked me if I was good to drive.

I wasn't sure. I hadn't had more than a single drink in months, and at the restaurant I'd had three or four. But I said something jovial about it being a straight shot home.

"I'm good," she said.

"To drive?"

She cocked her head. "Come on, I'll drive."

"Where?" I was genuinely confused. And what about my car?

"Come on, big guy. You're telling me you don't want this?"

"Want what?"

She stared at me, smiling slightly.

Oh.

The thing is? I did want it. I hadn't had sex in, well, let's just say a long time. I hadn't had *regular* sex with anybody since Ellen Kearney, my high-school girlfriend, pathetic as that is to admit, so the idea of having sex with Amy was very appealing to me, and I got a flash in my mind of a once-a-week rendezvous for spicy food, cheap wine and carefree sex. But to be asked in such a direct way left me speechless. There was also the issue of my bowels, which were roiling. And I hadn't stopped sweating.

"I'm sorry, Amy—"

She sighed. I felt badly.

"Let's do this again," I said.

"You need another drink or what? There's a place two blocks down. It's mostly Mexicans but the beer is cheap."

"Don't you have to go to work tomorrow?"

Amy sighed again. Then she put both hands on her forehead and made a soft moaning sound, and for a moment I thought she was going to collapse, but she just flung the butt of her cigarette to the ground, grabbed the keys out of her purse and clicked her car unlocked.

"I'm so sorry," I said feebly, following her toward her car. "The spicy food..."

After Amy got in her car and executed a three-point turn with surprising precision, I went inside a Mexican grocery at the end of the strip mall and bought a bag of day-old *pan dulce* for a dollar. I sat on the hood of my car, munching them, and soon they were all in my stomach absorbing the alcohol and lava-like Sichuan sauces.

When I got home I was looking forward to brushing my teeth to get the cigarette taste out of my mouth, but there was a package on the stairs of my condo.

A fat padded envelope.

Inside the condo, under the bright light that hung over my kitchen island, I recognized Mrs. McCutheon's drooping cursive. I opened the envelope, revealing a thin gray box identical to the one I'd received from her days before. I opened the box and was shocked to see the exact same 1987 Steve Stipanovich basketball card. Was this some kind of joke?

But the other items were less familiar: a Mr. T action figure missing one arm, a Kennedy half dollar, a marble. And the folded construction paper, which was blue, not red, said *"To me, From me"* in tiny neat cursive. I opened it, feeling some trepidation, and read the note:

> *Dear Me,*
>
> *I don't know when you'll get this or if you'll be a policeman. The policeman who came said you have to take a test. But the firemen have to take a test where they run fast and do a hundred pushups. The Army guy was kind of mean. Mike's dad says the brake box factory is okay but what about the guy who got his finger chopped?*

*Maybe you're married and have kids but I doubt it. Maybe you
have a mustache like Uncle Jeff.*
     Sincerely,
     Tim B

I read over the note several times, trying to convince myself that
Tim's desperation to see his own future was typical, not a sign of things
to come. I brushed my teeth and put on pajamas and looked at sports
scores on my phone for a while, but I couldn't fall asleep. I tried to think
of Amy, hoping to masturbate and get sleepy, but the feeling of my hand
around my soft penis made Tim pop into my head. That may sound
strange, and it is, so let me explain: I started puberty before Tim, and at
some point we were comparing anatomy, as kids do, when Tim asked if
he could touch it and I told him he could. I guess I was flattered. He told
me it was huge. It wasn't. Even now my penis is smaller than average, I
think. But he just held it for a while, admiring it. When it started to get
big—from the touching, I assured myself—I zipped up and we never
talked about it again.

To get Tim out of my head I thought about Ellen Kearney, who
remained my go-to in these situations. I had studied her Friendster photos
well enough to conjure them at will, and in my mind I could ignore
the fact that most of them were at little kid birthday parties and family
vacations to Disney World. I could edit out the children, her husband,
her aging parents whom I had loved and was pained now to see. What I
didn't edit was Ellen herself. If anything, she had gotten *more* attractive
with age, with a thinner face that set off her dark eyes. Now her hair was
going gray, and she wasn't coloring it even though the other women in
her photos had ridiculous dye-jobs and wore too much makeup. Ellen
had always had a defiant streak. In my mind, this mature, confident Ellen
was superimposed on my memories of the girl who'd allowed me to
reach under her shirt while we were kissing in the woods by the field
where we had our beer parties. The girl who'd stripped off her clothes to
have tentative sex with me—my first time, though whether it was hers I
never knew—in the back of her family's Dodge Caravan. Some of those
memories were so crisp, so delectably vivid, that I had to suspect, based
on the paltriness of the rest of my memories, that their crispness came
not from any particular fidelity to the past but from reliving them again
and again in fantasy. Who knew how much they resembled the actual
events of our two-year relationship. We'd spent holidays together, gone

on trips, but fully ninety percent of my memories of her were sexual. Is that what I chose to remember? I hoped not, because I can tell you damn well that I wouldn't have minded taking a nice vacation with Ellen Kearney right about then, or watching her father carve a turkey.

Wide awake, I took out my phone and went online. After checking my e-mail and Friendster, it wasn't long before I was on the Tuol Sleng Museum website, which had a database of hundreds of mugshots from its four years as a torture prison. I was looking for one in particular, of a young woman holding her baby. The photo had struck me so powerfully that I printed it on the color printer at work and put it in this special folder I keep for inspiration. It was against the rules to print on the color printer without entering a project number, and the photo was black and white so I could have printed it more cheaply, but everybody knows that black and white photos look better, almost chocolaty, on a color printer. In addition to the woman, my special folder contained photos of workers in rice fields, young soldiers standing in the streets of Phnom Penh, and hundreds of skulls stacked and bleaching in the sun.

At last I found the photo I was looking for. The woman, No. 246, had short black hair pulled behind her ears. She was so young that her round face didn't have a single line, and her wide, flat nose barely disturbed the smooth plane between her large mouth and dark eyes. What struck me most wasn't her neutral, almost peaceful expression, despite the horrors she had almost surely faced and would face again, but the fact that the baby in her arms, partially cropped at the bottom of the photo, bore the *exact same expression*. Thinking of Ellen Kearney and her own strapping children, I imagined a world in which No. 246 was born in America, where, in addition to not being killed, she might have had enough disposable income and leisure time to reach out to her child self. She might have been encouraged to do so by her son, who in my mind was fully grown and felt guilty about how little time he spent with the mother who'd given him everything she could. Would they know, deep down, despite the alternate present they occupied, what a blessing it was that they were alive?

Did *I* know?

Shouldn't I have been living every moment in thanks? Because compared to life in a torture prison, what was a blown date with a possibly unstable woman who might have had sex with me? What was a missing friend who I barely knew anyway?

I closed the browser, unnerved, and opened the e-mail confirmation I got from the online sleuthing agency. I called the help number, which went immediately to voicemail. A gravelly male voice apologized for being away from his phone and asked me to leave a detailed message.

"Hi there," I said, confused by the ambiguous voicemail greeting, "is this Double A Detection? If so, this is Mike Muhler. I hired you to find a missing person. Sorry to call so late, but I, uh, I'm just wondering how it's going. I'd love an update when you get a sec. Feel free to e-mail as well. The thing is? I have new evidence. I got this thing in the mail, and I was thinking maybe you could dust it for fingerprints? I don't know. That's your line, obviously, not mine. Just thinking aloud here." After thinking aloud for a while longer I gave my e-mail address and phone number, even though I had entered these when I signed up for the service, before concluding, idiotically, "Okay, talk to you soon!"

7.

The Atlanta child actor scene had boomed alongside the film scene, due mostly to tax breaks for production companies who deigned to shoot in Georgia instead of California. Marvel Studios was actually headquartered in Atlanta. There was enough work to create a cottage industry of extras, and none were more competitive than the child extras, whose parents thought of them as actors but were more like models: cute faces meant to look joyful and/or horrified, to say the occasional line, and to stay out of the way of the LA talent. Fortunately for us, these people were extremely available.

Carol Chen had set up the conference room with softbox lights and three cameras on tripods, along with a drapey-looking background of matte beige. Carol, who wore all black, was probably the most talented person at the agency but too reserved to look for other work or go into business for herself. On the few occasions she spoke about something other than the task at hand, it was on subjects like ekphrastic poetry and the violence of representational art. She let an intern named Drea deal with the children and their parents, who were lined up in the hallway. I tried to avoid eye-contact as I passed them on my way in, all of them overdressed and squirming. I joined Lizzie and Demarcus on chairs in the back of the conference room, where I hoped to say as little as possible.

Carol told Drea we were ready, and Drea led the first little boy and his mother into the room. The boy was wearing tight jeans and a faux leather jacket with many zippers, like something Michael Jackson might have worn. He went straight for the stool in the center of the room, swung his leg over it, and gave the camera a look that could only be described as sultry.

"Lose the jacket," Carol said from behind the camera, and the boy, confused, looked at his mother, who sped toward him and yanked off the jacket.

Carol took a few photos, went to her second camera and took a few more.

"Thank you," Carol said.

The boy looked at his mother again.

"That's it?" the mother asked Carol.

"Thank you," Carol repeated. "Drea?"

Drea, a friendly SCAD graduate who wore oversized glasses and mismatched outfits that looked to have been gathered from the closets of dead people, chatted quietly with the boy and his mother while leading them out of the room. Snacks were offered.

The next six shoots went just as quickly. The stage mothers, and in one case a stage father, ran the gamut from resignedly professional to outraged. One mother complained they had driven all the way from Kennesaw and offered to change her daughter's clothes. She started pulling out a portfolio. But Carol just stood in stony silence as Drea corralled the mother and son, offering snacks and bottles of water, until they were out the door.

The eighth child, a small boy with thick dark hair whose mother stayed in the hallway, elicited from Carol some actual coaching. When he smiled, she told him not to smile. She told him to relax. She told him to put his hands on his knees. All the while she shot photos from all three of her cameras. Before dismissing him, she turned to us and asked if we had any special requests.

"Can we have him stand up for a full frontal?" Lizzie asked.

"Clothes on or off?" Carol deadpanned.

"Carol!" Lizzie whispered, but the boy didn't seem to have noticed. He was staring through unfocused eyes into the middle distance, as though lost in thought.

"That's it," I said.

Carol and Lizzie turned to me.

"That's the expression."

But it was gone. The boy was looking at me now, his brow furrowed. "Can you cry on command?" I asked him.

Lizzie laughed uncomfortably.

I said to Carol, "Do they ever cry? Can you get them to cry?"

Lizzie was about to take me aside, I could tell, but then the kid wrinkled up his face and all we could do was watch. It wasn't crying exactly—more like he had drunk poison and was trying to retch, but in its aftermath, after he allowed his face to relax, there was something like sadness. We kept watching him, waiting for it to end, but the stillness of his face suggested a deep well of whatever memories were causing him to look the way he did.

"Thank you!" Lizzie said, breaking the silence. "That was great."

After Drea led the boy out of the room, Carol said, "That's the one, right?"

"I don't know," Lizzie said, "wasn't he a little dark?"

"You mean ethnic?"

"No! I mean, like, brooding?"

Carol took out her phone and scrolled through some photos. "And what would you call this?" she asked, turning the phone to show us our Time Windows mock-up with the face I'd drawn. "The kid looks like a refugee," she said, "and if that's what you want, we aren't going to do much better than—Drea, what was that kid's name?"

"Josh Feld."

"Josh Feld. Problem is," Carol told us, "child actors tend to have a healthy glow, like tycoons."

"I liked Josh Feld," I said. "Should we call it a day?"

"What? No way," Lizzie said, and so we spent the rest of the morning watching Carol shoot photos of preening children until, at the subsequent lunch meeting, Mr. Courtney chose Josh Feld. Josh Feld wasn't perfect, we all agreed, but he was close enough to approximate our concept for the sake of the client. So we gathered around Demarcus's computer and watched him fiddle with our mock-up until my drawing had been replaced with a misty photo of Josh Feld looking sad-eyed and vulnerable, and by the end of the day we were back in Mr. Courtney's darkened office watching him look at the new version of the ad projected on his wall.

"Well done," Mr. Courtney said at length.

"Thank you," Lizzie said, and she elbowed me so I said thank you. Then Demarcus said thank you.

Mr. Courtney turned on the lights and said, "The client meeting is set for tomorrow at nine. Tell Martha to bring in pastries."

"For real?" Lizzie asked.

Mr. Courtney nodded. "I went ahead and booked it. I had a feeling."

Lizzie turned to me, bright eyed, and I mustered a smile.

After staying late to prep for the client meeting, the three of us decided to treat ourselves to a drink. We'd never done this before and weren't sure where to go, but after wandering around midtown, which was empty—it was seven o'clock, well after the office buildings unloaded their workers—we settled on the patio of a swanky bar that specialized in the sort of cocktails I associate with black-and-white movies but which other people seem to associate with admen.

Demarcus had never been in a client meeting, so Lizzie told some horror stories about clients fooling with their phones the whole time, ignoring us, or rejecting our ideas right away and acting annoyed when there wasn't a second idea or third or fourth to be scrolled through like profiles in a dating app.

"Dang," Demarcus said, swirling his manhattan with a thin red straw. The drink was stronger than he'd expected. For my own part, I was almost done with my ginger old fashioned so I tried to slow down. I told Demarcus that Lizzie was exaggerating, but my voice may have betrayed that I was as nervous as he was. I wondered if I would meet Dr. Nol, and, if so, what would I say? Normally I would have introduced myself and launched quickly into a prepared joke about midtown traffic or the pastries, but the man had suffered so much!

"So, Lizzie," I said casually, "any word yet on who'll be representing Time Windows?"

"If I knew I'd tell you. Seriously, Mike, this is like the fifth time you've asked."

"Just want to know who I'm dealing with."

"Cambodian time-travel scientists."

"Of course, but there's a difference between meeting with a renowned scientist like Nol Rithipol and, I don't know, some office guy whose job is to keep the business stuff off Nol's plate. With a man like Nol, I mean, where would you start? Do we know the proper honorifics?"

"Honorifics?"

"Cambodia has a very hierarchical society. Words are chosen depending on who you're speaking to."

"And you got this from…?"

"The internet." I hadn't wanted to reveal just how much time I'd spent researching Cambodia and the Khmer language, but it was too late. "For instance, *Lok* is the term of address for an older male you respect, as in *Lok Nol*. But *Ayah-Dom* is used for a person of very high social status—"

I was interrupted by a buzz in my pocket. I took out my phone and saw that my mother was calling, which was unlike her. I let the call go to voicemail, meaning to get back to my disquisition on Cambodian honorifics, but I couldn't concentrate. What if she was calling to tell me my father had another stroke? Had to be committed? Was *dead?*

I excused myself and listened to her voicemail in the bathroom: "You'll never guess what Dad and I just saw. There were bulldozers and an honest-to-God wrecking ball. That big brick wall where the theater was went down like a chunk of cheese. I'll send photos." By the time I was in the bathroom she'd already sent the photos. Most showed clouds of dust but one, a close-up of the ground, showed bricks and hunks of concrete mixed together in little hills that reminded me of burial mounds. It was impossible not to imagine Tim in there, but I tried to put the idea out of my head. So my elementary school had been razed, what was the big deal? Better razed than turned into a torture prison. Tuol Sleng had been a girls high school before the Khmer Rouge barred the windows and surrounded the campus with electrified barbed wire. Brick partitions had been built inside the classrooms so they could accommodate more prisoners in solitary confinement. The prisoners had been awakened at four-thirty every morning and told to strip so the guards could check them for hidden objects they could use to commit suicide.

I ordered another round of drinks and carried them to the patio, where Lizzie was sitting alone.

"Demarcus wasn't feeling well," Lizzie said. "I think he's nervous."

I nodded and set down the drinks, wishing I hadn't bought them. Though she was too polite to say anything, Lizzie probably wanted to go home to what I imagined was a cozy, tastefully decorated apartment. I pictured her curled up in bed watching a favorite show or reading a stimulating magazine. Then I thought of my own home, tyrannized by the exercise bike.

"I shouldn't have bought these," I said.

"We're celebrating," Lizzie said.

As we sipped our second cocktails, Lizzie was unusually quiet, and I made a point not to fill the silence with empty chatter. Eventually she said, "Are you nervous?"

"I guess I am, yeah." I wondered if I should tell her about Dr. Nol, or about the connection between the child in the mock-up and a child from my past, a lost friend.

"Me too," Lizzie said. "I guess I worry the whole thing is a sham, you know?"

"You mean Time Windows?"

Lizzie frowned. "Let's not get into that again, okay?"

"But I thought—"

"I mean *us*."

I was confused. "You think we're a sham?"

Lizzie nodded, looking down at her drink.

"Courtney Associates might not be the most prestigious firm," I said, "but in the transportation sector—"

"I mean *you and me*, Mike. Tom put us on this because he doesn't care about the job. He loved what Dietrich did, and the fact that it didn't work, well, that tells him *nothing* will work. So he brings in the B-team and cashes one more check from Time Windows before they fire us."

"We're not the B-team," I said. "Sure, Dietrich and them made a splashy ad, but it didn't get results. Mr. Courtney said so himself. Now we're giving the client something different."

"It's different, alright."

"What's that supposed to mean?"

"No offense, Mike. The art is great. You know I think you're a real artist."

I didn't know that, and I composed a sober expression to disguise the fluttery feeling I got from hearing it.

"But the kid," she said, "it's like he's floating in outer space. He looks so sad!"

I nodded.

"It's not what I expect from you," she said. "Usually you're so level-headed. *We have to give people something they can trust*," she said, affecting my blustery voice. "Fat lawyers on desks, you know?"

"J.J. Deckle is one of our best clients. And he isn't that fat."

"He wears a girdle."

"Really?"

Lizzie told me Carol Chen had felt something hard and smooth while positioning Deckle on the aforementioned desk. "Carol thought he had, like, a prosthetic torso," Lizzie said, laughing, "and he noticed when she touched it. He winked at her!"

While I sympathized with J.J. Deckle, who was a vain but decent man, it made me happy to hear Lizzie laugh like that. It made me think that no matter what happened with Time Windows, or any other account, Lizzie and I would be okay.

While we split the watery manhattan I'd bought for Demarcus, Lizzie asked if I had given any more thought to what I would say to my child self. I told her I hadn't, which seemed to disappoint her.

"How about you?" I asked. "Do you know what you'd say?"

She nodded. "There was this guy."

"Hmm."

"In college," she said, "and I don't know, I think that maybe we should have stayed together. He was applying to law schools senior year and made it clear he expected me to move wherever he got in, and I was like fuck that, you know? But I only felt that way on principle. I could have moved to any major city and ended up doing what I do now, and who knows? Maybe I would have done something cooler."

I nodded, but Lizzie's story had made me think about Ellen Kearney and my increasing conviction that we, too, should have stayed together, maybe even gotten married. Ellen had been a year behind me in school. After I graduated and moved to Georgia we kept dating, but I would meet all these other girls when I was out drinking with the team, and I didn't want to cheat on Ellen so I broke up with her. I told her she had her whole life ahead of her and shouldn't spend it with an oaf like me. But I hadn't actually thought of myself as an oaf at that time, so now I felt as though I'd made a prophecy and fulfilled it.

"I didn't mean to imply that what we do isn't cool," Lizzie said.

"Pardon?" I said, still thinking about Ellen Kearney.

"When I said I could have done something cooler. I know how much you love our work."

I laughed. "I wouldn't say I *love* it. I guess I just feel lucky, professionally. I might not have had as much going for me as you did, growing up."

"What was it like where you grew up?"

The question took me aback. Lizzie's cautious tone made me think she suspected I'd grown up in a difficult environment, but I hadn't. My hometown was glum and seedy, but it wasn't in a warzone. None of my family was killed or tortured. I wracked my brain for something concrete I could share, but what popped into my head was a night some friends and I were cruising around and saw a black man getting beaten up outside the only bar in town. The parking lot was well lit and full of pickup trucks. One of the attackers, a white man, was swinging a plank of wood, and I remembered the ragged look of the thing, as though he'd ripped it from a nearby structure. The black man had been hugging himself and had his head down, to protect his face and the soft middle of his body. My friend hadn't stopped the car, I remembered, and I wondered if any of us had called the police, but that was before people like us owned cellphones. Surely *someone* had called the police, right? I almost asked Lizzie, but that would have required describing the whole scene, which wasn't appropriate—we were having a pleasant evening—so instead I told her about a drainage ravine where Tim and I rode our BMX bikes up and down a concrete embankment.

"I bet you were a funny little kid," Lizzie said, and I nodded. Then I listened to her describe camping trips and science projects and other escapades with her sister and father, who was the original goofball, she said, and still a practicing bankruptcy lawyer even though he was seventy and everybody told him to take it easy already.

I tried not to think about the black man or Tim Benahan or any of the rest of it. I tried to focus on Lizzie's words, and on the lovely features of her face, animated by memory. I hoped to lose myself for a little while.

8.

The Time Windows people were already forty minutes late by the time they called Lizzie to say they wouldn't be able to make it. Some kind of lab emergency, Lizzie told us, but they would call in a few minutes for a video conference. Demarcus started setting up the monitor. I considered clearing the carafe of coffee and plate of pastries off the table, since the clients wouldn't be able to smell the buttery croissants or reach out from the screen to grab a danish, but I had my eye on an oatmeal and currant scone. I was exhausted. I hadn't slept well the night before; I'd been so anxious about meeting Dr. Nol.

To pump myself up I imagined Dr. Nol's giant wizened face staring at me from the monitor and saying, "What you propose sounds risky," then pausing provocatively before adding, "so risky it just might work!" Or: "Your idea is so simple, so elegant, I can't believe it didn't occur to me myself. I must have been lulled into a stupor by the previous team and that conniving flatterer, what's-his-name, Dieter? Dirk?" Or: "I can tell by your appearance you're a man of seriousness. Your team respects you, as mine does me. I'm a little embarrassed to admit this so early in our relationship, but I can imagine, in a different life, having become great friends with you."

I started eating the oatmeal and currant scone.

By the time the video monitor chimed, I'd finished that scone and started another. A greasy napkin lay in front of me with crumbs all over it. I quickly balled up the napkin and started swatting at a fat fly that was buzzing around the table, not wanting Dr. Nol to see such a wretched scene. But the man who materialized on screen wasn't Dr. Nol; he had a bald head, bushy eyebrows, and a drooping, frog-like mouth. He said something in an Asian language (Khmer?) and someone off screen said, "Greetings. Thank you in advance for your time."

I wiped the crumbs from my mouth with the back of my hand. "It's our pleasure," I said, and introduced myself.

The man said something and the translator said, "I know who you are." Then the man explained, via translator, that Mr. Courtney had shown him my work before assigning me to the project. "Very tasteful," the translator said.

I could tell this man was all business so I dove right in. "Sir," I said, since he hadn't offered his name, "we have enormous respect for the service your company provides. It's life-changing, maybe even world-changing."

He said something and the translator said, "How do you know?"

"I guess I don't," I said, unnerved, "firsthand, I mean. But the opportunity to talk to yourself as a child, well, the power of that almost speaks for itself."

"Almost?"

"Yes. The power has to be made clear through presentation. That's where *we* come in."

I turned to Demarcus, who cued up the photo of Josh Feld's face shuouded in mist with "Time Windows" written below in an elegant sans-serif. Then Lizzie started in on our pitch, which was basically an expanded version of Mr. Courtney's idea about the closeness of the child self and the possibly reassuring feelings which that closeness might conjure. There was some new jibberjabber about "seeing the world like a child again," but I stopped listening. I fought the urge to ask where Dr. Nol was.

The bald man, for his part, watched Lizzie impassively. Sometimes he nodded. Sometimes a younger man (the translator?) leaned in and whispered in his ear. It was hard to tell if he understood Lizzie or if he needed the translator but didn't want to interrupt until Lizzie was through, out of politeness, but Lizzie kept going. I guess she was waiting for some kind of sign from him. She started riffing off-script about her childhood in Roswell.

I was about to butt in and ask the bald man what he thought, but then he stood up and left. Lizzie turned to me with an embarrassed wince on her face that broke my heart. She didn't deserve to feel embarrassed. She'd done a good job! I wanted to say something reassuring but we were still on speaker so I couldn't.

Demarcus said, "Where'd he go?"

The younger man poked his head sideways into the frame and said, "Dr. Chern begs your pardon." This was the translator, judging by his voice. "He needed a break."

I said, "Should we sit tight?"

The young translator squinted, confused. "Please stand if you like."

"I mean wait."

"Oh, yes, I'll wait." He sat down, looking antsy. He had a long face and wavy black hair. I was fairly certain he was Dr. Nol's son, having determined from my research that Time Windows was basically a family affair involving Dr. Nol, his adult children, his second wife, and an unnamed business partner who may have been this Dr. Chern character.

The young man said something in his native language to someone off-screen, gesticulating apologetically.

I cleared my throat to get his attention. "I mean should *we* wait?"

"Of course, yes. Thank you." He stood up and left.

We waited.

Fifteen minutes later Demarcus went to get Mr. Courtney, who turned out to be standing on the other side of the conference room door, listening. He spoke to us from outside the room, as though he were afraid to be seen by the clients. "Hang up," he whispered, "and if they call back say our video is on the fritz. That way it's our fault."

We hung up.

They didn't call back.

After a quick *post mortem* with Demarcus and Lizzie, I went to my desk and looked up Dr. Chern. For a fee I could be given the address and phone number of a Sirhik Chern in Monroe, Georgia, but instead I used a translation site to convert his name into Khmer script, and searching for *that* led me to several batches of text. Then *reverse* translating the shortest of the texts gave me a string of near gibberish that seemed to be an article or encyclopedia entry about faith healing. Or at least the words *faith healer* and *faith healing* appeared four times, in such phrases as "*faith healer medicine closed was sitting controversial.*" Was Dr. Chern some kind of faith healer? And what about Dr. Nol? I was confused.

When Mr. Courtney called us into his office an hour later, Lizzie was still rattled by the meeting, which she likened to a painfully awkward date, but I knew better. Men like Dr. Chern were hard to read. Probably he didn't care about the ads and was only watching our presentation to indulge the younger people at his firm, whose opinions he trusted. Probably he went straight back to his office or lab and forgot all about us. That's what I told Lizzie, anyway, but Mr. Courtney had such a troubled look on his face that I suspected Time Windows had fired us. After the initial sting of the idea, I felt relieved. The account was upsetting my equilibrium.

"Dr. Chern sends his apologies," Mr. Courtney said.

"Fuck," Lizzie said.

"Apparently he became emotional."

"What?"

"He had to excuse himself."

"Wow. I mean, that's a good thing, right?"

"It's a *great* thing." Mr. Courtney smiled, as though his troubled demeanor had been a little show for our benefit. "He wants you at the compound as soon as possible."

Lizzie clapped and gave Demarcus an enthusiastic high five. She was about to give me one then noticed my face. "Come on, Mike, this is good news."

"I'm just surprised is all," I said.

Mr. Courtney looked at me. "Must you be so black-hearted? The man was moved."

"Sorry," I said, and we all exchanged high fives.

If my high fives were less than enthusiastic, it was because going to the compound meant using Time Windows. There was no way around it. It was like driving the luxury car you were doing a campaign for. You couldn't write about the purr of a BMW or even the tight steering of a Mazda without feeling it for yourself. The senses had to get involved: the smell of the leather, the feel of the bucket-seat, the slight rocking of the chassis around tight turns. I tried to reassure myself that the Time Windows experience would be interesting, if nothing else, but was I ready to meet Dr. Nol in the flesh?

Lizzie and Demarcus left to share the good news with our coworkers, but Mr. Courtney asked me to stay behind. He shut the door on the rest of the office, which was already abuzz, and when he turned to me he had the same troubled look as before.

"I'm sorry I left you hanging," he said.

"Sir?"

"In the meeting."

"Oh, no worries, Mr. Courtney. I completely understand your—"

"Will you please not call me *Mr. Courtney* right now? Don't you think I feel old enough right now?" He shut his eyes and pinched the bridge of his nose, like he was waiting for a sneeze to pass.

"I stayed out of the meeting because I didn't want to screw things up," Mr. Courtney said. "I was so gung ho last time about that mother-daughter monstrosity. Fucking Deitrich."

I was happy to hear Dietrich cursed aloud, of course, and even happier that Mr. Courtney was confiding in me. It felt like the beginning of the relationship I had always imagined us having, as the two senior people at the firm.

"Tom," I said, liking the sound of his first name in my mouth, "I don't mean to be crass, but we get paid either way."

"It isn't all about money," Mr. Courtney said.

"Of course it isn't. We're artists first and businessmen second, like you always say. Why, just the other day I heard you saying to Demarcus—'"

"We aren't artists. We make bus ads."

"Well, sir, the simplicity of—"

"Do you think this is the life I imagined for myself?"

I tried to come up with something to say, but all I could think about was my own life. What had I imagined for *my*self, besides playing football in college, which I didn't get to do, and being a basketball coach like John Wooden?

Mr. Courtney stood up and started pacing the office. "I'm not like you, Mike. I don't live and breathe this work. I don't spend my off-hours networking with trial lawyers." He was referring to the time I got a drink with J.J. Deckle. When I told Mr. Courtney about it he had gone around the office telling everybody I was a *closer*, whatever that meant.

"It was only one drink," I said weakly. I didn't add that I had agreed to the drink in the first place because I thought Deckle and I might become friends. "It's hard to balance work and personal life. If you're good at one you just kind of stick to it, I guess."

"I should have gone to the Olympics," Mr. Courtney was saying. "I was almost an alternate on the crew team in eighty-four, but all the eights had gone to Yale together. I wasn't part of their little club."

I tried to come up with something to say about how he got screwed and Yale sucks, but my heart wasn't in it. I wanted to tell Mr. Courtney he shouldn't whine about not making the Olympic rowing team because if he'd been born in Cambodia he might have been a child soldier with a Chinese-made machine gun slung over his shoulder, or a rusty hoe. Then again, if my father had been born in Cambodia he might have died any number of ways and never have conceived me, so who was I to wring my hands over Tim Benahan and Ellen Kearney and whether or not I was a big fat loser? However frivolous the causes, our anguish was genuine. We had to comfort each other. I wanted to tell Mr. Courtney I admired his work, I really did, and that even though he could be cold in manner, and prone to fits of petulant anger, everybody in the office thought he was a great designer and, more importantly, a decent person who treated people with respect. But that seemed like a corny thing to say so I didn't say it. Instead I sat there nodding while he ranted about how rowing in the Olympics would have made him a celebrity in certain circles and opened literally hundreds of career paths. When he finally calmed down, he leaned against his desk and sighed.

"Sorry, I didn't mean to go off like that," he said. "Money is money, like you said."

"And you're the one who assembled the team. You made this happen."

"I guess you're right. It's just—I don't know, Mike—sometimes I wish we were using our talents, paltry though they may be, to do some fucking good."

"We do good for our clients. And it's not like Time Windows is a payday loan place. The men behind Time Windows, well, they're kind of heroes in a way."

Mr. Courtney squinted at me. "Heroic scam artists?"

"Pardon me?"

"It's a scam. You know that, right?"

I said nothing. I'd used the word myself, only days before, but now I found it almost profane. Why would Dr. Nol, who'd seen so much, who'd *done* so much, dedicate the final years of his professional life to a time-rip scam?

"Come on, Mike, putting you in touch with your child self?"

"Maybe it doesn't do exactly what they say it does, but it does *something*, don't you think?"

"Fortunetellers do *something*."

"But these people are real scientists, and they're charging a lot of money, so if what they're doing is a con, then somebody would have sued them, right? Their clientele—wealthy people, *bored* people—are extremely litigious."

Mr. Courtney just shook his head. He started going through papers on his desk, so I stood up and gathered my things. When I got to the door, I fought the urge to take a parting shot, defending Dr. Nol, but I hadn't even *seen* Dr. Nol. For all I knew he was back in Cambodia getting checks in the mail from Time Windows. In the end I said nothing. Later, I couldn't decide what surprised me more: that Mr. Courtney was so convinced Time Windows was a scam, or that I was entertaining the possibility it *wasn't*.

9.

To prepare for our visit to the Time Windows compound, we were given questionnaires about our personal histories. The personal histories, the questionnaire explained, were to help the Time Windows scientists "track down" our child selves using the patented Time Windows algorithm. I was tempted to make up a fake history, to stump the scientists and thereby avoid the whole thing, but we were also required to give our social media info, so they could have flipped to the oldest of my Friend-ster photos and seen where I went to high school and college, and who my friends had been. Personally, I didn't care if they caught me lying and thought I was a liar, but I didn't want to make trouble for my team.

I had all weekend to fill out my questionnaire but I dragged my heels. Despite Mr. Courtney's strident disbelief, and my own suspicions, I found myself asking for the first time, seriously, what would I say to my child self *just in case* it was real? More specifically, how would I reassure my rude name-calling child self that I wasn't a big fat loser? I hadn't lost weight on my new exercise bike, and I hadn't struck up a romantic relationship with Amy or anybody else.

I continued to have trouble sleeping. I tried to watch TV shows I'd enjoyed in the past. I tried reading self-help books until I was tired. I ate bananas. I drank Sleepy Time tea. I pedaled to the point of exhaustion on my fancy stationary bicycle. In short, I did everything I had ever done to make myself fall asleep, but every time I closed my eyes I pictured the Time Windows ad, only instead of Josh Feld it was Tim's face shrouded in mist. Tim's face swirling dreamlike in Thulerat with Mrs. McCutcheon's dead wife and Wilfred Johnson. With No. 246 and her baby, who in my mind had become Dr. Nol's wife and child. Tim's face whispering urgently to me of his father, his grizzled sex-offender brother, and his hopes for the future such as passing the test to be a policeman.

When I got Dietrich's contact info from Martha, I told myself it was because we needed as much information about Time Windows as possible, even if it meant breaking Mr. Courtney's rule about starting fresh.

Dietrich's cell phone had been disconnected, so I was forced to call his emergency contact: his (ex?) boyfriend, a friendly struggling actor named Tyrus whom I used to chat with once a year at the holiday party. Tyrus told me Dietrich had moved to Los Angeles. He gave me Dietrich's new number but warned me Dietrich had changed.

"How do you mean?" I asked.

"Are you Christian?"

"Not really."

"He's like one of those Christians who seem just a little too happy."

I wasn't sure what to make of that, but I called Dietrich's new number and left a friendly voicemail. Dietrich didn't call back, so on Monday I had Demarcus call Dietrich pretending to be an accountant with new information on the percentage vestment of his 401k. Dietrich called back immediately, and Demarcus transferred the call to my desk.

"Dietrich, it's Mike," I said.

Dietrich sighed. "Greed will be my undoing. And the 401k vestment?"

"Same as ever. Can I have a minute?"

"The clock is ticking."

"We need help, and Mr. Courtney says you're the only one who really understood Time Windows."

"Sure he did."

"And the Time Windows people speak highly of your work."

"The Time Windows people don't speak at all, Mike. You've got a meeting coming up and you're scrambling. I can hear it in your voice."

"Alright, alright." I explained how Mr. Courtney was keeping us in the dark, to make sure our ideas were original, but, now that the rubber was hitting the road, we needed more information, plain and simple. "You tried it, right? What's it like?"

Dietrich didn't reply. It was unlike him—unlike any of us in the business, really—not to answer right away, with confidence. "Sorry," he said. "It's just, I don't often talk about it. It's quite personal, really."

"Was it—bad?"

"It was glorious."

"Like, the effect? It's convincing?"

"It isn't an effect, Mike. It's real. Time Windows is real."

Like one of those crazy Christians.

"I was in a small dark room," Dietrich continued, "sitting in front of a sort of picture frame. The small person who began to appear on the other side of the frame was indistinct at first, like a mirage."

"But you knew it was you?"

"Think about how often you look at yourself in the mirror, how well you know your own face. Sure, our noses get bigger, our eyebrows bushier, but there's more to the human face than that. There's an essence to it. You should know that better than anyone. You're an artist."

"Oh, I don't know about that."

"Save the false modestly." He sniffed. "I used to think your whole life was like some weird performance art—those pleated khakis? I mean, come on. You're like William Burroughs or something."

I had no idea who William Burroughs was, but later that night when I found out he was some kind of junkie who shot his wife, I wasn't flattered. I *was* flattered Dietrich thought of me as an artist, though.

"God this is going to sound corny," Dietrich was saying, "but what do I have to lose? Mike," he said, "seeing myself, speaking to myself like that, it made me reassess my life. That's why I quit."

"You quit?"

He laughed. "Of course I quit. Did Tom tell you I got poached?"

"I don't know who said what, but that's what people think."

"Oh well, it doesn't matter."

"What was it doing?"

"What was what doing?"

"You. Child you. Was it, like, digging in a sandbox?"

"You mean *he*? Let's dignify me with a gender. Young Deitrich was, well, it was hazy, like I said, but I guess he was sort of sitting. I remember my face. We were looking into each other's eyes."

"Did you talk?"

"Of course."

"What about?"

"I don't know. We just talked. He said some zany stuff, like kids do. Look, Mike, I don't know what to tell you about Time Windows except it's real and it changed my life."

"But how? How did it change your life?"

"I guess it reminded me that I was just a kid back then. Before that, when I looked back at childhood, when I thought about it, I always imagined myself as having an adult consciousness. I'd think of the times I got in trouble or did something embarrassing and think, *why the hell did I do that?* I was so hard on myself. We all are. I'd forget I was just a kid."

"Just to clarify: was it the reaching back in time part, like the novelty of the time-rip experience, or was it just seeing a child version of yourself? Did you give yourself a secret message? Did you—"

"Mike, are you okay?"

"Of course. I'm just stressed is all. This account—boy!"

We hung up soon thereafter, and I came away from the conversation thinking Dietrich was a lot nicer than I remembered. Whether or not what he experienced at Time Windows was real, he believed it, and it changed his life. I had to prepare myself. I had to think of something to say.

Pay attention in school, big fella. You can be anything you want to be! But I *was* what I wanted to be, wasn't I? In terms of practical advice, I could tell him to quit football before senior year so he wouldn't get his bell rung too many times, but I knew he wouldn't do that, not after tasting glory his first three years. And anyway, without the football scholarship, he wouldn't end up in Georgia or at Courtney Associates. He might not even try his hand at design, and what then? The brake box factory? No, I decided, I should focus on personal advice. *Talk to girls,* I could say, *they're afraid of you too!* But I *did* talk to girls, or at least I talked to Ellen Kearney, and she was the best girlfriend I ever had. *Don't break up with Ellen Kearney.* Or maybe I shouldn't mention Ellen by name? I didn't want kid me to seek her out too young, when I wasn't ready, or, worse, start teasing her. I'd have to keep it vague. *At the end of high school you'll be dating a woman.* Scratch that. *At the end of high school you* may *be dating a woman, and you may have to date long-distance for a while. But even though it's hard, and even though people may tell you you're too young and have your whole life ahead of you, and even though"*—this was the hard part—*"you may lust after other women..."* But how would kid me react to the word *lust?* Had I experienced lust at that age? I remembered my dad catching me rubbing myself over-the-pants-style against the edge of a table one time and saying "Stop that!" But I hadn't even known what I was doing. I'd been watching a cartoon on TV. Something with a dressed-up dog.

Alternatively, I could focus on other people. The Tim thing was tricky, but what about Mr. Bruccoli, the music teacher who wrapped his Camaro around a light-pole? *Tell Mr. Bruccoli not to drink and drive,* I could say. *I'm serious now. Go to the music room and tell him you had a dream that he died in a drunk driving accident. He'll tell you you're a goddamned little weirdo but it'll do the trick.* But where would I go from there?

Tell Wilfred Johnson to be careful.

Tell Chappy Mendoza to apply his husbandry talent to non-fur animals.

Tell Tim—what?

I had no idea.

The night before we were scheduled to go to Monroe and try Time Windows, I was packing my bag for the overnight trip when I got an e-mail from Double A Detection: *"Dear MICHAEL MUHLER, We are sorry to inform you that the party you wish to locate TIM BENAHAN is deceased. Click here for more information."*

I clicked the link, my hands shaking, only to learn that getting details about Tim's death would cost extra. Disgusted, I shut my laptop. I paced the condo. I called my mother, but we hadn't talked since the elementary school got razed and that was all she wanted to talk about. She said she and Dad drove out to see the demolition, and that Dad had let slip a few silent tears about the whole thing.

"But I don't know," she said, sounding a little tipsy, "I think I may join that LA Fitness. They got those bike spinning classes I hear so much about." She paused. "Mike?"

"Yes?"

"Is that why you called? About the school?" There was something sad in her voice. Years ago, we had spoken almost every day.

"No," I said, feeling the name *Tim* bubbling in my throat but unable to produce it, for fear of crying. Curiously, what I saw in my mind wasn't my own face crying but my mother's, red and wrinkled, tearlessly weeping as she had when her own mother died. Her mother, my grandmother, had given birth to her as a teenager. The two were often mistaken for sisters.

"Just calling to check up," I said, "and also to let you know I'm going on a business trip."

"Ooh, where to?"

I tried to explain the nature of the trip.

"My goodness!" She shared the news with my father, who made no comment.

I went on to tell her about Time Windows, about the client meeting, and even about Dr. Nol and how I'd begun to admire him. It felt good to talk about my work with her. I told myself to do it more often.

"I don't get it," my mother said, "are the scientists in Georgia or Cambodia?"

"Georgia. They're *from* Cambodia."

At this point my father demanded to be put on the phone. He told me in a cracked voice that he had spent some memorably unpleasant months in Cambodia during the war, by which he meant the Vietnam War. "Be careful," he said. "Those Cambodians would have sold their mothers for a hot lunch."

I laughed uncomfortably. "That was a long time ago, Dad."

"It didn't surprise me what happened to them."

"Geez, Dad—"

"Listen to me. I want you to be careful over there."

"At Time Windows?"

"Cambodia. We were just talking about Cambodia. Don't tell me we weren't!" He put my mother back on the phone, grumbling. She apologized on his behalf.

"He's been very reflective lately," she said.

The conversation did nothing to put me at ease. I spent the night imagining different ways Tim could have died, and wondering if he died knowing he was loved, but *was* he loved? Did it count that I had loved him thirty years ago?

I opened the e-mail and let the cursor hover over the "*here*" in "*Click here for more information*" until I felt my gumption fading and made a frantic click. The screen changed, and I struggled to look at it.

According to Double A Detection, Tim died at thirty-six of an overdose. His body was found in an abandoned building in Indianapolis. He had a long arrest record, a mixture of vagrancy and possession and possession-with-intent-to-distribute. His first arrest had been at age twenty in Morgan County, where we grew up.

Tim's blood had contained heroin and fentanyl, the dangerously potent synthetic opioid. According to the death certificate, which I could view for an additional fee, wounds on Tim's arms indicated frequent, possibly habitual, intravenous drug use.

I told myself I shouldn't be so surprised. Overdose death was rampant where we grew up. But the thought of Tim among the grubby addicts I saw slouching around downtown whenever I visited, darting in and out of abandoned buildings, sleeping under the shelter of empty storefronts, was almost too much to bear.

At the bottom of the screen was a note that Double A Detection could contact Tim's next of kin, also for an additional fee.

10.

Monroe was only an hour away, but a car was sent to the office to drive us to the Time Windows facility. It was part of a new VIP package that the Time Windows people were hoping would lure customers from markets outside of Atlanta. In addition to the car, the package included a night of "luxurious on-site accommodation." The pickup was scheduled for five o'clock, so Lizzie and Demarcus spent the day chatting nervously about what to expect, and I spent the day avoiding Lizzie and Demarcus. I wasn't in the mood to chat, in the wake of the news about Tim, and I hadn't finished my questionnaire until the wee hours of the morning. By that time my answers had changed so much that I felt compelled to call someone at Time Windows to make sure what I wanted could be done. A woman there assured me it could.

An elderly Asian man buzzed the door at Courtney Associates. He was wearing a shiny dark suit and a sort of chauffeur's cap, and when he took off the cap to greet us I recognized Dr. Chern, the bald scientist from our meeting. He bowed and shook our hands, and we followed him to a Lincoln Continental with a younger Asian man behind the wheel. Dr. Chern opened the curbside door for us and we piled in the back.

The cushy back seat was pristine, but I caught an unmistakable whiff of old cigarettes, which got my mouth watering. I hadn't stopped wanting a cigarette since the night with Amy. While the driver delivered a spiel to greet us, Dr. Chern could be heard struggling to heft our bags into the trunk, and I fought the urge to go outside and help him.

"Welcome to Atlanta," the young man was saying, and I recognized the voice of the translator from our meeting. "In a moment I shall drive you to the facility in Monroe, a lovely city in its own right, with many gardens and paved walkways."

"Sounds great!" Lizzie said, playing along.

We sat in silence until Dr. Chern climbed into the passenger seat, huffing and puffing, and they spoke what I recognized by now to be Khmer. Then the translator said in English, "Dr. Chern asks me to tell you that he and Dr. Nol are honored to host you."

"The honor is ours," Lizzie said, turning to me. "Isn't that right, Mike?"

"Can't wait," I said. The mention of Dr. Nol made real the fact that I would be meeting the man, and I wanted to muster some excitement, some thankfulness—I'd rehearsed what to say to him!—but I was too nervous.

Throughout the monotonous drive out of town on I-20, the driver pointed out seemingly random landmarks like mega-churches and shopping plazas and a barely noticeable trickle called Shoal Creek.

I nodded and said things like "Ah yes, very interesting," to encourage him, but it was almost impossible to see the landmarks over the high acoustic walls of the expressway. Sometimes Dr. Chern got in on the act. He would say something in Khmer and the driver would say, for example, "Dr. Chern asks me to point out Stone Mountain of Confederate monument fame," then gesture vaguely at the window while the three of us nodded in back.

We got off I-20 in Conyers and entered an area of oversized strip-malls with vast parking lots that glittered in the sun. We followed a four-lane highway past business parks with angular glass office buildings, subdivisions full of pink brick houses, and finally, when the highway narrowed to two lanes, forests and fields. Dilapidated farmhouses stood in the distance. Horses roamed swishing their tails. Soon we turned onto a country road and sometime later were met by an iron gate. The driver lowered his window and lay his hand on a high-tech keypad. The gate slid open and we proceeded onto a long asphalt driveway. Live Oaks had been planted on either side of the road, and even though the trees were spindly and shaggy with random growth, there was something reassuring about them, as though the Time Windows people imagined their business would be standing here two hundred years from now, by which time the trees would have grown into the kind of massive, thick-limbed sentries made famous by plantation homes all over the South.

At the end of the driveway, atop a barely discernible hill, stood a low, flat-roofed building with large tinted windows and a wide front door made of expensive looking wood. Potted bushes stood here and there, and Japanese maples. The whole thing would have looked more like a ranch-style house than a place of business if it weren't for the parking lot, where there was a second black Lincoln, identical to ours, and a burgundy Buick.

After we parked, the translator took our bags out of the trunk and led us to the front door. I smelled cigarette smoke and wondered if Dr. Chern, who'd disappeared, was smoking somewhere out of sight. I glanced around at the campus. In the distance stood a few long, low-slung buildings that looked like chicken houses.

Inside, we were greeted by two Asian women, one young and another who looked about my age but might have been much older. I suspected they were Dr. Nol's daughter and wife. He'd met his second wife in France, years after losing the first.

The women bowed before gesturing for us to follow them into a sitting room, which was well appointed but vaguely institutional, like the waiting room of a doctor's office. Chinese-style ink drawings hung on the walls, between bookshelves full of leather-bound books and decorative items like gilded plates.

The driver offered us refreshments ("A cocktail, perhaps?"). I demurred, but Lizzie asked for a gin and tonic, which the driver mixed at a rolling cart. After he served her he said, "Doctor Chern apologizes to have left without saying goodbye, but he was needed by Doctor Nol.

Will you wait a moment?"

"No problem," I said, thinking *Dr. Nol is in the building*.

"If you need anything, please ring this bell." He indicated, on the small table between Demarcus and Lizzie, a counter bell of the type that might be found in a pharmacy.

After the young man left, Lizzie turned to me and said, "This place is so *nice*. It's like one of those salons where they serve you champagne. We're lucky. Everybody talks about this place but so few get to do it."

"Somebody does," I said, "or they wouldn't be in business."

"I don't know," Demarcus said. He'd picked up a *Golf Digest*. "This magazine is from two years ago."

"I bet the young ones are the kids," Lizzie was saying, "and the older lady is probably married to one of the doctors. It's quaint. Don't you think it's quaint, Mike?"

"For sure," I said absently, going through the magazines. All of them were out of date. The Time Windows people couldn't renew their subscriptions? And they couldn't afford actual drivers? Either money was tight or the business was so secret that no one but family could be trusted.

"The family angle might demystify the whole thing," Lizzie was saying, "make it more inviting. Demarcus, are you writing this down?"

Demarcus opened his laptop.

Lizzie kept brainstorming while Demarcus typed and I stewed in silence about what was coming. I thought of Dietrich sitting where I was sitting, not yet knowing that his life was about to change. I thought of the word *time-rip* and pictured it as a sort of fissure in the air. A fissure from which both past and future rose like clouds, with children's faces floating here and there inside them, peering at us, waiting.

When the translator reemerged, he took us to our bedrooms, which were spare but clean and had en-suite bathrooms.

The translator, whose name was Prang, told us dinner would be served at seven and we were welcome to join him and the doctors if it pleased us. He said he could also serve us alone in the dining room if we preferred our own company. "You've had a long day," he added, to give us an excuse to eat alone. The third option, he said, was for him to drive us "to an eatery of your choice such as Chick Fil-A."

"Ugh, no!" Lizzie said. "We'd love to join you and your family."

"Very well, I will bring a menu."

"No, please, we'll have what you're having."

Prang hesitated before smiling and telling us we were welcome anywhere in the building and that he would find us at seven.

I didn't bother unpacking. My bedroom had a sliding glass door that faced the back yard, and on impulse I opened it and walked outside.

The yard was full of azalea and rhododendron bushes. A trail of granite paving stones led to a bench under a tree. Near the bench was a big copper birdbath turning green. Some crows were splashing around in it, cleaning themselves or looking for the larvae of water insects, but when they saw me they stopped. They watched me wander the yard until I found a hole in the tall wooden fence. Through the hole I could see the long buildings I'd thought looked like chicken houses, but now I could make out small windows. They looked more like barracks.

I heard the flick of a lighter and moments later smelled a burning cigarette. I turned, expecting to see Dr. Chern, but the person I saw, on the opposite side of the courtyard, was a black man in coveralls. For a moment I thought it was Demarcus—they had similar faces—but the man was much shorter than Demarcus. He might have been a kid, but what was a kid doing outside the Time Windows compound smoking a cigarette?

When he noticed me he turned around, as though searching for an exit, but I strode toward him.

"Wait," I said, crossing the courtyard.

He turned to face me, and I was relieved to see he looked older up close than he did from a distance. Old enough to smoke, anyway, and be working here as a technician or groundskeeper or whatever it was he did.

"Can I get one of those?" I asked.

"Sure," he said, and he pulled out a cigarette for me.

I took the cigarette, he lit it, and we smoked for a while in silence.

I felt so lightheaded that I considered putting out the cigarette, but I told myself, as I had on the night with Amy, that I wouldn't smoke again for years and might as well make the most of this one.

"So," I said, "you work here?"

"Yeah," he said.

"Do you like it?"

He shrugged. "It's a gig. Wait—you're not a client, are you?"

"Why, you aren't supposed to talk to clients?"

He said nothing.

"Relax," I said. "I'm in advertising. We do ads for you guys."

"Cool," he said.

"Have you ever tried it?"

He shook his head. "I think it's more for older people."

"I suppose that's true. But tell me, how would you feel if an older version of you came back from the future to talk to you?"

"I guess it would freak me out."

"Would you run?"

"I guess not. I guess I'd be startled at first but kind of curious, once I got to thinking about it. I'd wanna see what I look like in the future."

"What if you were fat?"

The kid eyed me, perhaps sensing the nature of this question. "Better than bald," he said judiciously. "Seriously, though? I'd just wanna be happy. I guess I'd just hope I'm married or whatever, and that I have a job I don't hate."

One for two, I thought. "Would you listen to him? You know, would you take his advice?"

"I guess that would depend."

"On what?"

"If he seemed credible. I mean, if he was some kinda hobo without a tooth in his head would I listen to him? Probably not."

That made sense, and I at least *seemed* like a credible person, I assured myself. I was considering other questions to ask the young man, when Prang came through a set of sliding doors and told me it was time for dinner. I turned to my companion, to thank him for the cigarette, but he was gone.

The food was warm and spicy and buttery, the kind of food that makes you feel cozy at night while it sloshes in your stomach. It made me wonder if Cambodia was the Memphis of Asia. The whole experience, from the food to the stilted but friendly conversation, made me like the family even more, though I hadn't yet met its patriarch. The doctors were in the laboratory, according to Prang, preparing for our session the next day.

The younger woman had begun clearing our plates when Dr. Chern came trudging through the doorway, followed by a smaller man who touched the woman's arm as she passed him on her way to the kitchen.

Dr. Nol.

While Dr. Chern sat down and began serving himself lumps of food, Dr. Nol remained by the door, and smiled at those of us who'd noticed him. He looked older than I expected. He had to be at least seventy to have been in graduate school in France by the time the Khmer Rouge took Phnom Penh, but in my mind I hadn't disentangled the young scientist and renowned speaker from the old man living in Monroe, Georgia, running Time Windows. Even so, his gray hair remained thick and wavy, and there was something almost rakish about his clothes and manner: the tin necktie neatly tucked beneath his cardigan sweater, the way he bowed slightly upon making eye-contact, first with Lizzie, then with Demarcus, and then, finally, with me.

I rose abruptly, and the chair made a loud scuttling sound against the wooden floor as my big legs pushed it backward. I fought the urge to throw my hand across the table for a corny handshake. Instead I placed my palms together, raised the tips of my fingers to my eyebrows, and bowed my head.

"*Chom reap sour,*" I said. "*Susadei?*"

"*Susadei,*" Dr. Nol said, as though correcting me.

Confused, I tried to imitate Dr. Nol: "*Susadei.*"

Dr. Nol smiled. "*Susadei.*"

"*Soos-ah-day,*" I repeated, flustered.

Dr. Nol said something to Prang, who chuckled.

"My father wishes to tell you your pronunciation is excellent," Prang said, "but the proper response to *susadei,* as in 'how are you?,' is also *susadei:* 'I'm well.'"

Dr. Nol said something else.

"My father is flattered to be greeted as an elder," Prang said, "but you raised your hands to your eyebrows. That is a *sampeah* reserved for kings and monks!"

Prang laughed, so I did too. I didn't tell him I'd chosen the so-called "fourth *sampeah*" on purpose, after deciding that the third, for parents and teachers, didn't adequately capture my feelings about his father.

After we sat down, Lizzie gave me a discreet thumbs-up beneath the table, and the meal resumed.

Conversation was somewhat awkward because Prang had to translate almost all of what we said, though Prang's sister, whose name was Channary, sometimes spoke for herself or translated for the older woman, who was their mother and Dr. Nol's wife. Dr. Chern was the only person unrelated to the others, though he acted like a crotchety uncle.

Despite his need to be translated, Dr. Nol was the center of conversation. He asked lots of questions. Some were unexpected, and disconcerting in their directness. When Prang translated the question, "Have you ever suffered a trauma?" Lizzie laughed with embarrassment. Demarcus looked down at his food. For an instant I considered blurting that Tim was dead, but instead I mentioned that my elementary school had just been razed.

"I guess it's no big deal," I said, surprised to hear myself talking about it. I told them about the time-capsule and how my teacher had reached out to me, which brought me very close to the subject of Tim and the news of his death, but I backed away. "The place was closed years ago, but I don't know. It had a strong effect on me."

"The places of childhood are close to our hearts," Dr. Nol said through Prang, "and the time-capsule, what a delightful idea. Perhaps one day such capsules will not have to be buried but can be presented directly by the child to his future self." Dr. Nol was smiling as Prang said this to us.

"Years ago I met an old man," Dr. Nol continued through Prang, "an antiques dealer who was born in Poland and had lived for a time in Israel. The man scoured Europe for antiques that were pilfered from the Jews sent to ghettos and camps. He worked on behalf of their descendants, who believed, he said, that if items were restored to their proper places the years would be erased. When I asked what happened when he wasn't able to secure this or that cherished item, he gave a sly wink. He always found a way, he said." Dr. Nol laughed. "He asked if we might collaborate to perform a similar service for my people, and though I agreed in principle with his ideas about loss and the passage of time, I explained to him that in my country it was not possible."

"Why's that?" Lizzie asked.

I looked down at my empty plate as Prang explained without being prompted by his father that the cities in their homeland had been emptied of people, their contents burned.

Silence settled over the table. Then Dr. Chern made what I could tell, despite the language barrier, was a sarcastic joke, and the others laughed.

Dr. Nol smiled self-consciously and said something in Khmer, and Prang said, "My father asks you to pardon his gloomy anecdotes. He asks if you have any questions for us. Any anxieties, perhaps?"

All three of us had anxieties, I'm sure, but no one spoke so I said, "Yes, if you don't mind my asking, what led you from your initial time-travel research, with Mr. Vinegar and all that, to a commercial time-rip venture?"

Dr. Nol began speaking without waiting for the question to be translated, and Dr. Chern spoke as well. The two seemed to be discussing the answer to my question, which I had posed innocuously but was wrapped up in my mind with the fact that the Mr. Vinegar experiments were now, years later, shrouded in scandal.

Finally, Prang said, "My father is deeply regretful over having misrepresented the methods of the fruit fly experiments, but not the result. There *were* two fruit flies, but only because of a convenient time rip. Speaking now for myself, I must say I believe my father. I believe he was so thankful for his position at the Chinese university, after everything that happened, that he felt compelled to do whatever his superiors asked of him. But to answer your question, he was already researching time rips by the time of the Mr. Vinegar experiments, so Time Windows is simply an extension of that research."

I nodded, but the answer didn't quite make sense. Dr. Nol had left China on the heels of the minor celebrity brought about by Mr. Vinegar, and his speaking engagements on that subject had transitioned almost seamlessly to the subject of what happened to him and his people under the Khmer Rouge. So what had caused him to *return* to science, and in America of all places? And how did Dr. Chern, the sometime faith healer, get involved? But before I could formulate a tactful way to ask these follow-up questions, Lizzie said, "What happens if what you say changes the present? Do you ever worry about, you know, the butterfly effect?"

My ears perked up. I'd been asking myself the same question, naturally. It was a major concern in time-rip science, but the consensus seemed to be that we mostly *perceived* the past, and didn't interact with it in any significant way.

Dr. Nol nodded as though he understood Lizzie's question.

Prang smiled. "An important concern but perhaps overrated. I feel comfortable speaking for my father because I've heard his response, which is as follows: if the so-called butterfly effect took place, we wouldn't know it."

"How do you mean?" Lizzie asked.

"Everything would be changed," Prang said, "including our memories of the world." He waved his hand to indicate the room, the food, his own body. "Some of us might even cease to exist. Naturally, many of our clients want to reach back in time and tell themselves, for example, not to break up with a girlfriend or boyfriend, or to cherish their final moments with a beloved parent, or even the score of a sports game, for gambling purposes." He smiled. "Unfortunately, children don't seem to be very responsive to the experience. We aren't sure how well they can hear us." He shrugged. "And children do what children do."

Children do what children do.

I thought of the drainage ravine, the sloping concrete embankment where Tim and I did dangerous stunts on our bikes. One time I tumbled over my handlebars and sprained my wrist, which caused me to miss the basketball season in eighth grade. If I could catch myself the moment before I tried the dangerous stunt, I wondered, could I prevent it from happening? Would I play basketball that season? Would basketball become my best sport, not football, sparing me the concussions? Would I get good enough to walk on someplace small like IU Kokomo? Would I become a coach's favorite for my grit and hustle and then, upon graduation, start my coaching career as an assistant on his staff? Would I inspire generations of young people who'd gather to thank me at a tearful retirement ceremony, or, better yet, would I have a massive heart attack on the court and die doing what I loved?

But it was too late for such questions.

Dr. Nol and Dr. Chern excused themselves to prepare for tomorrow, and when they were out of earshot Prang said softly, "At the risk of bragging, I should say that my father is considered the grandfather of Cambodian time-travel science."

Lizzie laughed. "Does that make you its father?"

Prang appeared confused, but his sister, Channary, smiled.

"More like a bachelor uncle," she said.

After dinner, and after saying goodnight to Lizzie and Demarcus, I went out the courtyard again. I hoped to find my young friend and bum another cigarette, but he wasn't there. The crows were gone, too. I crossed the courtyard to the fence and looked through the peephole at the long low building. A few lights still burned, and the damp night air made the windows flicker like stars.

The next morning, Lizzie asked to go first. She wanted to get it over with, she said, and Demarcus and I made no objection. We were sitting with Prang in the waiting room, drinking coffee. The curtains were drawn and the lights were unlit, so the coffee didn't do much to make me feel awake. After Prang went to notify Dr. Nol and Dr. Chern, Lizzie reached over and squeezed my hand but didn't look at me. She seemed lost in thought. When Prang came back, she went with him down a hallway into the room where it would happen.

I tried to make chitchat with Demarcus, but he was listening to something on his hearing-aid headphones. I almost told him to lose the fucking headphones already, this was a big deal, but for that same reason—this *was* a big deal—I didn't bother him. Instead, I thought about what I would say. Then I tried *not* to think about what I would say. And then, finally, I decided I would say nothing. I would stare at him, trying to burn every detail of his face into my memory, and if he decided I was a creepy old loser and left, so what?

Five minutes later, Lizzie came back into the room wearing the dazed but happy expression of someone who had just gotten a deep-tissue massage.

"Mike, you were so right," she said dreamily, as though she were still seeing whatever she had just seen. As though she would be seeing it again and again for the rest of her life. "It was glorious. Just take it in!"

"I'm so glad," I said, turning to Demarcus. "Mind if I go next?"

Demarcus shrugged.

Prang opened his leather folder and flipped through some papers, confused. "This isn't your name," he said.

Lizzie looked at me, the euphoria draining from her face.

"On the website it says you can talk to a loved one," I said, "as long as the loved one is a child."

"True," Prang said. "I'm sorry, it's just—"

"Most people want to talk to themselves. I understand."

Dr. Chern emerged and said something quickly to Prang, who bowed and then turned to me and bowed again, more deeply. "Sorry for the confusion. The doctors have of course been able to honor your request."

"No worries. Thank you."

The look on Lizzie's face was less confused than offended, and I decided I would lie and tell her I had a brother who died. Or a sister.

Cancer. But for now I gave a wan smile of apology before Prang led me into the hallway.

The long, windowless hallway was painted black. Ambient music played softly from hidden speakers. At the end of the hallway was a door, which Prang opened with practiced fluidity: turning the knob with his left hand while ushering me through with his right, and with an expression on his face that was neither smiling nor stern.

We entered a room so dark that I couldn't tell how big it was or if there was expensive equipment here and there, but there was a sound like the low hum of a central HVAC unit. Other than that, the only impressions I got were of the hard floor beneath my feet and of Prang's hand on my elbow as he guided me into a stiff-backed chair.

"The window is very faint," Prang said, "so we'll take a moment for your eyes to finish adjusting. They should be dilated already from the darkened waiting room."

I nodded, and soon I began to see patches of color in the darkness. I wondered if the colors were the remnants on my retinas of whatever I'd last seen—Lizzie and Demarcus in the waiting room, Prang's peaceful face—or if the colors were afflatus from the rip in time and would coalesce into the image of a child.

"Here," Prang said, placing what felt like plastic sunglasses in my hand. "These will amplify what little light comes through. Please put them on when you're ready."

I put the glasses on my face, bending the earpieces to accommodate my large head.

Through the glasses, the room was even darker, but I could see a glimmer of something straight ahead of me, like headlights far in the distance on a nighttime highway. I didn't hear a door open or close, so Prang may have been standing behind me, but if so, I couldn't hear him breathing. I could hear only my own heartbeat and the low whooshing of blood in my ears. The distant light seemed to brighten slightly. The darkness had taken on a brownish quality, and a shape was beginning to differentiate itself from its surroundings. The shape seemed to have a head. The glint of eyes.

The voice that issued from the vicinity of the eyes was high-pitched and sounded like it was coming through a tank of water, but the words were unmistakable: "What's happening?"

"Don't worry," I said, thinking *earn trust, don't scare him.* "It's just me. It's Mike."

The boyish face that had gathered around the eyes looked confused.

"Mike?" he said. "But you're—"

"I can't believe it," I said, unable to control myself. "You're alive! Let me look at you."

The boy glanced around. He had the bowl haircut I remembered, and was wearing the kind of rugby shirt we all wore back then, with thick blue stripes and a floppy collar.

"I gotta go," the boy said.

"No, no, wait," I said. I hadn't even started my spiel.

"I'm not supposed to talk to strangers."

"Please, Tim, give me just one sec."

"But my Mom said—"

"You're going to die."

"What?"

"From drugs. Don't do drugs."

"I won't."

"Especially intravenous drugs."

"What's that?"

"Drugs you inject with a hypodermic needle."

"Okay."

"That's what you say now, but you're only a kid. Your life is going to get much worse." I worried this sounded harsh. "I mean, everybody's life gets worse. That's life. A sort of downward spiral, you know?"

Tim squinted.

"Even people whose lives are pleasurable, they might experiment with so-called gateway drugs for leisure purposes." This was part of the spiel I had practiced. "Some would consider alcohol a drug—wine, beer."

"I don't like beer."

"You've tried beer?"

Tim glanced over his shoulder, as though I were keeping him from something more fun he could be doing.

"Tim, listen," I said forcefully, "I'm from the future. I know it sounds crazy, but we don't have much time so just tell me you've heard what I said."

"The thing about drugs?"

"Yes. Promise me you won't try them."

Tim shrugged. "I won't."

"Great!"

"Can I go now?"

"No! I mean, don't you want to ask me a question about the future?"

Tim stared at me for a moment, squinting. I wondered how well he could see me. Then he said, "Will Steve Stipanovich make the all-star game this year?"

I almost laughed, the question was so trivial, but I had to answer. This was Tim's question. The answer was Steve Stipanovich would never make the all-star game, and would be out of the league with back problems before his twenty-eighth birthday, but I couldn't bring myself to say that, so instead I said, "I can't remember, but you keep rooting for him, no matter what happens."

"I will," Tim said. "I gotta go, though."

"No matter what happens you're a winner," I added quickly, "you and Steve Stipanovich both. Remember that, okay?"

He started to fade, and I almost cried out for him to ask another question, but then another child entered the frame. This one was larger and had a haughty look. He draped a big pale arm over Tim Behahan's shoulder and said, "Who's the dick weed?"

"Some guy," Tim said.

"Is he like a ghost or what?"

"Maybe. Maybe he's *your* ghost!" Tim squirreled out from under the big boy's arm and took off running.

"Wait!" I yelled, and I almost cursed the oafish kid for fucking things up, but he looked so happy! After a moment of watching his friend run, the big boy hollered and ran after him without casting a second glance in my direction. Maybe I, the ghost, had begun to recede, or maybe he didn't care either way. His carefree childhood wouldn't be affected by me, and neither would Tim's, I feared.

I sat there for a moment, wondering how I should feel. I'd just seen myself as a kid—a good-natured kid who loved his buddy Tim—but the moment passed and I felt the urge to fit the experience into ideas I already had about my child self and childhood. I seized upon the phrase *dick weed*. I'd been the kind of kid who called strangers dick weed.

When I came out, dazed, Demarcus stood up and left with Prang. I sat down next to Lizzie and told her I was sorry.

She shook her head. "I shouldn't have gotten mad."

"But the way we were talking the other night, I should have said something."

"Maybe if I let you get a word in! So who did you see, if you don't mind my asking?"

"This kid who died. We used to be best friends."

Lizzie reached over and took my hand. "Oh Mike, that's so sweet."

Sweet wasn't the word I would have chosen. There was nothing sweet to me about childhood. "I was there too," I said.

"Like, you saw you too?"

I nodded and tried to explain.

"Wow, what are the chances? You must have been real good friends."

"How do you mean?"

"When they tracked down the kid, you just happened to be there."

"Yeah, I guess it does seem like a long shot, now that you mention it."

Lizzie laughed. "Two for one!" Then she told me about her own experience. She'd started off asking questions, she said, but then child Lizzie had wrested control of the conversation and asked Lizzie what she did for a living and if she was married and whether a woman was President. The questions came fast but they were easy to answer, Lizzie said, and the way the kid was looking at her, it made her feel like a millions bucks. "I could have told her *anything*," Lizzie said, "and she would have eaten it up. She was probably just happy to have boobs. I guess I forgot what a good kid I was."

When Demarcus came out, I was still lost in thought, but Lizzie said, "How did it go, Demarcus? Wasn't it amazing?"

"That wasn't me," Demarcus said.

"What do you mean it wasn't you?" There was an edge to Lizzie's voice, a mixture of surprise and defensiveness.

"When I was a kid I had a cauliflower ear," Demarcus said. "They did surgery on it when I was fourteen. It cost a lot but my parents didn't want me to get picked on at the new school I was going to." He turned his head so we could see the ear. It was strange, with the appropriate number of folds but all of them slightly out of place, more like a sculpture of an ear than an actual ear. And it *was* a sculpture, I suppose.

"How can you be so sure?" Lizzie demanded. "Did you ask the kid to turn so you could see his ear? Is *that* how you spent your five minutes?"

"I would have," Demarcus said, "but he was crying. It was like he was scared or something. I told him it was okay, it was just me, you know?"

"I'm so sorry," Prang said, coming through the door. "I've spoken with Dr. Nol. The experience can be traumatic for the child self."

"Sure," Demarcus said.

"Dr. Nol would like to speak with you, when you're ready."

"It's cool, man. No worries."

"It isn't *cool*," Lizzie said. She was standing now. "The kid was probably crying because you rejected him."

"Will you chill?" Demarcus muttered, backing away from her.

Lizzie left the room, and Demarcus and I stood there until we heard her scream.

Outside, Dr. Chern appeared to be wrestling the black youth I'd bummed a cigarette from the night before. To break it up I ran over and got between them, planted a hand in each of their chests and pushed them away from each other. They seemed relieved to have an excuse to stop fighting. Dr. Chern staggered away coughing, but the boy stood next to me, as though for protection. He had shiny tear tracks on his cheeks, but he wasn't crying anymore; he was angry.

"Get that fucking guy away from me," he said, and Dr. Chern, whose shirt was torn, kept walking until he was hunched over a potted bush.

Prang came up to us, looking stunned. "What happened?"

"Fuck you," the boy said. "My mom's on her way right now."

"But in our agreement—"

"Keep your money. Fuck you people."

Prang went over to Dr. Chern, who had his hands on his knees and was coughing into the bush. The boy took out a cigarette and began smoking it, which seemed to calm him down. I asked if he was okay.

He shrugged. "I never should have signed on for this shit."

I nodded.

"I just wanna go back to Atlanta."

"We aren't far."

"Feels like a million miles away. Feels like I been here forever."

As we talked, it became clear was that the young man, whose name was Taurean, had been living down the hill in the barracks building along with other performers.

"He was my first guy," Taurean said, raising his chin toward Demarcus, who was lurking in silence near the doorway of the compound, his head hanging, "but I been practicing for days. What to say, how to say it, how to focus my eyes—sort of soft, right? But I don't know, man, when I saw him for real I freaked out. It's like I thought it *was* me. From the future. And the guy was so slick, with his shirt all pressed, his little necktie, and here I am in this fleabag joint, I mean, how am I gonna end up like *him*? I know it doesn't make sense, the guy isn't me, but with all the smoke and mirrors..." Taurean trailed off, and in the silence I worried he would start crying again, so I risked putting my arm around his shoulders, which seemed like an appropriately avuncular thing to do. He started shaking his head, looking at the ground and saying, "Damn, man, damn."

Meanwhile Prang was helping Dr. Chern pace around taking deep breaths, and Demarcus had sat down on a bench. I scanned the grounds for Lizzie, didn't see her, and wondered if she was somewhere inside, upset, but then I heard her yelling. She was across the parking lot with her phone at her ear. From the words she chose, I could tell she was yelling—screaming—at Mr. Courtney.

11.

Lizzie was yelling at Mr. Courtney because she had figured out, from Demarcus's ear story, that the Time Windows people hadn't chosen him (or me or her); rather, Mr. Courtney had chosen Demarcus, *because* of his ear deformity, to catch Time Windows in the lie that he, Mr. Courtney, had become convinced they were perpetrating. Over the course of our *post mortem* in his office, throughout which Lizzie scowled, Mr. Courtney made clear his theory that the Time Windows people paid child actor lookalikes to impersonate their clients as children. This cohered with what I'd gleaned from my conversation with Taurean, which was that there was an entire barracks of child actors down the hill from the facility. Taurean had told me it wasn't so bad. They watched lots of TV. But I found it hard not to think of them as semi-abandoned children who needed just as much attention as the children we were reaching back in time to see. Before we left, Taurean's mother had shown up in a haggard Pontiac with three younger children in tow. She'd seemed annoyed.

"A client signs up and they go through the headshots," Mr. Courtney mused, gesticulating at the window overlooking architects working at their high desks, and in that moment I wished I had chosen architecture. I wished I could have driven by a building I designed, laid my hands on the bricks. But the permanence would have been illusory, I knew. Even small-town elementary schools got bulldozed.

"And people are such windbags," Mr. Courtney was saying, "that the kid doesn't have to say much, just sit there nodding and looking cute. And it's kind of dark so the client can't get a good look, you know?" He turned to us, almost frantic. "You know?"

"I hear you," Demarcus said, "but my guy was like a midget or something."

"Sure, why not?" Mr. Courtney said. "There's only two places in America where they could pull this off: LA, obviously, and here. Think about all the movies they shoot here now, all the kids who come with their parents from all over the South to be in commercials and be extras in those fucking comic book movies, or on that zombie show. And for every child star there's a midget who does stunts, right?" He turned to me: "How about you, Mike? You got two of them, right?"

"Yeah," I said, "but I don't think they were midgets."

"How good were they?"

"As performers?"

"The likeness, I mean."

"Well, the one was a kid I hadn't seen in years, so who knows, and I guess I was too busy looking at that one to get a good look at the one playing me." This was a lie. The one playing me had fooled me completely. Then again, I never looked at photos from childhood. My mother had very few framed inside their tiny house, and the few she kept showed me on the football field, where in my helmet and pads I could have been anybody, or at least anybody who weighed two-fifty at sixteen. I was an easy mark, in other words. The person to ask was Lizzie, but Mr. Courtney didn't want to bother her. The way she was sitting there with her arms crossed, looking out the window instead of at Mr. Courtney, I wouldn't have been surprised if she stood up, left the office, and never came back. Days later, to keep her from quitting, Mr. Courtney would give Lizzie a raise and put her in charge of what remained of Deitrich's old team, the lead team of the agency, and the two of us would chat in the office but rarely work together again. Demarcus, for his part, would leave for grad school somewhere in Florida, where he was from. I envied him. I guess I wished I could have followed him there and started all over again. I would major in history this time. Maybe go to grad school. Clark University in Worcester, Massachusetts, offered a PhD in Holocaust and Genocide Studies.

For the moment, though, Mr. Courtney was too swept up in the success of his scheme to understand that he was digging himself a deeper hole. He kept asking Demarcus questions. Lizzie kept staring out the window. And for my own part I kept thinking about all the child actors like Taurean, each appearing in a commercial or two. Each feeling so good for having made his parents happy. But what happened when they aged out of the business and returned to school? By then they'd have missed a few grades. Runty to begin with, they'd be ostracized. My heart went out to them. What could be worse than professional failure so young?

Torture, for one.

Civil war.

The death of family.

"You know what I think?" I said, interrupting Mr. Courtney. He turned to me, and Lizzie and Demarcus did too.

"I think it doesn't matter if they're actors or not," I said.

Mr. Courtney made a snorting noise, but Lizzie and Demarcus kept quiet. They expected me to keep talking, to make sense of this thing, so I tried to explain that what I'd said to those two kids, to Tim and me, was true, and that it didn't matter if they were actors or not because I wasn't talking to them. Not really. I was talking to the kids inside me.

"And those two kids in front of me," I said, picturing their friendly young faces, "those kids were like a target. An excuse to point the gun of my feelings and shoot. You know?"

Lizzie nodded slowly, as though to say *yeah, keep going, you're nailing this!* Demarcus, who was staring at the floor, perhaps regretful of his role in the scheme, nodded too. Mr. Courtney paced around like he couldn't wait for me to be done talking but knew better than to open his mouth.

"The kid who's inside me," I repeated, thinking of a phantom child somewhere inside my head, floating around in a quagmire of concussion and embarrassment, "that's the one I thought I maybe got through to. That's the one who counted."

"That's what I said," Mr. Courtney blurted.

"Sir?"

"I said, 'It isn't about the effect you have on child you, it's about the effect child you has on you. Child you was the only person who ever really understood you.' Remember?"

"You're being an ass," Lizzie said to him, and then to us: "Guys, let's go get some fucking candy."

To our surprise, the Time Windows people wanted to move forward. They believed so strongly in our campaign that they wanted to use it to expand into the DFW and Charlotte markets and possibly reach a higher price point down the road. Their long-term goal, Prang explained in a phone meeting, was New York City. I didn't disabuse him of the idea that a national company could get by with billboards and train ads. I had always dreamed of putting an ad inside an MTA subway car.

Prang invited us to the compound so we could make use of their performers, as he called them, for a photo shoot. He said they wanted ads for boys and girls, black and white, and every other race under the sun. Kids in wheelchairs too. He said they envisioned the ads as a celebration of American diversity, and I said it sounded good to us. I wasn't ready yet to tell him that the *us* I referred to, the Time Windows team, had been winnowed to one, me, but I didn't think he'd care.

My conversations with Prang were full of awkward pauses, and it was impossible not to wonder if the thing meant to fill those pauses was a frank discussion of the nature of their business—of their scam, for lack of a better word—but I never brought it up. I didn't want to embarrass him.

During one phonecall, shortly before Carol Chen and I were to drive to the compound for a daylong photo shoot, Prang asked if he could put his father on the phone. I said of course, and there was a click as another phone was raised from its cradle.

Dr. Nol's soft voice filled my ear, and Prang began simultaneously to translate what he was saying. Sometimes I couldn't hear Prang over Dr. Nol, but the gist I got was of an apology, but not for the scam itself. Dr. Nol was upset that Dr. Chern had made such a scene in front of us. He insisted that Dr. Chern was not a violent man, certainly not one to "attack young boys," as Prang translated it. Dr. Nol explained that he and Dr. Chern had been childhood friends. More like brothers, really. Dr. Chern had grown up in a privileged military family like Dr. Nol's, but he hadn't been in France when the Khmer Rouge took Phnom Penh. He'd been in the capital with his large family, who'd scattered in pairs, disguised as beggars, while their father remained inside their home awaiting his fate.

Dr. Chern toiled for years in the countryside and was forced to marry a woman he barely knew. The woman miscarried again and again from malnutrition. Eventually she died giving birth, and this steeled in Dr. Chern the Buddhist faith he'd nursed in secret while working day and night in the rice paddies and suffering all manner of indignities. When the Khmer Rouge were ousted by the Vietnamese, Dr. Chern returned to Phnom Penh but never found the rest of his family. Having no interest in marrying again, he became a sort of healer. At first he traveled around with the usual herbs, barks and roots, but at some point he realized what people really wanted was an excuse to unburden themselves to him, and that, for many, he was a stand-in for someone else. Soon, he began making this proxy arrangement explicit. He told people he would shut his eyes and listen as closely as he could, using whatever power he had as a devout Buddhist to communicate with those who were no longer among them. He refurbished and decorated an old pedicab to be used as a special booth for this purpose.

Dr. Nol got quiet, and in my mind he rose from their dining room table to gaze thoughtfully at the courtyard with its birdbath full of shiny black crows.

"You see," Prang said, "many died where they are from, and to speak again to the dead was a great consolation."

"I understand," I said, and to control the confusing emotions I felt rising within me I took out my notepad and began jotting notes.

Prang explained that when Dr. Nol made money in the aftermath of the Mr. Vinegar experiments, he returned to Cambodia to help his family and friends, but few had survived, and it wasn't long before he tracked down Dr. Chern. Despite his misgivings, he tried his old friend's consolation service, and he was so moved that he decided to help Dr. Chern expand it. It was this decision, and not time-rip science, that led to Time Windows. But actualizing their vision was difficult under the repressive Vietnamese-controlled regime, and so Dr. Nol continued touring as a speaker, and the two eventually found their way to America.

Dr. Nol paused, said something softly to Prang, and Prang said to me, "Do you understand?"

I told him I understood perfectly well, but I heard the salesman's bluster in my voice and felt ashamed. I didn't want to treat Prang and Dr. Nol like clients. I wanted to let them say what they needed to say, and just to listen. And yet I wanted them to know what was in my heart.

"I sure do know what you mean," I said again, or something insipid like that, inwardly cursing myself, but I meant what I said. Many had been lost on my end, too: Tim, of course, but also Ellen Kearney and the rest of my childhood; and though I didn't know it yet, my own father would die later that year. At his funeral I would think of that long conversation with Dr. Nol and his son.

When I finally mustered the gumption to mention Tim, they told me how sorry they were. They said the years had done nothing to deaden the anguish Dr. Nol felt at the mention of lost children. He couldn't accept that children would be lost of their own accord, and so easily, in a country like this one. Today, he said, he understood that few are truly lost; that most simply go through periods of unhappiness, deep unhappiness, and will be reconciled if only they can persevere. He asked if I had children, and I said no. He told me I should have some, and not to worry: just because I didn't remember my childhood as being particularly happy didn't mean it wasn't, especially for my parents. He compared the child self to a chrysalis which the adult self sheds and then searches for until death.

I continue to work with Time Windows, which continues to struggle financially. Sometimes they request new work and I give it to them, but I don't bother running it by Mr. Courtney anymore. That puts them, as clients, in the same category as J.J. Deckle and the other corpulent white men.

Prang and I talk on the phone quite a bit. I always ask him how the grandfather of Cambodian time-travel science is doing, and he laughs. Prang laughs at all my jokes, which is about the best you can hope for from a client, or from anybody else, really.

ACKNOWLEDGEMENTS

As ever I thank my family: Andrea and Lenore; Cheryl and Wayne Bazzle; Vicki and Galen Sweigart; Sara, Jim, Max, and Maya Durnin; Tim Coveney and other Coveneys and Bazzles. I thank my teachers: Tony Ardizzone, Judith Ortiz Cofer, Mark Crotty, Art Kopit, Deb Margolin, Reg McKnight, Alyce Miller, Margaret Spillane, Maura Stanton, Samrat Upadhyay, and of course Kyle Galbraith, who started me down this road. I thank the editors who took up these stories: Bradford Morrow, Chris Fink, Michael Koch, Bryan Castille, Russell Scott Valentino, Joanna Luloff, and Wayne Miller. I thank Andrew Ibis and everyone at C&R Press, without whom this book would still be lurking unpublished in a seedy district of my mind. I thank Indiana University and the University of Georgia for fellowships that supported my writing. I thank Maceo Montoya.

For "The Beard of Human Weakness" I thank Adam Wells, who coined the title for a Trophy Dad show. For "The Milkman" I thank DW Gibson and Ledig House, where I wrote the first draft. For "The Mask of Cajolo" I thank Tripper Clancy and the inestimable Stephen Herek. For "Legendary Americans on Wheels" I thank Daniel Squadron, whose bracing performance in *The Franklin Thesis* has been rattling around in my head for half my life. For "Magellan" I again thank Adam Wells, whose *Western Canon Series, Part Three: Corruption* was my inspiration, along with several bold choices by Ian Cheney. Thank you, Ian. For "In the Presence of the Actor" I thank my former collaborators Matteo Borghese, Scott Hoffer and John Phillips, along with Mark Thomas McGee for writing *Fast and Furious: the Story of American International Pictures*, and Chuck Klosterman for "Crazy Things Seem Normal... Normal Things Seem Crazy." For "Fathers of Cambodian Time-Travel Science" I thank the writers of two other books: Sydney Schanberg for *The Death and Life of Dith Pran*, and Samantha Power for *A Problem from Hell: America and the Age of Genocide*.

Lastly, I thank the friends and fellow writers who read early drafts of these stories or inspired me with their own writing and performing: Chad Anderson, Catalina Bartlett, Tina Bartolome, Patrick Coleman, Jonathan Coveney, Juliana Crespo, Liz Cunningham, Johnny Damm, Will Dunlap, Lindsey Harding, Chris Johnson, Kelly Kennedy, Robert Latimer,

Raleigh Lee, Daniel Lockhart, Nina Mamikunian, Michael Manis, Neil Mascarenhas, Sean McBride, Jeff Miller, Danny Nguyen, Matt Nye, Raj Reddy, Kate Russell, Nathaniel Rich, Joanna Ruocco, Ashley Rutter, Andrés Sanabria, Lana Spendl, Matt Stolbach, Ryan Teitman, Alexander Weinstein, Marcus Wicker, and Sana Younis. I hope I haven't missed anyone, but if I have, and if that person is you, please know I thank you.

C&R PRESS TITLES

NONFICTION

Women in the Literary Landscape by Doris Weatherford, et al
Credo: An Anthology of Manifestos & Sourcebook for Creative Writing
by Rita Banerjee and Diana Norma Szokolyai

FICTION

Last Tower to Heaven by Jacob Paul
No Good, Very Bad Asian by Lelund Cheuk
A History of the Cat by Anis Shivani
Surrendering Appomattox by Jacob M. Appel
Made by Mary by Laura Catherine Brown
Ivy vs. Dogg by Brian Leung
While You Were Gone by Sybil Baker
Cloud Diary by Steve Mitchell
Spectrum by Martin Ott
That Man in Our Lives by Xu Xi

SHORT FICTION

Fathers of Cambodian Time-Travel Science by Bradley Bazzle
Notes From the Mother Tongue by An Tran
The Protester Has Been Released by Janet Sarbanes

ESSAY AND CREATIVE NONFICTION

Selling the Farm by Debra Di Blasi
the internet is for real by Chris Campanioni
Immigration Essays by Sybil Baker
Je suis l'autre: Essays and Interrogations
by Kristina Marie Darling
Death of Art by Chris Campanioni

POETRY

The Rented Altar by Lauren Berry
Between the Earth and Sky by Eleanor Kedney
What Need Have We for Such as We by Amanda Auerbach
A Family Is a House by Dustin Pearson
The Miracles by Amy Lemmon
Banjo's Inside Coyote by Kelli Allen
Objects in Motion by Jonathan Katz
My Stunt Double by Travis Denton
Lessons in Camoflauge by Martin Ott
Millennial Roost by Dustin Pearson
Dark Horse by Kristina Marie Darling
All My Heroes are Broke by Ariel Francisco
Holdfast by Christian Anton Gerard
Ex Domestica by E.G. Cunningham
Like Lesser Gods by Bruce McEver
Notes from the Negro Side of the Moon by Earl Braggs
Imagine Not Drowning by Kelli Allen
Free Boat: Collected Lies and Love Poems by John Reed
Les Fauves by Barbara Crooker
Tall as You are Tall Between Them by Annie Christain
The Couple Who Fell to Earth by Michelle Bitting
Notes to the Beloved by Michelle Bitting